SEQUOIA CHRONICLES

Guy and Mary,

I hope you enjoy the book as much as I enjoyed writing it!

Thank you!

Jim

This book is a work of fiction. The goodwill tour of President Carter is historically factual. Other historical events, medical terms, climate conditions, geology, security, aircraft and geography are depicted accurately. The Sequoia Lake depicted in this novel, located in Northern California, is fictional. There is no relationship, intended or otherwise, to a 77-acre privately owned and operated lake with the same name in Southern California. All other names, characters, places, incidents, and dialogue are drawn from the author's imagination. Any resemblance to actual events or persons, living or dead, is entirely coincidental.

A Horse With No Name
Words and Music by Dewey Bunnell. Copyright © 1972 (renewed) Warner/Chappell Music Ltd. All rights for the Western Hemisphere controlled by WB Music Corporation. All rights reserved. Used by permission of Alfred Music.

Time Passages
Words and Music by Al Stewart and Peter White. Copyright © 1978 Universal/Dick James Music Ltd., Frabjous Music and Approximate Music. All rights for Universal/Dick James Music Ltd. controlled and administered in the U.S. and Canada by Universal—Songs of Polygram International, Inc. All rights for Frabjous Music controlled and administered by Spirit One Music. All rights reserved. Used by permission. Reprinted by permission of Hal Leonard LLC.

Sometimes When We Touch
Words by Dan Hill. Music by Barry Mann. Copyright © 1977 Sony/ATV Music Publishing LLC, and Mann & Well Songs, Inc. Copyright Renewed. All rights administered by Sony/ATV Music Publishing LLC, 424 Church Street, Suite 1200, Nashville TN 37219. International copyright secured. All rights reserved. Reprinted by permission of Hal Leonard LLC.

Precious And Few
Words and Music by Walter D. Nims. Copyright © 1970, 1972 Sony/ATV Music Publishing LLC, and Emerald City Music. Copyright renewed. All rights administered by Sony/ATV Music Publishing LLC, 424 Church Street, Suite 1200, Nashville TN 37219. International Copyright Secured. All rights reserved. Reprinted by permission of Hal Leonard LLC.

Jackie Blue
Words and Music by Larry Lee and Steve Cash. Copyright © 1974, 1975 Irving Music, Inc. Copyright renewed. All rights reserved. Used by permission. Reprinted by permission of Hal Leonard LLC

Cherish
Words and Music by Terry Kirkman. Copyright © 1965 Beechwood Music Corporation. Copyright renewed. All rights administered by Sony/ATV Music Publishing LLC, 424 Church Street, Suite 1200, Nashville TN 37219. International copyright Secured. All rights reserved. Reprinted by permission of Hal Leonard LLC

East Of Eden
Excerpt(s) from East Of Eden by John Steinbeck, copyright © 1952 by John Steinbeck. Copyright renewed © 1980 by Elaine Steinbeck, Thom Steinbeck and John Steinbeck IV. Used by permission of Viking Books, an imprint of Penguin Publishing Group, a division of Penguin Random House LLC. All rights reserved.

The Great Gatsby
Excerpt(s) from *The Great Gatsby* by F. Scott Fitzgerald. Copyright © 1925 by Charles Scribner's Sons. Copyright renewed © 1953 by Frances Scott Fitzgerald Lanahan. Reprinted with permission of Scribner, a division of Simon and Schuster, Inc. All rights reserved.

It is believed that quotes by Orson Welles, Winston Churchill and Mark Twain are in the public domain.

This book is dedicated to my wife, Claudia.

She has loved, encouraged, patiently tolerated, indulged and humored me for more than 42 years. This book represents the latest example of her love and encouragement.

Thanks, Toots! I love you!

AUTHOR'S NOTE

This book is set in the 1960s and '70s. The book uses terminology, jargon, phrases, and slang in common use at the time.
Some of the language may be considered offensive to readers
with today's sensibilities and awareness.

"We're born alone, we live alone, we die alone. Only through our love and friendship can we create the illusion for the moment that we're not alone."
—Orson Welles

O N E

"Well I'm not the kind to live in the past. The years run too short and the days too fast…"—Al Stewart, "TIME PASSAGES"

Sequoia Lake—The breathless hush of evening
Just after 8:30 p.m.
Memorial Day, 1978

The lake is quiet. You could almost feel the calm falling on the water.

A short time ago, water skiers crisscrossed the lake for a last run under ideal conditions. The water was mirror smooth, like glass. Absolutely perfect for skiing.

Now it's quiet. No wind. No wakes. No waves.

Twilight. The passage of day into night. The end of another warm Northern California day.

All of this is lost on Jordan (Bobby) Laine. Near the middle of the lake, Bobby sits in a small rented fishing boat. He's putting on waders, the rubber overalls that allow fishermen to stay warm and dry while standing in the middle of a stream.

The Sequoia Lake Land Development Corporation was his brainchild, a planned community offering the prospect of owning the last lakefront property available in California. It had attracted millions of investor dollars—a magnificent concept that nearly sold itself. There were glossy brochures featuring artist renderings of a private community, sweeping vistas, golf courses, wide landscaped boulevards, spacious model homes and open spaces. There were TV ads in major markets in California. It was a work of art. Bobby's brainchild.

Not so terribly long ago, he had been the toast of the town. At one point, he owned the largest houseboat on the lake.

The "ship," as it was called in town, helped him host the investor presentations.

The "road show." Even the most hesitant or skeptical potential investor was sold after one of these trips. It was breathtaking: the scene, the sale, the pitch, the vision.

A "visionary" with a promise to change life around the lake forever. That was how the community looked at Bobby.

He set off the latest wave of fortune and progress for the area. 120 years ago it was the lure of gold. Then prosperity showed up with the coming of the railroad linking the town of Sequoia City to forests containing millions of virgin board feet of lumber. Then, construction of Sequoia Lake.

The promise of gold was fleeting. So, too, the railroads, the forests and the lake construction. And now: The Sequoia Lake Land Development Corporation.

In each case, the hope was real. Too often, so was the hype. In each case, the vision never quite panned out.

Now there were questions about the Sequoia Lake Land Development Corporation project. Parcel splits. Water quality issues. There were numerous district attorney investigations. "I didn't know I couldn't split those parcels," Bobby said when first asked by investigators. I think he even blinked his eyes with a hurt look as if to say, "How could you think I'd do anything wrong?"

A grand jury was already handing down indictments with more expected any day. The savings and loan handling the escrow accounts was under investigation by the Federal Savings and Loan Insurance Corporation (FSLIC). How did so much depositors' money get funneled into one development? The bank manager had a lot of explaining to do. The FSLIC would protect depositors' money and bail out the local bank. While the regulators didn't know the whole story yet, they were certain of one thing: Someone was going to pay, civilly and criminally.

"Too many cut corners. Not enough greased palms," Bobby thought. "I guess it really doesn't matter now anyway."

The ultimate insult came a few days after the D.A. issued the first subpoenas. The Chamber of Commerce office removed Bobby's portrait from the gallery of past presidents.

"As if I never existed."

Bobby stood up and as he did, the boat shuddered, causing him to briefly lose his balance. He laughed at his reaction, his fear of falling out of the boat. Then, without note or fanfare, Bobby Laine took a deep breath and stepped out of the boat.

The waders quickly filled with water.

The last thing he imagined—as he slipped below the waterline—was the perfect outline of the streets that were never paved in the development that was never to be. The vision was still impressive, and for one last time, still within his reach.

"The things you lean on, the things that don't last, well it's just now and then my line gets cast into these time passages..."

Bobby Laine's body sunk into the muck at the bottom of the 500-foot lake several minutes later.

The next morning, fishermen found the empty boat.

There was no sign of Bobby.

His banker was the first to suspect something was wrong. He and Bobby had a standing meeting every Tuesday morning at 9. He was usually early. Never late.

And never missed a single meeting.

His lawyer, Glenn Robert, was the next to know. Bobby met Glenn at 12 sharp for the Rotary meeting every week. If he was going to be out of town, he'd call Glenn and they would agree to meet for drinks later in the week.

The lead contractor at the housing development was also curious when Bobby did not appear on the construction site Tuesday. Bobby visited the project every morning. Actually, it was not unusual for Bobby to check on the progress several times a day.

Bobby's car was found in the marina parking lot, which in itself, would not have been unusual. Bobby's "ship" was anchored in the marina. To get to the houseboat required a water shuttle from the marina dock.

When a sheriff's deputy went to look, the "ship" was locked tight. No one had apparently been there for several days.

While none of the pieces fit together just yet, the Sequoia Lake project had claimed another life.

SEQUOIA CHRONICLES

"It was late in December, the sky turned to snow, all around the day was going down slow. Night like a river, beginning to flow, I felt the beat of my mind go drifting into time passages..."

Monday, December 18, 1978
Running Deer Campground
Little Grass Valley Lake
Near La Porte, California
Elevation 5,000
3:12 pm

I've been writing in this journal for three days and nothing makes sense.

There's a heaviness hanging over me.

I might be dying.

I thought there might be more to life than just 27 years. And I certainly never expected my life to end here, cold and alone.

My biography would be pretty short—I'm a small-town radio newsman. I report the news. Big deal. I'm writing a suspense novel, although it's hardly a great novel.

My life would not be a blip on anyone's radar.

When I look back, things have been spinning out of control for about a year. It's been unbelievably frightening, with more highs and lows than I could ever imagine. As a newsman and even as a would-be novelist, I find it all hard to believe.

If this were one of my newscasts, here's how I would report the events of the past year: "Let's recap what we know about this developing story so far. I've watched two people die violently. I worked with an undercover detective investigating a grisly murder. I've made enemies of a motorcycle gang and some local land developers. I have been threatened a lot. Even shot at once.

Elsewhere on the local scene: I lost several of my best friends this past year: Ed, Grandpa. And now Emma. Oh, and this is my last newscast, because I was fired last week."

God this is crazy.

I have spent a lot of time recently crafting alibis. Unusual for a guy who has only been in one fist fight in his life, doesn't own a gun and hates violence. Nothing seems real.

What if I am paranoid? Losing my mind? Is there really something to be afraid of here? Now?

The hair on the back of my neck is at full attention.

I feel like quite a disappointment right now, an assessment more than one person would agree with. If my father were alive, he would be the first to say I am a *profound* disappointment.

Normally there's 5 or 6 feet of snow here. Today, there are just a few small drifts in areas with a northern exposure. A California drought started two years ago. It was the fourth driest winter on record. This past year, 1977, was the driest year in more than 100 years of record keeping.

Everyone hopes it will end this winter, but it's not looking promising right now.

Just down the road in Forbestown, rainfall is running 10% of normal for the month.

Typically 75% of California's rainfall occurs between November and March. And most of that in the months of December, January and February.

Another slow start to the rainy season. Not promising at all.

God, it's cold here though.

When I came through La Porte a few days ago the store, Riley's Bar and the Union Hotel were pretty quiet. Unless there is a lot of snow this winter, the cross country skiing, contract road plowing and snowmobile business will be down significantly.

This Forest Service campground closed at the end of September. The paid seasonal campground host finished a final cleanup, drained the water lines and left on October 5.

The campground is north of the flight pattern of San Francisco International Airport. During the day, when it's quiet, you can hear the jets headed east. At night, if you stand on a picnic table and look south through a clearing in the trees, you might be able to catch the twinkling of aircraft lights as they approach cruising altitude.

But right now, right here, there's no one.

But no doubt more than one person is looking for me. It might be the sheriff. It could be someone else.

It doesn't really matter, I suppose. The only thing I know for certain right now is that I am really cold.

What a life: Nothing solved. Nothing resolved. Nothing at all.

Maybe my father was right.

"Years go falling in the fading light. Time Passages. Buy me a ticket on the last train home tonight…"

Sorry, I have gotten ahead of myself. I am really not thinking clearly. You need to know why I am here…what brought me here.

Let me start over.

"On the first part of the journey, I was looking at all the life..."
—America, "A HORSE WITH NO NAME"

T W O

"The Days of Wine and Roses"—Andy Williams

My name is Mark Keating. I was born May 10, 1952, in Schiller Park, Illinois, on a day when the temperature reached 61 degrees at O'Hare Airport.

I remember winters in Schiller Park were cold and summers were humid. Living within three miles of O'Hare, it was also noisy all the time.

My father worked for the Cook County public works department. He loved his job. And little else. I don't think he ever loved Mom. Or me. He was a very nasty man and very mean. To me and Mom.

We lived in a small apartment. My father smoked a lot. He said renting an apartment was cheaper than owning a home, because you didn't have to cut the lawn, rake leaves, shovel snow or paint.

My father was always yelling. He was angry at everything. The Cubs. The weather. The news. The mayor. His boss. My mom. Me.

The apartment walls were pretty thin. I heard him slap Mom more than once. I would hear her crying after he went to work or when he was asleep in his chair in front of the TV.

No matter how hard I tried to please him, my father found a reason to spank me every day. Every single day. For as long as I can remember. Some days it was a couple of swats. Other times, it was a first-rate thrashing.

It didn't matter the reason. If I was late getting home from a friend's house. If I didn't wash the supper dishes right away or the right way or put them away the right way. If I took too long in the bathtub. If I didn't make my bed right. If I didn't take the garbage out the instant he told me to. If my shoes weren't shined three times a week. If I didn't put the newspaper on his TV tray. Whatever the reason, he'd give me a whipping. Sometimes I would get into bed at the end of the day, relieved, thinking I had escaped, only to be yanked awake and turned over his knee.

I was afraid of him. And, as a result, nearly everything else. I never mentioned it to my friends. I thought everyone's life was the same. I thought it was normal.

My stomach was always in knots. I threw up a lot. I heard about ulcers. I was pretty sure I had one.

In a college psychology class, the professor said children grow up strong, healthy and secure when parents provide love and a feeling of safety. I wouldn't know. I had no experience with love or safety when my father was around.

I still get sick inside when someone raises their voice or yells. Until I was in high school, I would lie awake afraid. I could hear the blood rushing, pounding, in my ears. I'd often cry myself to sleep. The only time I let myself feel the rage inside was just before I went to sleep.

It didn't matter that Mom and my father got a divorce when I was 8. And it didn't matter that my father lived 2,000 miles and two time zones away.

Mom and I moved west to California to live with her parents.

THREE

"For What It's Worth"—Buffalo Springfield

It takes a lot of energy to live in fear, always trying to please people and hoping they won't lose their temper or be disappointed in you.

Fortunately, as I grew older, I was able to shut off my brain and shut out the rest of the world with sleep. By the time I got to college, it rarely took me more than a minute to fall asleep and I could take a nap any time of the day.

I also counted on music and the radio to be my constant companions and escape. They provided consolation and solace. I liked some classical, but mostly Top 40.

For the longest time, I thought I was going crazy. I felt like I was constantly on the verge of losing my grip. Like a character in a movie, hanging on to a ledge by a couple of fingers above a deep abyss. I felt like an inmate in the movie "Titicut Follies": When you are insane, how do you know it? How do you prove you're not unbalanced? What point of reference do you use?

My palms sweat a lot, too, which doesn't help my anxiety around other people.

I spent a lot of time developing and practicing verbal comebacks for situations that might happen, but never did. My heart rate would go up and my breathing quicken as I envisioned telling someone off and speaking my mind. The snappy retorts were always ready, if someone would just step into the right situation. I had been surprised enough in my life, so I tried to plan to prevent it from happening again.

I often envisioned myself rescuing someone from a wrecked car or a burning house. I would show no fear stepping into harm's way. I would be a hero. I think the song "The Impossible Dream" could have been my life's theme song.

On the other hand, I was afraid if I didn't keep my feelings to myself, it would be like a dam bursting. Like "all the king's horses and all the king's men couldn't put Humpty together again."

All my life, I had the radio on. Even when I slept.

I admired the disc jockeys and newsmen on the stations. So cool and confident. Never sounding afraid.

The more I listened, the more I knew what I wanted to do with my life.

I wanted to be a faceless, fearless voice on the radio. Someone people could admire without really knowing who I was or how frightened I was. I could be behind the microphone, trusted, authoritative and anonymous.

In college, I never thought of myself as a lover or a fighter.

Life is funny, though.
It turns out: I was both.

F O U R

A Horse with No Name

When Mom and I moved west, I fell behind at school and got held back a year. That delayed the start of my college classes, but I finally graduated from college in May 1975, with a degree in journalism and a minor in broadcasting.

After graduation, I spent my first summer working in a cannery in Woodland, California. Hardly an auspicious start to a journalistic career.

There's nothing like the smell of ripening, cooking and processed tomatoes to encourage a person to accept the first job offer that comes along. And that job was in northeastern California.

KBSC—Broadcasting for Sequoia City.

> *"...and the sky with no clouds, the heat was hot and the ground was dry but the air was full of sound..."*
> —America, "A HORSE WITH NO NAME"

F I V E

Sequoia River Headwaters

> *"Wherever the river flows, every sort of living creature that can
> multiply shall live, and there shall be abundant fish…along
> both banks of the river, fruit trees of every kind shall grow…
> every month they shall bear fresh fruit…their fruit shall serve
> for food and their leaves for medicine."*
> —Ezekiel 47: 1-12

Civilizations thrive near the water. Situated next to great rivers or along seashores, commerce developed. Interactions between cultures and societies blended first along the world's waterways.

On a clear day, if you could climb the tallest tree in the area, you would see Lassen Peak to the southeast and Mt. Shasta to the northwest. At this spot, you are close to where the Sierra Nevada meets the Cascade Range. To the south, the Sierra is characterized by large granite features, like Half Dome and El Capitan in Yosemite. Granite lakes, cliffs and boulders are found throughout the Sierra range. To the north, the Cascades are mostly volcanic from Lassen Peak to Mount Rainier and into Canada.

Almost indiscernible and below that tree are the headwaters of the Sequoia River. Unless you knew what to look for, you could walk over the spot and not notice. Fed by snow melt and groundwater, oozing up from the forest floor in tiny rivulets, feeding into small streams and creeks, merging with larger streams, it becomes the Sequoia River.

The Sequoia City has two branches: the north and middle forks. There is no south fork. Before the reservoir, the forks converged into one large river a few miles east of the town of Sequoia.

The north fork was the easiest to follow into the foothills. The middle fork was so covered with boulders and framed by steep cliffs that it could not be accurately surveyed from the ground. It was not until the late 1940s—with the use of aircraft—that map makers were able to produce a moderately accurate picture of the middle fork.

The Sequoia canyon has another unique feature. Most canyons in the Sierra run east to west. Canyon Creek in Butte County and the Sequoia River canyons run nearly north and south. Because the prevailing winds in the Sacramento Valley are from the south, fires can be especially treacherous in these canyons and difficult to control.

For 5,000 years, native American cultures lived and evolved along the banks of the Sequoia. In the summer, tribes moved east from the hot valley to the cooler temperatures in the foothills and mountains. In late fall, the migration reversed.

But always, along the banks of the river.

The natives stayed close to their lifeblood.

S I X

Sequoia City, California

Sequoia City sprang to life during California's gold rush.

Right now it has a population of 7,200 in the city limits, with 20,000 more people living within 10 miles of the town center.

Sequoia City has five bars and four churches. More bars than churches, a constant issue with local pastors. The bars are a holdover from the dam construction years before. There are three gas stations, a funeral home, two pharmacies, one physician (a G.P.) and the U.S. Post Office.

Sequoia City has four stoplights in town, all synchronized to 25 miles an hour. If you make the first light and drive 25 miles per hour, you'll make the next three lights. There aren't any parking meters in town. Years ago, the city council discussed installing meters and hiring a parking enforcement officer to enforce a two-hour limit. The proposal was quickly dropped. There were serious, loud and often profane objections from the business community. The city manager who brought the proposal to the council quickly found employment elsewhere.

Like most small towns in rural California, Sequoia City has a branch of the Bank of America and United California Bank. The city hall and the municipal court are in the downtown business district. There are feed and hardware stores as well as two grocery stores: a Holiday market and a local family-run operation.

There is a Mode O' Day store downtown—one of 700 franchise operations in the country. The W.T. Grant store downtown closed a couple of years ago and the building is still vacant. The W.T. Grant chain started in 1906. At its peak, the company had 1,200 stores and more than 80,000 employees. A short time after the Sequoia City store closed, the entire W.T. Grant chain filed for bankruptcy. When it ceased operations, Business Week called it the most significant bankruptcy in U.S. history. It was the largest business failure since the collapse of the Penn Central Railroad in 1970.

There's a saw and tool shop, a used car dealer, a small five and dime, one radio station, one newspaper and a travel agent. Sequoia City also has a couple of attorneys, helping to confirm Mark Twain's contention that "One attorney in town will starve, two will prosper."

Sequoia City also has a movie theater, a Sambo's Restaurant just off the highway and a small coffee shop downtown.

I came to Sequoia at the end of September 1975, just a year after the reservoir filled and the dam was dedicated.

The massive construction project was still winding down when I pulled into town. At the time, temporary housing for the construction workers was being dismantled and shipped to the next major construction site. Some of the workers, though, stayed behind and bought these quickly constructed housing units to convert into permanent housing. Cheap but comfortable. With lots of remodeling ahead. They became inexpensive versions of the Winchester House in San Jose, California.

I came to work for KBSC in the "News Department." It was a "department" of one. I'd never met my new employer before that day. He hired me over the phone after listening to an audition tape I'd mailed a couple of weeks earlier.

The first day I showed up at the station, I wore a long-sleeve shirt and a tie. Until I introduced myself, he thought I was some punk inspector for the Federal Communications Commission. I was probably the best-dressed guy in Sequoia City that day. My necktie was actually tied, too, not a knit clip on.

I never wore a shirt and tie to the station again.

My job was pretty routine: news interviews with the public officials, covering the city council, board of education plus the police log. I also taped a weekly interview with the superintendent of the local school districts. "Inside the Classroom" played twice on the weekend.

Scintillating radio it wasn't, but that was my job.

My predecessor thought arrests for "drunk and disorderly" were newsworthy.

When he left, the newsroom was a mess—old stories, no files, no source phone numbers or addresses. I wanted to do stories that affected the most people. Kind of high handed when I think about it now. It's not like I was changing the world or the course of the universe from Sequoia City.

The teletype machine clattered all day and night. Along with CBS radio network news, delivered via phone lines, it was our only connection to the outside world. The "Big News" events were signaled by a number of bells on the teletype—the more bells, the bigger the news event.

In the early morning hours after election night in 1976, the teletype banged out several bells followed by the words FLASH and the headline "CARTER ELECTED PRESIDENT."

It had been a very close election and a very long night. I kept that teletype story somewhere in my stuff at home. It was the only time I ever saw the word "Flash" cross the teletype.

The station was licensed by the Federal Communications Commission. It operated with 1,000 watts in the daytime and 250 at night. We were on the air 18 hours a day.

The station also owned the Penny Pincher's Gazette—a free shopper newspaper, published every other week and filled with want ads. There were between 12 and 18 pages of ads in the Penny Pincher. It helped pay the bills.

Charlie Dillon was the station's morning "personality" responsible for signing on the station at 6 a.m. The first quarter-hour was a daily syndicated church program, followed by the California Farm Bureau report and a five-minute legislative update whenever the state Senate and Assembly were in session in Sacramento. The rest of the year, the update would be either a series of features of statewide interest or a Sierra and Mt. Shasta ski report. Charlie played music until my first newscast at 6:45. I had six 10-minute newscasts per day. I recorded the last two newscasts.

Unless some major news development happened after I went home at 2 p.m., the recording would play at 4:45 and 5:45.

I never did get used to hearing my own voice. It didn't sound like me.

The station signed off at midnight with the U.S. Air Force Band rendition of "The Star-Spangled Banner" or Kate Smith's "God Bless America."

The station owner believed it was important to get the name of every person in town on the radio at least once a year. That was easy when you reported on new businesses, high school football games, scholarships, city council or county supervisors meetings and Chamber of Commerce events. But eliminating "drunk and disorderly" stories made the job more challenging.

My job also included publishing a daily recap of the top local stories: The KBSC Bulletin. I composed the recap around 7 a.m., mimeographed the finished product and got it ready for distribution by a high school student before school started.

I loved the smell of that mimeograph.

Copies of the KBSC Bulletin were placed in the local coffee shop, the Five and Dime, the jewelry store, the feed store, Sambo's restaurant and the gas stations. If the business wasn't open, copies were simply left at the front door, held down with a rock.

Circulation of the KBSC Bulletin was about 300. Nice way to get some additional promotion for the radio station. And the Penny Pincher's Gazette.

I also provided stories for the Sacramento Bee and for United Press International.

UPI, along with the Associated Press, was one of two major news services in the U.S. In the news business, I was known as a "stringer." These stories gave me some additional spending money and occasionally a byline in the Superior California Section of the Bee. The Bee paid me by the column inch, extra if the story was moved to the front section of the paper and more yet if there was a photo. I had to keep track of the stories and file for reimbursement at the end of the month.

All of the stories were phoned in. You were assigned an "editor" who decided whether or not the story was newsworthy. If it was, the editor helped with wording and style. He would often ask questions to add a dimension to the story.

It wasn't Shakespeare.

UPI paid by the word. It's amazing how much detail you include when you are paid that way.

The station featured local phone-in talk shows. The most popular was "The Barter Bureau": a call-in show that allowed folks to advertise items for sale or trade.

It was amazing how much stuff people in a small town had to sell. The show ran 15 minutes Monday through Friday.

The music format featured what the broadcasting industry called "Middle of the Road" (MOR) music—not quite elevator music, not quite Top 40. It was also called Adult Oriented Radio—(AOR). Employees at the station thought AOR stood for "All

Over the Road."

The owner liked to call the music format "Bright and Happy." We called it "Light and Sappy."

I don't think the station owned a single record by the Doors.

Police news came from my radio scanner. Running day and night, the scanner would alert me to car accidents, robberies, burglaries and the like. If something piqued my interest, I would follow up in person the next morning at the police substation before my 6:45 newscast.

I'd have to go in person to read the report. If you phoned for information, police dispatchers were trained to say "nothing happened." There might have been a multiple murder, an explosion, a major derailment or a 12-car pile-up on the highway. Still, if you called, "nothing happened" was the standard dispatcher's reply.

In every town there are unofficial sources of news that keep no written record: barber shops, beauty salons and coffee shops. While beauty salons and barber shops had set hours of operation, in every town there's some place to have coffee at all hours of the day and night.

There was Sambo's Restaurant where tourists stopped. Visible from the highway, it was next to two gas stations.

Melva's Cafe was where the locals went. The coffee was always on and the food was pretty good. It was open 24 hours a day.

Melva's was fairly small. It had a long counter with 12 seats and six booths along the wall. There was also a large round table in the rear of the cafe. A tightly packed, full house was 40 people. That was pretty rare.

Melva's overnight cook, John, was wiry and tough. Great sense of humor. Great source of news, too. You knew John had been "around the block" a few times.

John quickly decided whether he liked you or he didn't. Fortunately, he liked me. For a while, John also served as KBSC's alarm clock. Charlie Dillon was known to oversleep. John got in the habit of calling Charlie 30 minutes before the station was supposed to sign on. A couple of weeks of John's crude, profanity-laden phone calls convinced Charlie to get up when his alarm clock went off. And to call John and tell him he was awake.

John showed me a Billy club he kept under the counter. He pointed out where he had slammed the club into the counter a few times to calm the occasional rowdy drunk who might stumble in. "That gets their attention, but I've never had to actually hit anybody."

Drop in on a coffee group and in no time you'd find out who was planning a run for office, whose wife was sleeping around, what the price of beef on the hoof was and, of course, a joke or two.

It was like a Boy Scout meeting without adult supervision.

Many of the jokes were about the town, of course. Like, "Before the lake, Sequoia City was too small to have a town drunk, so we all took turns." Then there was "Sequoia City is so small the 'Welcome' and the 'Thanks for Visiting' signs are on the same post." "If you turned on an electric razor, the trolley downtown would stop running." And, "In Sequoia City, 'formal wear' is a freshly washed and pressed pair of Levi's."

My predecessor attended one group every morning at 5 at Melva's. The group included a couple of businessmen (one who worked in Redding with a long commute), loggers and maybe a highway patrolman or sheriff's deputy.

Occasionally the city manager or a councilman would drop in.

A reporter showing up at a coffee group quickly stifles any conversation. The first time I showed up, it felt like a Western movie scene where someone walks into a packed bar: Everything goes quiet, the music stops, everyone stares at the newcomer and someone says "stranger in town."

Within a couple weeks of that initial "welcome," all I had to do was bring some local gossip, a great joke, agree to never report anything I couldn't verify elsewhere and I was "one of the guys" by the end of the month.

There were newspapers lying around on every table. The San Francisco Examiner (yesterday afternoon's edition) the San Francisco Chronicle (this morning's early edition), the Redding Record Searchlight and the Sacramento Bee.

Our group could sit absolutely quiet for 15 minutes while we read the papers, looking for a topic to start a conversation or an argument. Most coffee groups have one member who is a self-proclaimed expert on everything, who believes every crackpot theory and buys into every harebrained, get-rich-quick scheme. He's also the one who has never had an unexpressed thought. In our group it was Lou. We called him "Professor Lou" or "Dr. Lou." We tolerated the Professor because we could easily convince him it was his turn to buy the coffee. He obviously never kept track, because he got stuck with the tab twice as often as anyone else.

You'll put up with a lot for free coffee.

Occasionally, we'd find copies of The Spotlight on the newspaper rack near the counter. The Spotlight touted non-traditional medical treatments like laetrile for cancer. There were also articles on how to deal with the IRS and the "fact" that Gerald Ford and Jimmy Carter were hand-picked for their jobs by the Council on Foreign Relations and the Trilateral Commission. Both organizations were funded by the Rockefellers who supposedly wanted to create a one-world government. So, Spotlight readers were not surprised when Nelson Rockefeller was selected to be Gerald Ford's appointed vice president.

Not surprised at all.

The Spotlight believed the CIA was behind President Kennedy's murder in Dallas in 1963. The paper repeatedly called for reopening the investigation of the assassination.

The Spotlight was probably the most read newspaper in Sequoia City. That's why it took weeks for copies to make it to Melva's and the pages with the mail-in coupons to subscribe were usually missing.

S E V E N

Sequoia City
Cameron Evans

Cameron Evans owned the Clement Funeral Home in Sequoia City and served as the deputy county coroner. The county seat was 45 miles away, so it made sense to have someone other than a full-time county employee assigned the duties of the coroner in Sequoia City.

Cameron was among the first people I got to know in Sequoia City. There had been a terrible fatal traffic accident in the hills above the city early on a Saturday morning two weeks after I arrived in town.

The accident details were pretty straightforward. It happened around 2:30 a.m., involving a 33-year-old husband and father of two and a single, 23-year-old female companion. The accident occurred on a dark dirt road at a very high rate of speed. Added in to the mix was a borrowed Jeep, a nearly empty 12-pack of beer, a sharp corner and a 35-year-old Douglas fir tree just off the road. The result was two fatalities. Followed by an ugly scandal.

I talked to Cameron the next day and got as much information as I could for my radio story. It would be old news by the time the paper put out its next edition.

The local newspaper printed afternoon editions Monday through Friday. The Saturday paper was a morning edition. There was no Sunday paper. Saturday's paper was prepared the night before by reporters and staff who could wrap up by 10 p.m. and have the rest of the weekend off.

As a result, all of the newscasts on the station through Monday afternoon led with the headline "As we reported first on Saturday morning." I loved to poke at the newspaper. ("If you hear it, it's news. If you read it, it's history" was our favorite off mic comment at the station. The newspaper guys countered with "Radio is the media for people who can't read.")

Cameron was a great resource in town. He would call me if there was a story brewing or one I would be interested in. Cameron was a likable guy for a funeral director.

He also had an irreverent sense of humor. Once you got to know him and depending on where you saw him, he would take out a tape measure and say, "It's been kind of slow at the office and you're not looking so good. How do you feel?" Or, "We're running a 'turn yourself in' special down at the office. You ought to check it out." Or, "We're having a two-for-one sale on funerals this week. Know anyone you'd like to spend eternity with?" And sometimes, "We have a great family plan—one big casket, one huge hole in the ground and one hell of a big discount. Of course, you all have to die in the same week, but it is really a great discount."

Cameron was married with two children: a son, Herb, and a daughter, Eileen. Herb was 19 and attending college in Nevada on a football scholarship. Eileen was married and living in Phoenix.

E I G H T

The Playlist of My Life

I have music and song lyrics in my head. Always. I will be somewhere or see something or be doing something and the name of a song or a few lines of lyrics will pop into my head. They were all there.

"All Music. All the Time" is how radio stations promote their programming format. For me, the "All Music. All the Time" format was in my head. Nat King Cole. Santana. Henry Mancini. The Carpenters. Buffalo Springfield. My constant companions. In funny situations or serious or boring or frightening or stressful situations. They were all there in my head. The names of songs. The lyrics. The names of artists. Gordon Lightfoot. The Beatles. Todd Rundgren. Frank Sinatra. Lobo. I always have music and song lyrics playing in my head. It can be very distracting. My daily life was a radio playlist of "All Time Favorites." I never needed an imaginary friend. "The Greatest Hits of All Time" was the internal music of my life and often my best friend.

When I look back, the big and small events in my life all seem to have had theme songs. And it wasn't just situations that would bring a song to mind. I could meet someone for the first time and they would immediately remind me of a song or the lyrics or an artist.

By the time I got to high school, I had a record collection of more than 300 LPs and 45s. It was the envy among my few friends. My library was alphabetized, so I could find an artist quickly. I listened to music constantly. If anyone asked, I could tell them the song title, the artist's name and the year the song was popular. I would have been a champ on the "Name That Tune" game show.

Songs summed up highs and lows of my life. Once I actually wrote down the songs and the artists that played most often in my head. I'm sure with a little more thought I could develop a Top 100.

As the disc jockeys would say, "And the hits just keep on coming…"

I've learned "making love" is a lot more than just haunting and romantic lyrics or a powerful physical release. So much more, but that story comes later.

N I N E

My Apartment
North Bristlecone Street
Sequoia City, California

I lived in an apartment upstairs in a large family home at 1270 North Bristlecone Street. There wasn't a South Bristlecone Street.

The house had been in the family of Jim and Joyce Healy since it was built in 1910. Made of sturdy redwood and pine construction, the "craftsman style" house smelled old and comfortable.

The house was set back from the street in a neighborhood of other large, well maintained and vintage homes on large lots. The Healys came from "old money."

Until the early 1960s, one of the last narrow-gauge logging railroad lines in California ran just across the street from the Healy home.

Grandfather Horace (Mick) Healy was in the timber business. He owned the sawmill in town and the logging railroad. The mill processed hundreds of millions of board feet of virgin timber logs every year. The railroad brought the logs from the woods high in the foothills. Once processed, the finished product was then loaded onto standard-gauge rail cars for shipment throughout the West.

When I got to town, the sawmill was operating two eight-hour shifts, six days a week. The mill workforce was down a third over the past five years. The sawmill still used a "tepee" to dispose of wood scraps left over from processing logs. The tepee was a cone-shaped, multistory metal building with a fire burning inside 24 hours a day. The fire was fed by a large conveyor belt from the mill. Local residents could also scavenge wood scraps for firewood prior to disposal in the tepee. At night, the metal top of the tepee glowed red. Growing up in Sequoia City, one resident said she thought "hell" was inside the tepee, since you could see fire and it belched smoke day and night. The air in town, particularly when there was no breeze, smelled like a campfire. In its heyday, with the mill operations running 24 hours a day, the noise level in town was always high. Residents said they had no problem sleeping through shift whistles, log dumps off trains or trucks or the constant hum of the massive steam boiler and enormous saw blades running at incredible RPMs. But, if plant operations shut down for any reason, everyone in town woke up.

My apartment was carved out of the top floor of the home. Jim and Joyce, now well into their 70s, no longer wanted to trudge upstairs and had arranged their living quarters on the first floor.

The apartment at the Healys was the first place I looked at. I paid $75 a month rent including water, garbage, electricity and gas heat in the winter. Jim and Joyce appreciated having someone younger living in the house. Money was not an issue in their decision.

My apartment was at the top of the main stairs, located just inside the front door. My room had been their daughter's until she married and moved out of town. When she moved, Jim and Joyce remodeled the room, added a small kitchen and added a closet, which was built in front of a window. I suppose it was cheaper than covering up the window or provided better light.

The bathroom only had a tub, no shower. I would have to give up the idea of a "quick shower" in favor of a not so quick bath.

I had been living in a room above the radio station. While it had a bath and kitchen, it was clear this arrangement was temporary. The station owner indicated the more temporary the arrangement the better. The apartment was reserved for the station's out-of-town partner who lived in the San Francisco Bay area.

So, the Healy apartment was perfect. Except it had been their daughter's room and was a vision in pink. With pink wallpaper. And roses. And lace curtains.

. Joyce said they would re-paper the walls and paint the apartment any color I wanted. I chose dark blue for the bedroom, a light blue for the bathroom and a pale yellow for the kitchen. Boy were those fancy choices for a guy. Every other place I lived, including the dorms at college, offered three color shades: ivory, white or egg-shell.

The lace curtains were replaced with pull down window shades.

It took a couple of weeks before the redecorating job was done, so I decided not to invite anybody over until then.

There was also a stairway in the back of the apartment at the rear of a large, enclosed sun porch. The back staircase led to the Healys backyard, which was fenced with a gate. At the bottom of the stairs, the back door had a window and the entry was protected by a small overhang. Perfect for coming and going in all kinds of weather and at all hours.

Most of the time, I used the back stairs although I did have a key to the front door.

The sun porch was added on to the house about 15 years before I moved in. In the late fall, winter and early spring, the sun porch was great. Large screened windows could be opened to let fresh air in. Even on a cold day, the porch was comfortable.

The architect and contractor apparently never considered the western exposure of the porch. In the summer time, with temperatures at or near 100 outside, the porch became an oven. Jim and Joyce eventually installed two doors as a cushion between the porch and the inside. They also installed a couple of air conditioners, one in the window in the bedroom and one just off the area that was now the kitchen.

My buddy Ed Thatcher was a regular visitor. We spent a lot of time together during the week and on the weekends.

On more than one occasion, on early evenings with a heavy wind blowing, we would open all the windows, put towels around the bottom of the apartment doors and smoke a couple of joints. On those nights, I made sure I had plenty of Granny Goose potato chips in the cupboard. It's amazing how many chips you can eat when you're stoned.

Still, it was pretty risky in a town like Sequoia City. Some Sundays in the late fall, we'd sit on the porch on a couple of patio lounge chairs and listen to an Oakland Raiders game on the radio. We would drink a jug of Gallo Hearty Burgundy and eat whatever was in the refrigerator.

We'd talk about town politics, sports and all the women we'd never slept with.
Just lazy afternoons.
The sun, the wine and the drone of the radio made it easy to nod off.
When we woke up, we kidded each other that "we had just slept together."
It was just a joke.
We weren't queer.

T E N

Sequoia City Bulletin
Ed Thatcher

Ed Thatcher had gone to journalism school at San Francisco State. It was just after the period of campus riots. The riots led to the rise of S.I. Hayakawa, the school dean who would be elected to the U.S. Senate in 1976.

Ed was a year younger than me. We were both single and got to know each other covering the same news stories and at civic meetings.

Ed's predecessor at the paper was usually drunk when he showed up for the evening city council meetings. The council had a "press table" for the two of us, located between the audience and the council. The last time I saw Ed's predecessor (Tim?), he showed up late, drunk, and in a loud voice said to me and, as it turns out, everyone within earshot, "I would have been here sooner, but my girlfriend and I were screwing."

Apparently a call from the mayor to the paper's editor the next morning ended Tim's (?) career at the Sequoia City Bulletin. At least I think the guy's name was Tim. I guess it really doesn't matter now. Ed showed up to cover the next council meeting.

Ed lived in a converted caboose next to a trailer park. The rent was really cheap. Neither of us was sure if the caboose was actually a legal residence, but he did get mail delivered and there was a rural electric company meter outside.

The rear of the caboose was a great place for Ed's hibachi.

It was also a great place for our first and only venture into the criminal underworld. We tried growing some marijuana plants from seed. Later, we decided that probably wasn't too smart. Besides, the plants didn't do so well, so we tossed them in the garbage. We stuck to drinking Miller Lite and smoking the occasional joint from a dime bag.

Ed loved hiking and rock climbing. He had gone on a number of field trips in college and got hooked. The foothills east of Sequoia City were perfect. Sometimes he would go with another buddy, sometimes he would go alone.

He and I hiked in and around Burney Falls east of Redding. Teddy Roosevelt said Burney Falls was one of the Eight Wonders of the World. We also took the 7-mile round trip hike into Feather Falls east of Oroville.

We hiked Lassen Peak, which has tough, non-technical climbs to the summit. Lassen Peak has an elevation of just over 10,000 feet at the southern end of the Cascades.

Twice we tried to climb Mt. Shasta. It's the fifth-highest mountain in California and second-highest mountain in the Cascade Range. At 14,179 feet, it's just 250 feet lower than the summit of Mount Rainier.

Like the other peaks in the Cascade Range, Mt. Shasta is a dormant volcano. It has three dormant volcano cones making up the summit.

If you get an early enough start from a base camp located around 7,000 feet you can make it to the summit of Shasta and back to base camp in one day. You have to hustle, but it can be done. Both times, though, bad weather cut our climbs well short of the peak.

Ed and I camped out whenever we could. Those were fun times.

After dinner, we'd sit around a campfire drinking Kahlua or smoking a joint and talking nonsense until 2 or 3 in the morning. "Getting high and talking shit" was what we called it. When we weren't laughing, we knew our alcohol-or pot-inspired "deep" conversations put us on the verge of changing the world.

On one of our trips, I must have shared more about my upbringing than usual because Ed made a comment that really struck me. I don't remember the exact context but it stuck with me nonetheless.

"Weak parents," he said, "raise strong children. Strong parents raise weak children. Weak children can only become strong when their parents step back and let them become the heroes of their own lives. Like it or not, Mark, you were raised by both kinds of parents: weak and strong. You grew up. Now you can be the hero of your own life. You're free."

At the time, I played down the comment, kidding Ed that he sounded like Keith Carradine on the "Kung Fu" TV series. "Yes, Grasshopper, you are wise beyond your years" I said and the conversation moved on.

But his statement stayed with me.

Ed was the best friend I would ever have.

E L E V E N

Sequoia City
Gerry Apte

"Jackie Blue"—Ozark Mountain Daredevils

The first thing you noticed about Gerry Apte was his eyes.

They were nearly a transparent blue gray. Striking. His hair was silver and he was always ready with a smile. Combined with a persuasive and charming personality, many women considered him one of the sexiest men in town. He loved the role and played it well.

Gerry (Gerald was his legal name) was what Southerners might call a Carpetbagger. He and Bobby Laine showed up when there were only preliminary discussions about the Sequoia Lake project. How Gerry and Bobby originally got acquainted was a local mystery, although the phrase "birds of a feather" comes to mind.

Bobby was the "face" of the Sequoia Land Development Company. He was president and, as such, signed the documents of incoporation. He also oversaw all of the financial disclosures, minimal as they were, and the disbursements from the corporate checking account. He was active in the community, serving as president of the Chamber of Commerce Board of Directors and as treasurer of the local Rotary Club.

Gerry, on the other hand, called himself the "silent partner" in the corporation, quickly adding "the one with the money." He and Bobby were equally involved in every aspect of the operation although there was very little paperwork actually linking Gerry to the corporation's activities.

Gerry and Bobby funded the Sequoia Land Development Corporation with $75,000 each. Bobby funded his half with liens against his home and other assets. Bobby often said he was too broke to file bankruptcy. He would often smile and ask, "If you owe a million dollars, does that make you a millionaire?"

Gerry's contribution came from a signature line of credit set up through a local savings and loan.

Then, working illegally with state land surveyors, they identified parcels near the shoreline of the proposed reservoir. Gerry said it was easy to find a willing surveyor. "It all boils down to money and everybody needs or wants more than they have," he said.

It didn't matter to Bobby or Gerry that California law required development setbacks from a reservoir. In some cases, the setbacks extended more than a mile from the shore.

They would buy options on a square mile of land, 640 acres, for $75 an acre. Market prices for similar land at the time were $50 per acre. Gerry and Bobby gave the owner $10 an acre as a down payment. The seller was always paid in cash and was convinced to defer future payments for at least a year. After that, Gerry and Bobby might pay a few dollars a month but not enough to make a dent in their bank accounts or the $48,000 purchase price.

Most of the owners had inherited their land, with some deeds going back to the Gold Rush days. These owners were pleased to have anyone interested in buying their land. Because of the terrain, most of the property was useless even for cattle grazing.

When the lake filled, Gerry and Bobby had options on three square miles of land, just under 2,000 acres.

At the same time, through an intricate system of fraudulent maneuvers, Bobby and Gerry divided the land into smaller parcels, circumventing a California legal process known as "4 by 4." State real estate law requires a subdivision map to be submitted after a parcel, regardless of size, is divided into four separate lots.

Subdivision maps detail the availability of water and utility services, access to the property and building site possibilities, including whether the land would support a septic system.

When the original 640 acres was split into four 160-acre parcels, any further division by the same owner would trigger the requirement of a subdivision map.

To get around the subdivision map requirement, Gerry and Bobby developed a process of making up names, using distant family relations, names of towns, even paying members attending AA meetings to sign deeds. They repeatedly transferred ownership back and forth. Each fraudulent "new" owner was then allowed to split a parcel four times. Once the splits were completed, ownership would be transferred to a new fraudulent owner who could then split the parcels four more times.

Cooperative or, in some cases, coerced employees at a local title company would notarize dozens of these property title transfers without ever witnessing the signatures of the "owners." Title companies are supposed to oversee property transfers and protect buyers, but hundreds of phony deeds were notarized without a single question being asked. When the house of cards fell, these same title companies would pay significant fines to state and local agencies. Some employees served prison time.

When all the final splits and transfers were complete, Gerry and Bobby owned 640 one-acre parcels. They advertised in newspapers throughout Southern California and Nevada acreage property "with lake views" or "within walking distance of California's newest lake."

Selling price was $750 for one acre or $2,500 for five acres.

The ads asked for a $100 down payment and monthly installments of $10 per month. Most buyers never visited the property or requested a legal description. Years later they would discover their parcel might be on a 35-degree slope or there was no road access or water or the soil would not "perk" to support a septic system. Many were stunned to find out utility services or the lake itself were miles away.

Similar land fraud schemes were springing up in Nevada, New Mexico and Arizona.

Gerry and Bobby 's minimal investment for 640 acres was quickly recouped from the down payments of out-of-town buyers. The remaining payments received on the parcels, with interest, would yield them at least a million dollars.

Later, when everything unraveled, there were questions about whether the IRS was aware of these "transactions." "Unlikely" was the most common answer.

California penalties for land fraud are severe. Most are felonies and carry jail sentences. Each time a parcel was split and the deed recorded fraudulently, a felony was committed. State law does not allow these crimes to be charged as misdemeanors. The state Legislature's intent was to emphasize the severity of land fraud crime in California.

Sequoia City at the time resembled a boom town of the Old West. Legitimate real estate agents balked at the process Bobby and Gerry employed, but seemed powerless to stop them.

No one was quite sure where Gerry or Bobby got their money in the first place.

Some said Gerry had been a developer in Southern California building large housing tracts or shopping centers. Others thought he inherited his money or ran a chain of liquor stores in the San Francisco Bay area. Some even thought he might be "connected."

By the time the first land surveyors completed their measurements for the Sequoia Lake reservoir, Gerry and Bobby were on their way to being major landowners. The lake project quickly drove up the value of their land.

Gerry Apte: a carpetbagger.

He said he was married, although no one had ever met his wife. Gerry said she lived in Southern California. Gerry said her "business interests kept her in the L.A. area. Once she is out from under those, she'll be moving up here."

That was his story anyway. If he did have a wife, theirs was truly a marriage of convenience. There was probably too much money and too many illegal activities between them to bring into open divorce court.

I suspected Gerry's wife was running guns or was a major drug dealer.

Neither was probably true, but since no one had ever met her, it certainly made her more interesting.

Gerry didn't wear a wedding ring and certainly never acted as if he were married. He usually had at least one girlfriend in town. He was never ashamed or embarrassed to be seen in public with them. And it was obvious they were more than just "company" to Gerry. For a woman to be seen with Gerry could either enhance or ruin her reputation.

He was the only person I knew with a key to the Playboy Club in San Francisco. Gerry was 64 years old. He could be very charming, but he could also make you feel uneasy. "A little too slick" or "a little too Hollywood" was how longtime residents described him.

You often wanted to shower after being in the same room with Gerry. Kind of the way Jimmy Stewart reacted after shaking Lionel Barrymore's hand in "It's a Wonderful Life."

Gerry and Bobby had a business office downtown in a building nicknamed by town residents "Alibaba's Place—the Den of 40 Thieves." Gerry also owned a bar called The Rip Roarin' a couple of blocks away. The Rip Roarin' had a full liquor license, but most patrons ordered beer and wine. During the hot months, the bar did a lot of business in wine coolers.

The Rip Roarin' had sawdust on the floor everywhere except the dance floor. It was supposed to be swept out and changed every day. I don't think that ever happened and I doubt anyone ever checked. Or cared.

The Rip Roarin' served sandwiches, pizza and hamburgers. On weekdays, before 5, there was one waitress on duty and a bartender who doubled as the cook. It did a brisk lunch business Monday through Friday. On Thursday, Friday and Saturday nights, there were usually two bartenders and two waitresses. It was not unusual to wait at least 25 minutes for your food order.

The Rip Roarin' was "the place" in town. It had a band every Friday and Saturday night. Mostly Western music, but sometimes rock and roll. Great place for a good time. Or a fist fight. In addition to his business office downtown, Gerry had an office on the second floor of The Rip Roarin'. When you walked in, the bar was to the left, the stage and dance floor were straight ahead. There were square and circular tables scattered around the room. To the right were stairs leading to Gerry's office, with a small landing at the top.

Gerry's office was quite large and the windows allowed him to keep an eye on the bar activities and patrons below.

He could spot a woman looking for company or drowning her sorrows from his office window. He'd be downstairs in a heartbeat, buying her "another" one and chatting her up. Often, Gerry would escort her upstairs.

They'd be gone a while.

> *"You like your life in a free form style. You'll take an inch, but you'd love a mile. There never seems to be quite enough floating around to fill your loving cup."*

It never bothered Gerry, or he didn't care to notice, that they might be married. As long as they were over 21, Gerry was "on." One of the regular band members was convinced someday a jealous husband would shoot him instead of Gerry in a case of mistaken identity. "The husband always assumes it's a guy in the band that's banging his wife," he said.

> *"Don't try to tell me that you're not aware of what you're doing and that you don't care. You say it's easy, just a natural thing, like playing music but you never sing..."*

Smooth when he was involved with a fraudulent piece of undeveloped land or on the make with women in his bar. A little too slick to everyone else.

American humorist Will Rogers once said he never met a man he didn't like. He'd never met Gerry.

> *"...Lives a dream that can never come true. Making love is like sifting through sand...it slips through your hands..."*

T W E L V E

The Great American Novel

Someone said there's a book in everyone, even if it's only their autobiography. I know a lot of folks whose autobiography would not be a book. It would be a very short story, in a pamphlet, about the length of a religious tract.

Like most reporters, I believed I was a budding mystery writer. In college, I heard a review of Robert Ludlum's "The Scarlatti Inheritance" on a PBS radio station and couldn't wait to get a copy. After that, I was hooked. Ludlum had a knack for intertwining historical facts and a fictional story line and making it believable.

Plots, scenarios, mysteries, conspiracies. They all flooded through my brain. They competed and often overlapped with the lyrics and music in my head.

I bought lots of books on writing. The books stressed that a writer should have the end of the book in mind before starting. The writer also needs to keep track of characters, the timeline of events and locations, the personalities of the villains and heroes all the while making sure they are always "true" to themselves. It was recommended that an author make an outline of the story line before committing a single word to paper.

I didn't think I had time to do all that prep work. So, I pulled out the Hermes typewriter I got for graduation and started work on what I knew would eventually be a best seller. My book would involve an exotic, mysterious foreign country, political intrigue and the president of the United States. It was the perfect combination for what I knew critics would one day hail as The Great American Novel. So, I decided to use Mark's Great American Novel as the working title for my book, at least until I can come up with something more creative. And original.

Mark's Great American Novel begins and ends in India.

MARK'S GREAT AMERICAN NOVEL
Chapter One

Rajasthan, India
May 10, 1957

The protagonist in my book is a young man named Zia Dhawan, a Sanskrit name that roughly translates to "messenger on the field of battle."

Zia was born in Rajasthan, India, on May 10, 1956, five years to the day after I was born. The temperature on the day he was born reached an all-time record in Rajasthan: 123 degrees.

When he was older, Zia heard stories, probably fables, about the day the heat record was set. In the fields, he was told, the ground was so hot that millions of insects burrowed to the top of the ground only to perish in the blistering heat on the surface.

The state of Rajasthan, India, is the largest in the country, covering more than 10 percent of the land mass. Rajasthan literally means "Land of Great Kings" or "Land of Great Kingdoms." It is slightly smaller than the state of Illinois.

Rajasthan became a state in India on November 1, 1956.

The Great Indian Desert in Rajasthan forms a natural boundary with Pakistan and is located in the northern part of India. The desert covers more than 80 percent of Rajasthan and is characterized by huge, shifting dunes. Rainfall in the area runs between 4 and 20 inches annually, falling primarily in the monsoon season between July and September.

In spite of the harsh conditions, agriculture accounts for about a quarter of the state's economy. There are two growing seasons. Winter crops are planted in October and November and include wheat, barley, rape, mustard and oil seeds. These are harvested in March and April.

The other growing season starts with planting in June and July and the crops are harvested three months later. Maize and ground nuts are among the chief crops.

The land is harsh and the growing conditions fierce. Zia's father etched out a living in the fields.

Zia was one of nine children, although six of his siblings died before they were 10 years old. Zia remembered lean times when food and water were in short supply. He remembered the smoky fires in the kitchen, built on the dirt floor of the house and fueled by dried cow manure. The smoke helped keep the flies out of the kitchen and with a side benefit for the cook who rarely had eye infections. The smoke in the air kept their eyes constantly watering.

He grew up in a small nondescript village, one of more than 30,000 in Rajasthan. He was personable, outgoing and intelligent, although some saw him as manipulative and cunning. Heartless at times. Even ruthless. There always seemed to be something simmering just beneath his affable appearance.

Zia liked to win: at cricket, at games of chess or in debates with his parents, classmates or siblings. He was aggressive on the playing field, occasionally injuring a fellow player. Zia could calmly walk off the field as if nothing had happened, never even looking back or showing any concern. Zia remained unfazed or even surprised to find out the severity of the other player's injuries.

In debates, his arguments were compelling and convincing. If he sensed he was losing, he was not beyond overwhelming his opponents with an aggressive verbal strategy, often bending the rules of fair debate.

It was evident early on that Zia would be the first person from his village to go to a university.

Whatever insecurities he might harbor were never evident to family, friends or strangers. He appeared comfortable in every setting but adopted a rigid, chiseled personal life.

He never talked about his background.

In college, when asked, he simply said, "it doesn't matter where I was born, it only matters where I am now."

It was at the end of his second year of studies that friends and family noticed a change in his personality. He became more outspoken and often argumentative. He challenged everyone on almost every subject: the weather, soccer matches, crop yields but especially politics. On more than one occasion, his father or mother would tell him to rein in his opinions and lower his voice.

His personal habits became even more ascetic.

During that second school year, Zia worked part time at a five-star hotel near the university. The sharp contrast between the wealth of the guests and the poverty of those employed at the hotel festered in his thinking.

He started a journal and wrote about work, his studies, his bitterness, the unfairness of modern life, the difference between the rich and poor and so on. Everything made his journal.

At university, he gravitated toward others who shared his views about the inequalities in the world. They were particularly angered by the toxic impact of western culture. India had won its independence from Britain in 1948, when the country was divided in two: Pakistan and India. Vestiges of two centuries of British rule were everywhere: social clubs, dirt-covered squash courts, polo fields, railroads and the architecture of public buildings.

At home on holiday, he would spend hours writing in the journal. He shared a bedroom with two younger brothers, but was careful to take the journal with him at all times, even to the toilet. During meals, he sat on the journal, much to the amusement of his brothers. His parents would exchange glances and simply roll their eyes.

During his junior and senior years, he was even more radical in his views and angrier.

He found more excuses and reasons not to come home during holiday or class breaks.

Midway through his junior year, the idea on how to meaningfully change the world occurred to him.

Zia developed a close relationship with fellow student Johar Kaniyar, who also worked part time at the hotel. In Sanskrit, Kaniyar translates to "those who calculate." Their friendship evolved during long, often lively conversations about the way things are and the way they should be. On more than one of these occasions, their conversations, beginning at an evening meal, ended when the sun came up the following morning.

At the university, it was easy to find others passionate about changing the world. As their friendship deepened, Zia and Johar devised a system to determine the sincerity and commitment of others who might be interested in an evolving and potentially violent plan. Initially, Zia would casually, carefully drop hints to friends or classmates as a way of sounding them out. Johar would then meet with them separately and talk some more.

Their responses would determine if there would be a next step in the relationship.

The system Zia and Johar developed was similar to aviation holding patterns.

When weather or other factors force delays at an airport, incoming flights are stacked into holding patterns. These patterns space airliners out for miles and at different altitudes. Depending on weather or conditions on the ground, air traffic controllers can expand or contract holding patterns, shortening or lengthening the time the flights remain airborne. Unless a pilot declares a low fuel warning or fuel emergency, planes take their place in the pattern and eventually work their way to the front of the line for landing.

After numerous meetings, alternating between light and serious discussions, eventually there would be one final intense interview. At that point, Zia and Johar would determine if a person could join their group or remain in a holding pattern.

After members were selected and the team was finalized, they agreed they would meet and stay at a low cost tourist hotel in Delhi. There would be weeks of planning ahead.

Their plot was set. The timetable already in motion.

They would change the world.

50

THIRTEEN

Schiller Park, Illinois

I went back to see my father once when I was 13. He had remarried. She was an equally horrid woman. At least they married each other and didn't ruin two other families.

"Sit Down Young Stranger"—Gordon Lightfoot

The week I was there, the only spare time he had for me was at dinner. On Sunday, he dropped me off on the Magnificent Mile, told me to look around, meet him there in four hours, and emphasized, "Don't be late."

I got his meaning. He hadn't changed.

On the last night of my stay, at dinner, I quickly figured out what was going on. I'd seen it before: The dirty looks across the dinner table, the short, angry demands to pass him something and answering questions with a grunt or two. Then there was the way he attacked the food on his plate. I'm surprised he didn't break the plate the way he jammed his knife and fork into it.

I knew what was coming. He was going to spank me tonight.

I finished my food and excused myself. I felt very, very warm—hot actually—from the inside out. I felt as if my head was about to burst into flames. Blood rushed and pounded in my ears. There were no melodies in my head now. It sounded more like a rock band and an orchestra tuning up at the same time. The noise was excruciating.

I'd never felt this way before. My hands were visibly shaking, too.

I helped clear the table, washed the dishes and went to my room. While I was packing, my father came in, slammed the door, started screaming something about my attitude. When he grabbed me, I shook him off. Actually, I fought back.

He was stunned.

When he grabbed for me again, I turned away and slammed my elbow into his ribs, followed by my fists. I punched him several times. Hard. I knocked the wind out of him.

I was screaming obscenities. I was out of control and couldn't stop hammering him with my fists. It was an uncontrollable fury.

I never hit him in the face. Grandpa told me that hitting someone in the face only bruises their ego because they have to explain to everyone what happened. And they heal quickly. Besides, a son hitting his father would lead to a lot more questions and probably an arrest. Hitting someone in the ribs and stomach is a lot more effective way to kick somebody's ass. They remember it longer—like every time they cough or laugh or sneeze. For weeks afterward.

Our wrestling match couldn't have lasted 25 seconds. My father broke down and left the room sobbing.

His little boy had grown up.

I heard him in the living room for the next 20 minutes ranting: half crying, half shouting about what a son of a bitch I had become.

"He's probably not even my kid, his mom was always sleeping around."

For the first time ever in his apartment, I locked my door. He could kick the door down for all I cared. He wasn't going to get another opportunity to hit me tonight. Or, for that matter, ever again.

I wondered if he had a gun. If he did, he would probably kill me.

This was just like the old days. I don't know why I came to see him. Why did I think it would be different this time?

Over the years, Mom and Grandpa encouraged me to call him every couple of months on a Sunday, when long distance rates were the lowest: three minutes for a dollar. Our conversations were short, never sweet and pretty one sided. I never had to worry about spending more than a dollar on our conversations.

All I ever wanted to hear was, "Sounds like things are really going well," or "How are you doing?" or, for that matter, to show any interest in any aspect of my life. But there was nothing. Just a couple of noncommittal, "That's nice." It seemed he was anxious to get off the phone.

So once again tonight, in my father's apartment, I was alone and afraid. But I wasn't afraid of him anymore. Now I am afraid of what's bottled up inside me. While I was hitting him, I was out of control. I couldn't, didn't want to, stop. I felt like a boxer in a ring with his opponent on the ropes.

I think I could have killed him.

What was also unsettling was that my new fear was accompanied by a profound sense of relief.

Later in college, a professor I knew said that beating a pillow with a tennis racket was a good way to release built-up tension and anger.

Tonight I found another way.

The previous few minutes, though, were a blur. I was breathing and sweating heavily. Tears were running down my cheeks, but I refused to cry or sob out loud. He would never see or think of me as weak again.

For a few moments, I thought I was going to throw up or pass out. Physically and mentally exhausted, I collapsed on the bed and went to sleep in my clothes. I don't think it was even 8 o'clock.

The next morning my father left for work without telling me goodbye.

My father and I never spoke again.

His wife barely acknowledged my departure when the cab arrived to take me to the airport.

As I left, I thanked God neither one of them ever insisted I call that woman "mom."

When I got home, I found all sorts of reasons to avoid calling him. Only once, months later, did Grandpa press me to ask why. Sensing there was no answer I was willing to share, he didn't pursue the matter and dropped it altogether.

When I think about it, I saw my father twice on that visit: the first and last time. Ever.

Less than a year later, he dropped dead of a heart attack. I didn't go to the funeral but I did sleep better at night. My father took the secret of our fist fight to his grave. For a long time I never mentioned it to anyone either. I was sure I would get arrested.

Years later, Grandpa told me that no matter what kind of relationship you have with your parents, you will miss them when they're gone.

I think that was the only time Grandpa was ever wrong.

Grandpa, though, was a great guy. After we moved in, the first time he raised his voice, I burst into tears and cowered, waiting for him to hit me.

He must have talked to Mom, because after that Grandpa never raised his voice to me again. And never laid a hand on me. Not once. When I did something wrong, he would sit me down and talk to me. Sternly. Clearly. He would make me look him in the eye, but he never yelled again. He made his points directly. There was no chance of misunderstanding him. There was no "wiggle" room in these conversations.

I did my best not to disappoint him. He seemed more like a dad than a grandpa.

Fridays we would go to a movie or work in the garage. Most of the time I think I was just in the way, but he never seemed to mind. Sometimes we would go to the dump and see what we could find. Amazing the perfectly good stuff people throw out.

He always seemed to find the right moment to bring up serious stuff: like school or homework, college plans or sex. Grandpa seemed to know as much about sex as the guys at school.

The most daring thing I ever did in high school was sneak into a hotel swimming pool with another kid from my class. It was during an unusual hot spell. We were caught after 15 minutes and asked to leave. They never asked our names or called Mom or Grandpa or the police, but I still felt like a criminal. I was on edge for days believing my "crime" would come to light and I would end up disappointing people.

Grandpa was a nice man, but not very physically affectionate. I only remember him hugging me once in my life. In retrospect, I guess that didn't matter much, because I never really trusted another adult man, before or since.

FOURTEEN

I loved going to the movies. Like sleep and music, movies were a great escape from the reality and fears of life.

There were three theatres within a mile of my grandparents' house.

The Coronado Theater showed the big box office, first-run movies like "Sound of Music," "Dr. Zhivago," "Lawrence of Arabia," and "Cleopatra," on 70 mm film with stereo sound. They were billed as "World Premier Events", unveiled at the same time at exclusive theatres throughout the country.

The theater would have two showings a day, seven days a week. I still get turned on thinking about the scene with Omar Sharif and Julie Christie in bed for the first time in "Dr. Zhivago." Pretty hot scene for the time. My teenage hormones were in full bloom.

For at least eight weeks, tickets had to be purchased days in advance for the showing you wanted to attend. Seats were assigned and reserved. It was expensive, too. Matinées were $5. Evening performances were $7.50.

In the lobby, before the show, large glossy souvenir programs were available for purchase. The programs had features on the stars and a behind the scenes look at the production of the movie. There was usually a story about the planning needed to bring the story to the big screen. I saved a number of the programs. They are in my apartment somewhere.

The movies at The Coronado always had an overture with highlights of the score. The overture was usually five minutes long. The theater lights were dimmed slightly at the start. The theater got progressively darker throughout the overture and would be completely dark when the film started.

Throughout an intermission, there would also be music playing. The Coronado also had the best popcorn in town. And you never found gum stuck on the bottom of the seats or on the floor.

It was exciting to go to shows at The Coronado. It felt like a Hollywood premiere, with searchlights outside the theater at night. Most of the time the audience applauded at the end of the film. It was also a theater you didn't go to unless you dressed up a bit.

If the film was very popular, the newspaper ads said things like "Held over for two more weeks" or "Performances sold out until next week" or "By popular demand, schedule extended indefinitely."

Art Gilmore could be heard on the radio advertising for these blockbusters. You could also hear his voice on the upcoming movie trailers. He was the voice who introduced the "Red Skelton Show." He seemed to be everywhere. What a voice!

The Orpheum Theater showed current first-run movies a few weeks after their exclusive "World Premiere" ended at the Coronado. These were shown in 35 mm at The Orpheum and didn't require special sound or projecting equipment. Tickets were less expensive and the popcorn was OK. Normally, The Orpheum would show films three or four times a day, advertised as "Continuous showings throughout the day."

Tickets were cheaper prior to 6 o'clock. And ushers cleared out the theater at the end of every showing.

The Encore Theater was the one I went to most. These were movies that were popular 12 to 18 months earlier. Admission was the cheapest in town, usually $1.50 per ticket, but Saturday and Sunday showings started at 10 a.m. and ticket prices were 75 cents until 2 p.m. I went to The Encore a lot when I was growing up. The floors were always sticky.

When I got to Sequoia City, the one movie theater was a bit of a letdown, but I still spent a lot of time there. Saturday afternoons. Sometimes on Wednesday and Friday nights.

It was easy to lose oneself in the story lines, characters and scenery and not have to deal with the world outside for a couple of hours. It was a shock walking out of the dark air-conditioned theater after a matinée, into the bright, hot sunshine.

FIFTEEN

In late June, our coffee group solved, at least in our minds and in the minds of local authorities, one of Sequoia City's great mysteries: what happened to Bobby Laine.

The story of Bobby's disappearance was, of course, big news in Sequoia City. His picture was on the front page of the Sequoia City Bulletin several days running with the latest details of the ongoing search. Detectives were looking into every possible lead, even checking with airlines serving Redding, Chico and Sacramento to see if Bobby had booked a flight out of the area.

Jack Reynolds of the Creekside Bait and Tackle Shop provided the best, although for some, not the definitive clue as to Bobby's last hours on earth. Jack was an occasional drop-in to our group, usually in the late spring and summer months, when his business was booming and the store needed to be open early.

Bobby's disappearance was being discussed one morning when Jack casually mentioned he'd sold fishing waders to Bobby in the late afternoon on Memorial Day. Jack remembered Bobby because he came in just as the store was closing. Bobby was the first customer Jack had seen in more than an hour. Most of the shop's business was done by 10 that morning as the "weekend fishermen" were wrapping up their trip and heading home.

Jack said Bobby obviously knew nothing about fishing, had no interest in finding where the "fish were biting" or even the best places to catch sturgeon, stripers or steelhead in the river. He didn't care where to find trout or bass in the lake either. Jack said he could not engage Bobby in any conversations about bait, rods or reels. Nothing. Not even whether he needed a fishing license. At the time, Jack said, the only thing that interested Bobby was the selection of waders the store displayed.

Bobby chose the largest and loosest fitting waders off the display shelf. Jack suggested better fitting, smaller waders. Bobby said, "These will be fine," but Jack could still not coax an answer as to where Bobby intended to fish. Bobby bought the waders for $33.95. Including the 6 percent California sales tax, the total was $35.99. Jack said Bobby paid him with a $50 bill, took the waders and didn't wait for a receipt or change.

"Except for some great fishing spots over the years, it was the best tip I ever got from a customer in this business," Jack said with a smile.

For a brief moment, the group sat in stunned silence, then looked, in unison, at Jack.

"What did I say, guys?" Jack asked. "What? Really, people don't tip me. It was the biggest tip I'd ever gotten."

I'm not sure who spoke first, but someone finally said, "Jesus, Jack, did you think to tell the cops that story about the waders? That might be a pretty important clue, don't you think, Jack?"

Jack looked bewildered. Apparently, it hadn't occurred to him until just now. Perhaps he'd been selling bait too long. Or night crawlers. Whatever it was, some of Jack's brain cells had definitely "gone fishing."

I was able to report this new clue and connection during my 6:45 newscast that morning. I literally was typing the last words of the story when the theme music for the news started to play on the air. I was out of breath which made the story sound more dramatic.

My opening teaser was a classic: "New clues this morning indicate Bobby Laine may be at the bottom of Sequoia Lake. Details coming up right after this." The station went to a commercial break after a rundown of the morning headlines. The sponsor in that slot that morning certainly got their money's worth.

Just after 8 o'clock, I called the sheriff's office to bring them up to speed, but a detective heard the newscast and was in the process of tracking down a 19-year-old marina employee named Everett.

It would take a few days to piece together what apparently happened although some people were never satisfied.

The mystery began to clear up when Everett was questioned at length. No, he hadn't taken anyone by shuttle to the houseboat in several weeks. He was pretty sure Bobby rented one of the marina's boats around the time of his disappearance, but Everett needed a photograph to make a positive ID.

"Yeah, that's the guy. He rented the fishing boat around 7 or so." Everett said Bobby paid cash, didn't wait for his change and said he would be back before dark.

Everett didn't think anything of it when Bobby didn't return the boat by the time he left work at 9. "Where was he going to go? Once in a while, we have folks rent boats and keep them overnight, even a couple of days. They just pay the extra rental fee when they come back. Where was he going to go? I didn't have to work for a couple of days after that and the boat was in the rental slip when I did come back."

Investigators had lots of questions. "Was he alone? Did he seem intoxicated or under the influence of drugs? Did he look clean cut or disheveled? Haven't you seen any of the newspaper stories or picture?"

When asked, and after thinking a moment more, Everett said Bobby could have had something under his arm. "I'm not sure. He might have had waders when he rented the boat." The boat was empty when it was recovered.

The sheriff's officer met with the D.A. and the deputy county coroner. Unless he "surfaced," Bobby couldn't be legally declared dead for seven years. Nonetheless, the agencies involved were satisfied and announced the case closed two days later.

Whatever their personal suspicions or the reasons surrounding Bobby's disappearance, there was no evidence of foul play. His death was ruled an "accidental drowning."

While the mystery of Bobby's disappearance was not completely solved, local bankers, originally lured to underwrite seemingly profitable loans on the property around the lake, scrambled to repackage their loans. Our radio station was inundated with large advertising buys touting great deals on "the last waterfront property in California."

With the legal clouds hanging over the Sequoia Land Development Corporation, it was hard to imagine anyone being able to get clear title to the property. With the FSLIC still in town, that was less of a concern to the local bankers who wanted to be rid of the problem before it got worse.

Since a body was never recovered, the lines between those who knew Bobby and those who didn't became clear very quickly. His friends and business associates took the "official line" of an accidental drowning.

"He's at the bottom of the lake. How else do you explain the empty boat?"

When asked about the possibility of suicide, their response was universally the same: "It had to be an accident. There was no suicide note. He had everything to live for, why would he kill himself? He was going to beat the D.A.'s and the grand jury charges."

Others weren't sure. The rumors in town started immediately.

Some speculated it was an elaborate ruse on Bobby's part: "I heard he bought property in Australia (or Idaho) (or Canada)" they said "and staged his death to escape trouble with the law."

What better way to start a new life than by disappearing in an "accidental drowning?" After all, no one saw him in the boat after he rented it. He could have parked a car on the other side of the lake earlier and driven out of the area to God knows where.

Some locals suggested law enforcement look for land or lake developments in Australia, Idaho or Canada. They were sure Bobby would be close by.

"I'll bet he just took the money and ran," went another. And, of course, "I heard there was a lot of 'east coast money' in the project and was mixed up with the mob. If he thought he could change his mind about working with them, they took care of him. The mob has a retirement plan that doesn't include a pension. They'll never find him now."

What a statement about a person's time on earth: You are the toast of the town one day, then when you mysteriously disappear many people are convinced you're not dead.

MARK'S GREAT AMERICAN NOVEL
Chapter Two

New Dehli, India
November 1977

President Carter's visit was still weeks away.

Secret Service advance teams, numbering almost two dozen, were already on the ground in India, coordinating with Delhi Police and Indian Security officials. Every minute of the president's trip would be intricately planned.

Similar security units were on the ground working with Polish, Iranian and Saudi officials to oversee protection of the president and first lady during their time in those countries.

There would be alternate evacuation or escape paths planned along the president's motorcade route. Marine helicopters and Special Forces units would be on standby in the each of capitals.

Several meetings would be held with all groups assigned to the president's security. In New Delhi, even air traffic control systems would be subject to security oversight when Air Force One was nearing Indian airspace. The oversight would continue until President Carter's plane left India on its way to the next stop in Saudi Arabia.

Security officials took over an entire floor of a hotel in downtown Delhi to coordinate their planning efforts. Prior to the president's arrival, agents would make an additional sweep of the motorcade route. Manhole covers would be sealed while traffic and parking would be prohibited along the route in the hours before the Air Force One landed.

The visit to India would be in the middle of the longest presidential trip Mr. Carter would take during his first two years of his administration. This trip would begin at the end of December in Warsaw, Poland. The president was scheduled to meet with Polish First Secretary Gierek. Gierek, a Communist Party organizer, assumed the duties of first secretary just before Christmas in 1970. He promised to improve living conditions in the country and re-evaluate the government's economic policies.

As a reformer, Gierek introduced legislation to expand trade with the West and relax travel restrictions on Polish citizens. He attempted to reduce favoritism in governmental operations and hiring.

President Carter's visit was part of Gierek's efforts to open the country to foreign leaders, businesses and industries.

The president and Mrs. Carter would be visiting seven countries in Europe and the Middle East on this goodwill tour.

On December 31st, the president would depart Poland. His next stop would be in Tehran, Iran, for meetings with the shah of Iran and the king of Jordan, then on to New Delhi.

S I X T E E N

My Real Dad

I thought a lot about what my father said the last night I was in Schiller Park, the last time I saw him.

I spent a lot of time wondering if I really was his kid and if Mom had an affair while they were married.

For years, I never mentioned this to Mom. But I did spend a lot of time envisioning my "real" dad: some dashing hero like a fireman, soldier or a powerful executive of some kind. I pictured him as strong, caring and loving. Someone confident and enthusiastic about life. Interested in everything and everyone, including me.

Then I imagined he never knew about me or had been killed in a tragic accident before I was born or moved away or had a family of his own when he and Mom got together for a passionate weekend. I often wondered if I had any half brothers and sisters.

I wondered if Mom ever saw him again or if they kept in touch. I wondered if Mom ever regretted not running away with him and staying with my father instead.

My real dad must have been something.

I envisioned my real dad taking me to Cub Scouts and helping me build a car for the Pinewood Derby. I could see him talking to my teachers on Open House nights at school. I envisioned my real dad and me playing checkers on Saturdays or afternoons after school. He would have been a big help with my homework. I'm sure he would have taken me to a baseball game or two every season. We would have been great Cubs or Cardinals fans.

I'm sure he never would have hit me.

"Oh for God's sake, Mark." Mom was really irritated when I mentioned it to her on the weekend I graduated from college. We were sitting in her motel room the afternoon of my graduation.

For a moment, I thought I was finally going to hear the whole sordid story about my "real dad." The whole truth, laid bare for me to deal with once and for all.

"I heard that crap for the nine years your father and I were married. He was insanely jealous and suspicious of every man I ever met or talked to: the mailman, the milkman, the principal at your school, the building superintendent, the gas station attendant, the guy selling shoes at the department store. For God's sake, he wouldn't even let me pay the paperboy without him being around. Before we were married, he grilled me about guys I dated in high school and anyone I had seen when I was out on my own. I had been single for a number of years before I met your father."

Then, with that no-nonsense look only a mother can give, said, "Your father was your father. Period. There was never anyone else. I never want to hear that again. Is that clear."

It was a statement not a question.

It got very quiet in the room. Cars on the street outside and the hum of the air conditioner were the only sounds for several seconds.

Mom was lost in thought, distant and suddenly melancholy. She wasn't really talking to me when she said softly, "Do you think I would have stayed with him if there was someone waiting for me? For God's sake, Mark. We left when I couldn't take it anymore: the yelling, the hitting."

She had tears in her eyes. "I'm sorry. I never protected you. He was an awful, awful man. He treated you terribly. I never knew what to do. I was so afraid of him. Finally I got up the nerve to leave."

Another pause. "Mark, why do you think I never dated since we left Illinois? I was never going to put you in a situation like that again." Tears were running down her cheeks now. "I'm so sorry. You never deserved what happened. What he did to you. I just didn't know what to do."

"It's OK, Mom," I said, giving her a hug. "It's OK."

It was quiet again.

Then she was angry and glared. "Just when the hell were you going to mention this, Mark? And why today? Why did you wait seven years to bring it up? My God, what kind of woman do you think I am?"

I was embarrassed and just looked at the floor. I didn't have an answer. Tears were now running down my cheeks too.

I stayed silent.

I was saying goodbye to my "real dad."

"I'll miss you Dad."

SEVENTEEN

Little Grass Valley Reservoir
Saturday morning
December 16, 1978

"King of Nothing"—Seals and Croft

Cowboy coffee.

That's all I've got this morning, although it's not too bad with a shot of Jameson's.

You don't need a percolator or a filter for cowboy coffee. You just throw a handful or two of ground coffee into a pot of boiling water. Then you continue to boil it until it looks dark enough to drink, pull it off the fire and wait a few minutes for the grounds to settle. Then you use a cup to scoop out a serving. I was a little too impatient this morning and my cup contains a lot of coffee grounds. Grandpa would say it's the kind of coffee that would "put hair on your chest." Or as John at Melva's said, "That's what we call 'coffee with full body.'"

I allowed myself two luxuries at my apartment. Michelob beer on the weekends. Weekends, according to their ad slogan, were made for Michelob. I drank Miller Lite the rest of the week. I also loved Yuban coffee in the morning. But this morning, even Yuban couldn't improve the taste of cowboy coffee.

Yuban is short for: YU-letide BAN-quet. Why in the world would I remember that now?

The Forest Service shuts off the campground water supply when it closes for the winter. I spilled water on my shoes this morning, hauling water from the lake for the coffee. It's quite a hike from the campsite to the lake because of the extremely low water levels. I am pretty winded, too, because of the elevation. Right now, my shoes are drying next to the fire. My socks got wet too, but I've got an extra pair.

My feet are still cold. I should have packed another pair of shoes.

At the apartment, I usually have General Mills Breakfast Squares or Egg Beaters for breakfast. I'm not so fortunate this morning. Breakfast is Kellogg's Frosted Flakes in a small box that you split up the middle and add milk. These came in a variety package of 10 cereals. My mom called these "camp cereal breakfasts," since all you needed was milk and a spoon and there were no dishes to wash when you finished.

I didn't have any milk this morning, so I added water.

It's not quite the same.

I didn't sleep well last night. I woke up several times thinking I was in my apartment, laying next to Emma. When I do sleep, I'm having terrible dreams: I see Gerry at the Rip Roarin'. I picture "Dick Tracy" in the canyon.

What's the matter with me? My head is so muddled today. Random thoughts are coming in at me from all directions.

It's funny. For the life of me at this moment I can't remember "Dick Tracy's" real name. And God, four months ago he tried to kill me.

Maybe I can rest some more later this morning. Get my bearings. Clear my head. If this is what it's like to be "on the run," it's not as much fun as they make it out in the movies.

Oh wait, that's right, how could I forget "Dick Tracy's" real name: It's Greg Olman.

Of course. Greg Olman.

EIGHTEEN

Sequoia City
Greg Olman

Greg Olman worked for Gerry.

He grew up in Sequoia City and went to work for Gerry as his "gofer." He would be what crime bosses called "muscle,"although Greg didn't have any.

He was only about 5'5". He walked with a swagger. He talked in phrases. I don't think I ever heard him speak a complete sentence. His hair was always a little greasy and his clothes never looked new. Or the right size.

Greg carried a gun and displayed it like an appendage.

The gun was legal. I checked. He had a permit.

Nonetheless, it was hard to take him seriously. He said he did some "investigative work" for Gerry. By that I guess he meant he followed Gerry's partners when they were in town. He also kept an eye on Gerry's girlfriends: past and present. In my mind, he was nothing more than a paid "peeping Tom."

Greg often bragged that he and Gerry were business partners, which was laughable. He ran errands for Gerry. Taking paperwork to city hall. Checking out rentals or collecting rents on the apartments Gerry owned.

You'd see Greg at civic meetings, community picnics or Chamber of Commerce gatherings. You had to look for him, but he was there. Lurking in the background. Greg worked very hard to look sinister.

Growing up, Greg was probably the kid who got beat up on the playground all the time. I considered a number of nicknames for Greg. At first I thought "Lurch" from the Addams Family. No, he was actually more like "Dick Tracy."

People I knew agreed. "Dick Tracy" was a perfect nickname.

No one knew much about Greg. Growing up, his family was poor, did not socialize much and moved away when Greg was in the seventh grade. He returned a couple of years ago. No one could remember if he had brothers or sisters and no one ever asked. To be honest, no one cared.

He loved horses and did a lot of back country hiking and trail rides. In the spring, phantom waterfalls appeared after heavy rains or during the snow-melt. The canyons were filled with wild hyacinth, dogwood and trees just budding out with bright green leaves. It was not unusual to come across huge nests of ladybugs. Hundreds of thousands, usually near a small creek or stream.

Greg would organize a group of a dozen riders to follow a trail and see the canyon at its most spectacular. He would point out old logging sites, miners' cabins and Indian grinding rocks. For millennia, Indians in the area ground acorns for food on huge flat rocks. Over the years, the grinding wore deep holes in the rocks—sometimes several inches deep.

Greg charged for the horses, saddles and lunch on the trail. He did quite a bit of business during the spring, partnering with the Chamber of Commerce. He also occasionally ran small ads in Sunset and the California AAA magazine, so many of his customers were from out of the area.

I took one of the rides the spring after I arrived in Sequoia City. The canyon was unbelievably beautiful. Every twist or turn in the trail brought a new vista, shadows and sunlight. Huge boulders, sharp cliffs and rushing water everywhere. The air was fresh and intoxicating, like standing near the ocean.

A camera could not do justice to the sights. It was a half-day ride and all of us returned exhausted and exhilarated.

Back at the stables before the group dispersed, Greg handed out a list of other trail rides he offered individuals or small groups. The rides, throughout the foothills, ranged from half-day to full-day trips and were tailored mostly for novice horse riders. The longer day trips included a sack lunch, canteens of water and a soft drink. The list included a price sheet and his phone number.

I took one of the fliers.

I loved history and geology. The foothills east of Sequoia City were perfect for the exploration of both.

For a couple of hours that day, Greg actually seemed interesting.

MARK'S GREAT AMERICAN NOVEL
Chapter Three

> *"One day the great European War will come out of some
> damned foolish thing in the Balkans"*
> —Otto Van Bismark (APRIL 1815-JULY 1898)

Early in his teenage years, Zia looked for ways to change the world. Even considering his living conditions and life circumstances, Zia's focus on making a difference was laser like: He would change the world.

He was not unlike most young people in their teens and early 20s who believe they are destined to make the world a better place. Within a few years, though, nearly all are absorbed into the routine of daily life consisting of family and work.

During his freshman year at university, Zia's discovered the man who would become his life's hero and role model: Gavrilo Princip.

Zia pored over every article, book and encyclopedia he could find containing information on the events of June 28, 1914, in Sarajevo. It was the event historians pegged as the beginning of World War I.

Two shots.

Perhaps more than the American Revolution, the two shots in Sarajevo that morning were not only heard around the world, but also shaped the world in the 20th century. The roots of World War II and the Cold War can be traced to the shots fired that morning.

World War I resulted in the loss of 10 million lives—military and civilian.

Gavrilo Princip, a 19-year-old fanatic, belonged to the Black Hand society, a group fiercely committed to independence. Their goal was simple: break away from the Austro-Hungarian empire and unite with Serbia. Serbia provided the assassins with guns, training and ammunition.

Princip was one of seven assassins stationed along the parade route of Archduke Franz Ferdinand and his wife, Sophie. Each member of the group would be alert for the chance to assassinate the archduke.

Whether out of arrogance or ignorance, the archduke and his wife chose an unusual day for an official visit to Sarajevo. It was the anniversary of the First Battle of Kosovo in 1389, the day the Turkish Empire defeated Serbia. Passions about the defeat were still strong more than five centuries later. It was also St. Vitus Day, one of the holiest days on the Serbian calendar.

It was an odd day, indeed, for an official visit and an odd day to inspect troops stationed in a hostile region.

The archduke and Sophie were celebrating their wedding anniversary that day and Sophie was pregnant. Ferdinand's last words to his wife were, "Sophie, Sophie. Don't die, stay alive for our children." Sophie, however, died instantly. The Archduke succumbed moments later.

Two shots.

Within a month, the world was at war.

NINETEEN

Sisters Cascade Waterfall
Above Sequoia City

Greg's trail ride took us past a number of waterfalls.

The most interesting was the Sisters Cascade waterfall. At first glance, from a distance, it looked like one waterfall instead of three.

The Sisters Cascade waterfall was not particularly high—a drop of less than 95 feet. What made it a local landmark was the drop into deep pools at 20-and 30-foot intervals.

The waterfall was fed by one of the seven main tributaries of the Sequoia River. The many "phantom" waterfalls that appeared elsewhere in the watershed usually dried up by late May or early June.

The Sisters Cascade waterfall ran year round, and the water was always very cold.

In the 1950s and 60s, the pools were the place where high school and college students attended a beer party or went skinny dipping for the first time. By the 1970s, it was the place to smoke their first joint.

It was also the destination for moonlight horseback rides by the local young horseman's association. Early on the day of the ride, organizers would hang mannequins in trees, dressed like cowboys. That night, during the ride under a full moon, one of the adult riders would tell ghost stories about sinister events and murders that occurred in the area a hundred years earlier. At just the right moment, a chaperon would shine a flashlight into the trees and spotlight the hanging mannequin. The screams of the riders could be heard half a mile away. Even riders who had made the trip for years were startled when the light shone on the "victim" of frontier justice hanging in the trees.

The Sisters Cascade was ideal for beginning rock climbers to gain experience. A missed foothold simply meant an unexpected dunk into one of the cold water pools. Even so, there were only a few months out of the year when the rocks could be scaled—either because they were too slick and cold or too hot to climb.

When the weather was too warm, there was also the chance a rattlesnake might be hiding in the nooks where your hand went.

Late fall and early spring were the best: not too hot, not too cold and little chance of snakes.

I got my first experience with rock climbing at the Sisters Cascade. Ed showed me as best he could, but I still ended up in the water a few times before reaching the top. The weather was pleasant, but I still let him climb ahead of me. Better for him to find snakes than me.

Only later did it occur to me that if he found a snake, he would toss it down and out of the way. And it would probably land on me.

MARK'S GREAT AMERICAN NOVEL
Chapter Four

Washington D.C.
December 29, 1977
7:35 a.m.

President Carter made a statement to the press at the White House just before he and Mrs. Carter boarded a Marine helicopter for the seven-minute flight to Andrews Air Force Base.

The presidential helicopter took off from the south grounds at 7:38 a.m. This would be the first international trip of Carter's presidency.

At 7:58, Air Force One took off from Andrews Air Force Base for the eight-hour, 17-minute flight to Okechie International Airport in Warsaw.

A little over an hour into the flight, just after 9 a.m., President Carter made a two-minute phone call to a congressional liaison.

At the same time, in a nondescript building in the nation's capital, the Secret Service received constant dispatches and updates from the overseas locales the president and first lady would visit. Coordinating security with overseas intelligence agencies began months earlier and now ramped up significantly with Air Force One airborne and en route to Poland.

When Air Force One landed in Warsaw at 10:15 p.m. local time, the president and first lady were greeted on the plane by the U.S. ambassador to the Polish People's Republic, Richard T. Davies. Also on hand was the chief of protocol of the Polish People's Republic, Janusz Lewandowski.

The president and Mrs. Carter stepped off Air Force One at 10:25 p.m. and participated in a ceremony lasting until just after 11. The ceremony featured a review of troops, greetings by various U.S. and Polish delegations and floral bouquets presented by four Polish children.

Then came brief remarks by the president and First Secretary Edward Gierek.

The presidential motorcade left the airport at 11:02 for the 28-minute drive to Wilanow Palace, where the presidential party would be staying while in Poland.

Wilanow Palace is a luxurious baroque design royal residence. Construction began in April 1677 and took nearly two decades to complete. The palace floor plan expanded from a single-floor residence to a project that would include an aristocratic house, an Italian garden villa and a Louis XIV-style French palace.

In 1805, Wilanow Palace was converted to one of the first museums in Poland.

After a short reception at the palace at 11:30, president and Mrs. Carter retired to their private quarters in the palace at 11:42.

At 12:10 a.m., before turning in for the night, the president left a message with the White House signal operator to wake him at 7 a.m.

MARK'S GREAT AMERICAN NOVEL
Chapter Five

I don't know if you are supposed to write a book from beginning to end.

I wonder if authors start with Chapter One and simply continue writing to the conclusion? Do they write the chapters in order, the way a reader eventually sees it?

Or is it like a movie that is filmed out of sequence and spliced together later?

I hope it's the latter. As ideas come to me, I scribble notes on whatever paper I have at the time. I have notes on napkins from Melva's, on deposit slips and even on envelopes from the mail I just opened.

Then, at some point, I sit down and develop the ideas on paper. I find myself writing chapters and paragraphs in no particular order. Sometimes I hammer out a couple of pages in one sitting. Other times, it will be a paragraph or two, but at least the thoughts are down in writing.

Writing the chapters out of order does allow me to rearrange them later in an effort to expand the plot, develop the characters or build tension and drama. Without numbering the pages, however, I have to be careful not to drop the manuscript.

I know how the book begins and ends. Filling in the middle narrative is the hard part.

TWENTY

Jordan (Bobby) Laine

Jordan was his given name, but everyone called him Bobby.

I met Bobby shortly after I came to town at a "meet and greet" event at a local business. He introduced himself as Jordan, but added "people call me Bobby." I got to know him better a few months later in February at the annual Chamber of Commerce banquet. He had been elected president and the banquet was the beginning of his two-year term. He was likable and interested in my job at the radio station, my education and my family. He was very engaging and knew a few details about the Chicago area, the university I attended and so on. I overheard one woman describe him as "charming."

Born in Yankton, South Dakota, in 1936, Jordan's family moved west to Reno in 1942. Jordan's father worked at the Crystal Peak mine north of Reno. The mine produced tuning crystals for radio equipment during World War Two.

Jordan attended Reno High School. Established in 1879, it is the oldest high school in Reno. The school mascot is the Husky and the school motto is "Reno High—Older than Reno."

Legalized gambling came to Reno in 1931 along with some of the most liberal divorce laws in the country. Reno flourished during and immediately after the war and lived up to its trademark: "The Biggest Little City in the World."

Jordan couldn't remember who called him "Bobby" first, but the name stuck, starting in preschool through grade school and high school and into the professional world.

While he never played sports in school, he was good looking, fit and very popular with the opposite sex.

Bobby developed a knack for charming his way into whatever he wanted and whenever he wanted it.

He was first, and third, in his class to "score." His first sexual conquest occurred a couple of weeks before he turned 16 in 1952. His second was the week he turned 16. He stopped counting after five, sometime early in his junior year.

He didn't mind bending the rules. He said rules were like rubber bands: stretch them as far as you can without breaking them. In the words of more than one female classmate, he could be very "persuasive." Although personable, Bobby quickly earned another nickname: "a bad boy."

Parents and teachers, on the other hand, described him as polite and courteous.

Years later, people who knew him were convinced he was the model for Eddie Haskell, the two-faced character on the "Leave it to Beaver" TV series.

MARK'S GREAT AMERICAN NOVEL
Chapter Six

Air Force One
SAM 27000

The Air Force One used by the Carters was a Boeing 707 delivered to the U.S. government six years earlier.

Prior to that time, previous versions of Air Force One could be used by any high-ranking administration officials as well as the president. The aircraft used by the Carters was designed for travel and use solely by the president of the United States. The plane entered presidential flight service in 1972 and was designated with tail number SAM (Special Air Mission) 27000.

Protecting Air Force One in the air is a constant challenge and concern for Pentagon and security officials. During the 1970s, a brand of terrorism involving the hijackings of passenger planes called for new security precautions on SAM 27000.

The plane was equipped with an infrared countermeasures system which was designed to protect Air Force One from heat-seeking missiles. The Pentagon worried surface to air missiles could be launched from a shoulder pack near an airport or on the flight path of Air Force One.

President Carter wanted to portray a less "regal" presidency to the nation and the world. The president often carried his own luggage. Critics speculated that the president's luggage was empty at the time and he simply carried it for a photo opportunity. The president occasionally planned out of town trips with an overnight stay in a private residence. On these occasions, the president even made his bed before he left the following morning.

At his order, the "V" (for VIP) was removed from Air Force One tail designation as well as from other official aircraft stationed at Andrews Air Force Base. He ordered the markings of Air Force One toned down along with other VIP transports.

During his campaign for president and before taking office in January 1977, Carter indicated he wanted to minimize the use of Air Force One.

President Nixon was the only sitting president to fly on a commercial airline flight. It was on a United Airlines flight on December 26, 1973, and was meant to emphasize the need for energy conservation. At the time, the U.S. economy was struggling with a Middle East oil embargo.

The president, his wife, daughter Tricia and a contingent of Secret Service agents arrived unannounced to board United Flight 55 from Washington Dulles to Los Angeles International Airport. The flight was scheduled to leave Dulles at 5:30 EST and arrive in Los Angeles at 8:05 PST.

The presidential party flew first class to California. The nonstop United flight aboard a DC 10 was designated "Executive One." For security reasons, however, that call sign was not used with air traffic control. As it turns out, the gesture was entirely symbolic. The actual Air Force One had to be flown to California, empty, for the Nixons' return flight to the nation's capital.

T W E N T Y - O N E

KBSC Radio

Everyone who met Charlie Dillon knew this was the height of his career in radio.

"Baker Street"—Jerry Rafferty

He signed on the radio station Monday through Saturday.

Charlie always had great plans. All the things he was going to do when he "made it." He read all the trade publications he could get his hands on. He subscribed to joke services offered to radio stations for use by on-air personalities. He listened to disc jockeys, news commentators and talk show hosts from as many major market stations as he could tune in. He sent audition tapes to other radio stations. He was "honing his skills" he said, although I didn't think his shows ever got any better.

He had signed up for the Army during the height of the Vietnam War. A nagging case of psoriasis kept him out. The humidity in Southeast Asia would aggravate the condition. He liked to tell how brave he was to sign up for the service when everyone else was looking for ways to dodge the draft.

Even though he was married, he often took advantage of his local celebrity status. Any woman who gave him any encouragement usually ended up in bed with him.

Or in the back seat of his car. Or on a secluded beach down by the river. Sometimes just once. More often, the "romance" lasted for days or weeks.

He told us he was "well endowed." We took his word for it. None of us needed proof.

He was the only married guy I ever knew who kept a package of rubbers in his desk drawer.

Everyone at the station knew when he had a new girlfriend. She would call the station and ask for him by name, usually in a somewhat hushed or throaty voice. Several times a week.

Sometimes she would come by the station. We all wanted to get a look at her, even though we all pretended to be doing something else when she came in.

It was nauseating. His wife never seemed to mind or never caught on.

He bought breath mints by the case. Worst case of bad breath any of us ever experienced. When he was done with his show, you'd have to air out the control booth.

I wondered how his "romantic flings" could ever kiss him. But, then again, that too was more information than I wanted to know.

TWENTY-TWO

Sequoia City
Emma Robinson

I met Emma at the Rip Roarin' on a Thursday night.

Monday through Wednesday, Happy Hour was 5 to 6. Ed and I went on Thursday because it was "Happy Hour" from 5 until midnight. The drinks were cheap: $1 well drinks, $2 for name brands and pitchers of beer.

On Thursdays, the bartender stopped the clock at 6 p.m., so that "Happy Hour" could go on for six more hours. It was a Rip Roarin' tradition for a decade or more.

As the sweep hand on the clock above the bar approached 6 'clock, customers would start a countdown from 10. At exactly 6 o'clock, a cheer would go up from the crowd. Unplugging the clock, the bartender would shout "Welcome to Thursday night Happy Hour at the Rip Roarin'," which was followed by another loud cheer. And more than a dozen drink orders.

"Diamond Girl"—Seals and Croft

Emma was a waitress at the Rip Roarin'. There was a spark between us right away. One of those "catch your breath" moments when we first laid eyes on each other. It was just a look, just for an instant and it was an incredible turn on. I think for both of us. Throughout the evening, I would watch her move throughout the bar. Once in a while, we would catch each other's eye, then quickly look away—like it was an accident. But there was definitely a spark.

Emma was born in Sequoia City. Her folks were divorced and had moved away. Emma stayed. "I didn't see any point in leaving, since my biggest problems broke up and moved out of town," she said with a laugh.

Emma and I got better acquainted months later when the Sequoia Parks Department sponsored a community garden.

"Dance With Me"—Orleans

There were 10 other "gardeners" in our group. Most of us lived in apartments and were single. There was one married couple in the group. They looked like "refugees" from San Francisco's Haight-Ashbury district. To most of us, it appeared the '60s had been good to them. I think they still lived there.

Our group borrowed a truck and picked up a load of horse manure from a local stable. The Parks District earmarked a vacant parcel of land for the garden. We spent every Monday evening tilling, weeding, tending, spraying and harvesting vegetables of all kinds. We took turns watering the garden during the week. Occasionally we would have a work party on Thursday night or on a Saturday morning. It was just something to do.

We usually all met at the garden site after work. After a couple of hours of hard work, we would meet for a beer at the Rip Roarin'. Most nights, of course, it ended up being four or five beers.

Emma and I hit it off right away. She laughed at all my jokes, even before she had anything to drink. I liked her a lot. She was fun to be around. And she really turned me on.

"Make It With You"—Bread

It was after one of these community garden work nights that Emma came home with me for the first time. Over drinks that night, our group had been kidding a lot about sex. Emma and I kept looking at each other. When the group broke up, Emma and I stayed behind. After some more small talk, she said she would love to see where I lived.

I never realized how long it took to drive home from the Rip Roarin'.

We went in the back door and up the stairs to my apartment. I never asked Jim or Joyce if it was OK to have "company" in the apartment. I wasn't about to go ask them now, either, although I was sure Jim would be OK with it.

"Rock Me Gently"—Andy Kim

We didn't sleep much that night. When I left for work the next morning, Emma was finally asleep.

I have trouble with intimacy. The mechanics of sex are easy, but not so the emotional attachments that go with it. Grandma and Grandpa were occasionally affectionate but seemed embarrassed if I walked into a room and interrupted them kissing or holding one another. My father and mom were never affectionate. Emotionally, I was probably more like my father: stoic, "manly," indifferent and pretty shut down.

But unlike my father, I never hit anyone I cared about.

I envied guys who seemed more comfortable with their emotions. And comfortable being around women and talking to them. I often felt very alone. Even around people I knew.

For years I thought intimacy was simply sex. Too late, I realized intimacy is being completely understood and honest with someone else. Eventually, Emma would be the only person in the world to see my emotional side, but honestly, there was not much to see.

Emma and I saw a lot of each other in those first few weeks. Like most guys, though, I thought I was dating someone far above my station in life.

Emma told me she had dated Greg Olman for a very short time. She appreciated the "Dick Tracy" nickname.

"Our first date was run of the mill," Emma said. "You know, a movie followed by a couple of drinks afterward. He just was someone to be with."

She looked at me and laughed. "Boy does that sound desperate!"

"A week or so later, he invited me to what he termed a 'candlelight' dinner." She paused, and rolling her eyes, said, "Trust me, it's not what you think."

"He bought a couple of hamburgers and a six-pack of beer, picked me up, and found a place to park down by the river. He lit a very small votive candle and put it on a paper plate on the dashboard. About the time we finished dinner, the candle burned out. Greg took that as his cue to try to get it on with me. He never got 'lucky'. As a matter of fact, he never made it past first base. I've made out with horny guys before and knew how to handle them. I'm not naive and I certainly wasn't a virgin at the time."

She shot a glance for my reaction, almost as if she thought she might have said too much.

I smiled. "Me neither."

"He was kinky and got a little rough. I don't know whether he thought I was easy, but we broke up after that."

Her voice trailed off.

"He still gives me the creeps when I see him. And the way he looks at me..." she shuddered a bit.

Then she chuckled and said, "he probably stole the votive candle from the Catholic Church."

MARK'S GREAT AMERICAN NOVEL
Chapter Seven

The U.S. Secret Service was formed in the 1860s and is among the oldest federal law enforcement agencies in the country.

The Secret Service was organized to investigate, prevent and stop frauds against the government. The Secret Service investigated mail fraud, bootleggers, the Ku Klux Klan, land fraud and counterfeiting. The counterfeiting of U.S. currency was widespread in the years following the Civil War.

Beginning in 1894, the service provided informal, part-time protection for the president. Seven years later, following the assassination of William McKinley -the third U.S. president to die at the hands of an assassin—protection of the president was expanded to full time.

The initial presidential detail consisted of two agents. The exact number of agents assigned to presidential security today is classified. The agency provides security for the president, vice president, major political candidates for the office of president and coordinates security for foreign dignitaries visiting the U.S.

The Secret Service coordinates and assists with security when the president travels to foreign countries.

MARK'S GREAT AMERICAN NOVEL
Chapter Eight

Wilanow Palace, Warsaw Poland
New Delhi, India
December 30, 1977

President Carter received his 7 a.m. wake up call from the White House. He and Mrs. Carter went to the Palace dining room an hour later for a "working breakfast" with administration officials. The breakfast included Secretary of State Cyrus Vance, Assistant for National Security Affairs Zbigniew Brzezinski, U.S. Ambassador Richard T. Davies as well as the president's physician, the personal assistant to the first lady and a special assistant for appointments.

At 8:43, the president met privately with Brzezinski and Vance for about 20 minutes. The trio was joined by Ambassador Davies just after 9 a.m. and the group then took a tour of the palace and museum.

The Secret Service assigned more than a dozen agents to the president's personal detail overseas. The teams worked around the clock, coordinating with local security in countries on the president's itinerary. Two agents were assigned to sift through the latest briefing information on the potential threats in New Delhi. Alternate routes for the presidential motorcade in Delhi were already in the late stages of planning.

The president and Mrs. Carter left the palace at 11:38 for the 20-minute ride to the Tomb of the Unknown Soldier. The president and first lady were greeted by a delegation of Polish officials. The tomb was constructed after World War I. The president placed a wreath at the tomb, signed the memorial book and greeted a group of Polish veterans.

The next stop on the president's schedule was the Nike Monument: a monument to the Heroes of Warsaw. In Greek Mythology, Nike is the Goddess of Victory. The Nike Monument in Warsaw is dedicated to the thousands of Poles who died during World War II, including those who died defending the city in 1939, the tens of thousands who died in the Jewish Ghetto Uprising in 1943 and the citywide uprising against the Nazis in 1944.

At 12:36, the president and first lady traveled to the Ghetto Memorial to place a wreath. The president also greeted members of the public, then traveled to the Parliament Building.

For Zia, getting details of the president's schedule of activities was difficult. New

Delhi was getting ready for the New Year's celebration. For centuries, India celebrated the New Year's Day on March 1. Sometime during the British occupation of India, the country phased in the use of the Gregorian calendar. Widespread acceptance of the Gregorian calendar occurred in the 1940s.

In some regions of the country still using the Hindu calendar, New Year's Day is still celebrated at different times of the year.

January 1 is known as a "restricted holiday" in India. Individuals are allowed a limited number of "restricted holidays" during the year. For Zia and his team, it was important to know on this "restricted holiday," though, most businesses, government offices and public transportation services would be open and operating.

TWENTY-THREE

Sequoia City Sheriff's Office
The Police Log and Sharon Longnan

Sharon Longnan was a sheriff's dispatcher for nearly 20 years. Sharon was married but had no children. She preferred the overnight shift because not much happened.

Sharon usually worked Tuesday through Saturday nights. Her counterpart on her days off was a tough, burly woman named "Mickey." Most of the time "Mickey" would hardly acknowledge my presence. She was immune to any effort to start a conversation and mostly grunted answers.

Ed said I shouldn't feel picked on. Mickey wasn't any more friendly to him.

We consoled ourselves by joking about her.

"She puts gravy on her hands to get her dog to play with her," I said. Ed added, "She's the kind of person who could brighten up any room…just by leaving it." "I'll bet she has marks all over her body from being touched by 10-foot poles." "She has trouble making imaginary friends." To which I added, "No, no, her imaginary friend only wants to play with the kid across the street" and "I'll bet she slaps the crap out of her inner child every day."

It also helped us deal with "Mickey" when we decided "Mickey" was really "Michael" who liked to dress up as a woman in a police uniform. And since she was the first person I talked to on Monday mornings, the thought of "Mickey" being "Michael" always helped me greet her/him with a smile.

There was only one deputy on patrol duty, except Fridays and Saturdays. Then the overnight police "presence" in this part of the county doubled to two deputies.

During the week, the deputy assigned to the overnight shift was usually a rookie.

The rookie deputy was thrilled to have anything to investigate. In the Sequoia City area, if there was any call at all, it would be a report of "shots fired" or "loud party" or "speeding cars" or "barking dogs."

Sharon and I got along great. When I came by in the early morning to check out the police log for my newscast, she would point out anything that might be a story or worth following up on later. If anything had happened before she came on duty at 11, she would have pull the written reports for me to look through.

Occasionally, there would be an entry on the log that read something like "officer stopped car weaving on road." There would be no license plate, no driver's name, no make and model; in fact, nothing except that one-line entry. It was understood some elected official or prominent businessman had been stopped, obviously drunk. The deputy would give a verbal warning to the driver, who was then told to drive straight home. Ed and I usually found out who it was, but as a matter of courtesy, we never released the names. We were also able to figure out if someone prominent was with someone other than their wife at the time of the traffic stop. Drinking wasn't the only reason a car would be weaving, slowing down or speeding up.

The only time we did report the name was when a self-impressed deputy public defender, in town for a prolonged trial, decided to head home for the weekend after more than a couple of drinks. The report of the incident was quite funny. Apparently Harold Sweet had run over something on his way home and flattened all four tires. A Highway Patrolman was writing a traffic ticket to someone on the side of the road when Harold approached. The sound of four flattened tires at 55 miles per hour was quite loud.

When the patrolman caught up with Harold a mile or two down the road, Harold literally fell out onto the pavement when asked to step out of the car. It was only then that Harold noticed the flattened tires and asked the patrolman: "What did you do to my tires? Those were brand new tires." He apparently kept repeating the question all the way to his booking at the jail.

The same Highway Patrolman told me about the time he observed a drunk driver traveling in the opposite direction on the highway. The driver was a "serial" drunk who always managed to avoid being caught and arrested. The patrolman alerted the local sheriff's deputy on duty and the Sequoia City Police, but by the time they caught up with the car, the driver had pulled over to the shoulder, shut off the motor and promptly passed out. With the car parked and the engine off, officers could not cite the driver for "driving under the influence." Frustrated, one of the officers reached inside, took the keys out of the ignition and tossed them as far as he could off the road into the brush.

Now that was a story! You couldn't make this stuff up. Not even a great potential writer could have come up with a tale like that!

Once I got to know Sharon, I could occasionally call rather than stop by in the morning to find out if there was anything newsworthy. I didn't abuse the privilege, so I didn't run into the "nothing happened" answer.

One morning she said, "Nothing much going on overnight. But there was an odd entry from yesterday afternoon. Apparently someone backed into a Mexican fellow in the parking lot at the hardware store. The driver said he knocked the fellow down. The driver said the guy was scuffed up on his head and arm and his leg was bent in an odd way. The fellow got up, told the driver there was no problem and limped over to a truck from Timberline Orchards. The truck drove off, despite efforts to get some information or take the guy to the hospital. A deputy followed up at Timberline's office, but there was no information on the injured man. That's where it ended. Kind of odd, huh?"

TWENTY-FOUR

Timberline Orchards
3,500' elevation

Apple orchards are labor intensive and require a lot of attention nearly year round. Most commercial orchards have more than 20 trees to the acre. The trees need pruning in winter, honeybees in the spring, herbicides to keep the weeds down and fertilizers, applied at just the right time, to enhance blossoming and setting of the fruit. Then there is harvesting, packing, shipping and marketing. There are gophers, birds, sometimes bears and moles to contend with in the orchards too.

In particularly heavy fruit set years, thinning of the fruit by hand is necessary to insure adequate size and sweetness.

Many commercial attempts at growing apples fail because of lack of capital and labor. The first marketable crop usually occurs five years after planting. In the meantime, the expenses of watering, pruning, fertilizing and weeding continues.

There are no mechanical apple harvesters. Harvest averages between 8 and 10 bushels per tree, with a bushel weighing about 40 pounds.

The Timberline Orchards in Sequoia County were first planted by Piero Giordano in the late 1800s and have been managed by his family since. The 35-acre orchard is at the perfect elevation for apples, about the same elevation as Apple Hill in Placerville, California. Apples need a few hundred hours of freezing temperatures during the dormant winter months and 150 frost-free days during the growing season. They thrive on long hot days and cool nights.

Timberline Orchards developed a marketing agreement with the Wentz/Holiday markets in Redding for exclusive distribution of their annual crop of more than 100 tons annually.

At the time, consumers were just beginning to consider "organic apples" with Joni Mitchell's "Big Yellow Taxi" their anthem.

At Timberline Orchards, the joke was "You know the difference between regular farmers and organic farmers? Organic farmers spray at night."

TWENTY-FIVE

Sequoia City

I ran into Cameron downtown and mentioned the incident at the hardware store parking lot.

"Timberline needs lots of farm workers to pick the fruit. Many of them are here on temporary work visas. Others are simply here illegally. If you're not supposed to be in the U.S., you certainly don't want to go to the hospital or get medical treatment," Cameron said.

"Gerry Apte and the owners at Timberline are pretty close. I'm sure there's a story there. But hey, you're the news guy. And," laughing he said, "I'm sure Gerry would just love to talk to you."

Cameron went on. "You oughta check in with Ken Morgan at the D.A.'s office. He works closely with the Immigration Service. He could provide you a lot of information. But hey, as I said, you're the news guy."

TWENTY-SIX

The D.A.'s Office

Ken Morgan grew up in Sequoia City and attended Hastings College of Law at the University of California in San Francisco.

UC Hastings College of Law was the first law school in California. It was established in 1878 and funded with a $100,000 gift from Serranus Hastings, the first Supreme Court justice of California. Hastings' gift stipulated that the school must remain in San Francisco forever and be governed by an independent board of directors, not UC regents.

After World War II, Hastings College started the Sixty-Five Club. The school began hiring Ivy League professors forced into mandatory retirement at age 65. As a result, the college boasted a preeminent faculty of experienced teachers, jurists and legal experts "too old" to work elsewhere.

Ken Morgan graduated from Hastings in 1972. Ken often said his invitation to San Francisco's "Summer of Love" apparently got lost in the mail and in any case, arrived over a year late. For Ken, a personable, good looking and athletic young man, that meant there were no extraordinary distractions for a single guy attending law school in the city.

Morgan was excited to talk to me about the illegal workers at Timberline. "You know, some of those guys have been arrested and deported four or five times. They get arrested and processed at the county jail. We feed and house them, at county expense, for three or four days until the Immigration Service comes to pick them up. Then an Immigration Service officer escorts them with a one-way bus ticket to Mexico and drops them off at the border."

Morgan went on. "It's very frustrating. Those same folks are often back working at Timberline within three weeks. So then we start the process all over again. It would be interesting, though, to know how they actually make it back from Mexico to here in such short order. Is that something you're working on?"

I told him it was an area of interest to me and to my listeners. I didn't tell him my interest was less than 72 hours old and the result of a minor mishap in a hardware store parking lot.

He chuckled. "I wouldn't be surprised if Mexican officials are waiting at the border to give them a return bus ticket back to the U.S."

As I got up to leave, Ken said, "Let me know what you find out. If you need any help or more information, just call me."

TWENTY-SEVEN

Flash Point in Sequoia City
A Letter to the District Attorney

Nuclear scientists use the term "critical mass" when a combination of elements at the right instant triggers a detonation. Chemists call it "a flash point" when ingredients mix at an exact temperature and explode into flames. Cookbooks caution about "the boiling point" where water starts spilling out of a pot. Architects define it as "the breaking point" when the stress of weight and gravity overcomes the design of a structure. My mother would simply say "it was the straw that broke the camel's back."

In Sequoia City, "the straw" was a letter addressed to the district attorney. The letter, from Chad and Beverly Martin, weighed less than an ounce and was postmarked in El Segundo, California.

In recent months, there were an increasing number of letters addressed to either the "District Attorney" or "Consumer Department" or "Real Estate Division" or similar variations.

All of the letters came from out of the area and contained similar complaints about property purchases around the lake: Deeds never delivered, a seller who couldn't be located, parcels that weren't accessible or couldn't be found on the county property tax rolls.

Unhappy as they were, some individuals acknowledged they could have done a more thorough investigation about the land before sending money. They privately acknowledged ignoring the caveat: buyer beware. Some had made payments for more than two years before getting queasy or curious. A few letters were profane and angry. Others were resigned to the fact that "there's a sucker born every minute" and, apparently, it was the minute they were born.

The Martins took a far more active approach.

Chad and Beverly Martin operated an ice business in southern California for more than three decades. At first, Chad held a full-time job in addition to the ice delivery business. Chad worked as a school janitor from 3 to 11 p.m. He would be home by 11:30, eat a quick meal and squeeze in a few hours' of sleep. Chad would get up and be at the ice plant by 4:30 a.m. The plant turned out 20 to 30 tons of ice every 24 hours. The enormous ice blocks would be carved into smaller chunks and directed to either a crusher and bagged or sliced and packed as ice blocks. Chad filled his truck with several hundred pounds of block and crushed ice. Until the mid-1960s, the truck was insulated, not refrigerated, so deliveries had to be made early and quickly.

When Chad started in business, water was frozen to make the ice blocks. Years later, ice shavings would be compressed into blocks. This process reduced waste at the plant but injected large amounts of air into the compressed blocks. These compressed blocks melted much quicker, which, in turn led to more ice sales.

Chad delivered to supermarkets, gas stations, family grocery stores and liquor stores. Finishing by 10 or so, he'd head home, eat something and do some book work for the business. He was usually able to get at least an hour's nap before starting all over again. A couple of days a week, Beverly would crawl into bed and keep him from napping for a few minutes.

Chad also serviced a number of ice machines he and Beverly owned outright. In the 1970s, the coin-operated machines dispensed 25 pounds of block or crushed ice for $1.25.

The ice machines required constant attention. Located along busy streets, they were subject to excess heat, dirt and debris. Coin slots jammed, delivery chutes malfunctioned and the machines, though well-lighted at night, were occasionally tampered with or vandalized.

During the summer months or on long holiday weekends, the challenge was to "guesstimate" the demand for ice. Chad discovered quickly it was better to have more ice loaded into the machines than risk running out during peak periods.

Extra ice was stored in a large walk-in refrigerated area at the rear of the machine. Chad checked on the operation of the machines several times throughout the weekend and restocked them as needed.

For the Martins, vacations were short and usually in the winter when business was slow. The rest of the year, ice deliveries were a seven-day-a-week job. Hours like that, Chad told friends, "went with the territory."

In the early years, Chad and Beverly posted their business phone on each machine in case a customer encountered a problem. The business phone was also their home phone. Occasionally there were calls from people claiming the machine "stole" their money and didn't dispense any ice. There were also 2 a.m. calls from drunks who wanted to know where to get change for the machine or why the ice wasn't free or if there was a liquor store nearby.

Chad and Beverly's business blossomed from one employee and one truck to eight trucks and 12 drivers. No one worked seven days a week anymore. As their business grew, the Martins transferred their home phone to the business and got an unlisted number for their personal use.

With retirement in sight, the Martins planned to sell the business and their home of 38 years. Three years earlier, Chad responded to an ad in the local newspaper and purchased 10 acres of "view property" close to the nearly completed Sequoia Lake reservoir. Chad sent a down payment check for $1,000 and mailed $100 checks every month thereafter.

Chad and Beverly met with designers and architects and drew up plans for building their dream home on the property.

The week after Thanksgiving in 1976, they drove from El Segundo to see their dream property for the first time.

Except the Martins were unable to find their property. Not at the title company, nor at the county assessor's office and not through any Realtor in the area. It was as if the property simply didn't exist, as though the property only existed in their dreams.

Chad Martin was a businessman and was not one to simply lick his wounds and move on. Over the years, he negotiated tough contracts with the Teamsters union. He could tell you to the penny which ice machine generated the most profits for the company. His accountant said he was the only business owner who took the time to go over, in excruciating detail, every expense and deduction on his tax return. He would spend hours poring over the company profit and loss statement looking for any opportunity to enhance the bottom line.

His business sense told him someone was getting away with theft on an enormous scale. And public officials in Sequoia City were obviously looking the other way.

Chad was embarrassed and fumed on the way home. He and Beverly hardly spoke during the nearly 12-hour drive home.

Two days later, Chad mailed his letter to the Sequoia City D.A. In it, he promised to visit every elected official, every legal expert, every county department having anything to do with property sales. He would attend every supervisors meeting and use the five minutes available for non-agenda items to detail his case. He planned a visit to the Department of Real Estate in Sacramento. And the Attorney General's Office. He would also visit with every newspaper, radio and television reporter in Northern California.

The flash point had been reached in Sequoia City, delivered by an ice man.

Chad decided to put off building his dream home for now. Which was OK since he wasn't sure where the property for his dream home was located.

With Chad's letter in hand, the district attorney impaneled a Grand Jury.

TWENTY-EIGHT

Little Grass Valley Reservoir
Saturday late afternoon
December 16, 1978

Something's definitely not quite right today.

I napped fitfully for a couple of hours. Even in the sleeping bag, I was very cold.

The fire, or what passes for one, is generating lots of smoke but not much heat. Ed said the Indians had a term for a smoky fire that didn't put out much heat: a white man's fire. I'll look around for more pine needles and twigs. Even if they are damp, they will throw off a burst of heat when they eventually dry out. Maybe enough to keep the logs burning a little longer.

I forgot how early it gets dark in the foothills. I don't think the temperature even got into the 40's today. A cold day followed by another cold night.

My journal writing is very confused and I am having trouble focusing. What if no one finds this journal? Or me? Would anyone be able to sort through this and make any sense of it? Or would it simply be written off as the ramblings of some "nut case" who wandered off and got lost in the wilderness.

I'm going to have to figure out something to eat for dinner soon, too.

I really didn't think this "escape" through. My Boy Scout leader would tell me I forgot the Scout motto "Be Prepared." I also haven't done so well lately with the Scout slogan either: "Do a Good Turn Daily."

T W E N T Y - N I N E

The Forests above Sequoia City

If marijuana cultivation could ever be considered "benign," it would have been in the mid to late 1960s. Most growers cultivated two or three plants. Larger marijuana "plantations" might have 75 to 100 plants.

It was not unusual for these larger grows to be planted on U.S. Forest Service land. The plants could be grown off private property and were protected from aerial view by the canopy of tall trees. These were usually planted near creeks or streams. Growers at the time rarely protected their groves with guns or booby traps and seldom gave any resistance when arrested.

All of that changed in the early 70s. Gangs including the Motorcycle Masters discovered rural California. Criminal gangs like the Masters found rural counties like Yuba, Lake, Humboldt, Butte and Sequoia ideal places to cultivate plots of several thousand plants. These groves were protected with guns, trip wires and booby traps, including pit traps.

Cultivation was now big business.

Remote counties have small law enforcement agencies with thousands of acres and hundreds of square miles to patrol. Gangs could also cook methamphetamine, undetected, on a large scale. The labs were often located within several hundred yards of a rural road that provided access and easy transport of both raw materials and the finished product.

The counties were a perfect place to dump the bodies of rivals, errant gang members or marijuana "pirates." Pirates were folks who raided marijuana grows just before harvest time. Like the friends of "The Little Red Hen" in the children's fable, these "pot pirates" let someone else cultivate all season and then steal the plants and enjoy the fruits of someone else's labor. Once the gangs moved in, pirates rarely lived long enough to enjoy the early harvest.

Bodies were dumped down the abandoned mine shafts that dotted the foothill and mountain landscapes. Sometimes the shafts were dynamited to keep the secrets for eternity. In a pinch or a hurry, lye and sulfur were dumped down the shaft on top of the bodies, which were then left to decay. It was unlikely they would ever be discovered.

There were fruit orchards and forest lands owned by gang or family members.

Equipment like backhoes on these parcels could be used to excavate large burial plots. Animal trails in the forest were a great place to leave bloodied victims or their dismembered remains. Nature would take its course from there.

MARK'S GREAT AMERICAN NOVEL
Chapter Nine

December 30, 1977
Warsaw, Poland

During the morning, first lady Rosalyn Carter and National Security Adviser Zbigniew Brzezinski met with the Catholic archbishop of Warsaw, Cardinal Stefan Wyszynski. Wyszynski was often referred to as "the uncrowned king of Poland.".

Ordained a priest in 1924, he was active in the Nazi resistance in World War II and elevated to the position of cardinal by Pope Pius XII in January 1953. In September of that year, he was imprisoned for three years for resisting a Soviet crackdown on the church. While imprisoned, Wyszynski witnessed the brutal treatment and torture of fellow prisoners. He was released three years later.

Wyszynski continued his efforts to make the church part of everyday life in Poland. In 1966, he celebrated the Millennium of Christianity in Poland commemorating the baptism of Poland's first prince. Polish authorities, however, refused to allow Pope Paul VI to attend. Officials also prevented the cardinal from traveling outside the country to participate in other celebrations around the world.

President Carter's afternoon consisted of a working luncheon with First Secretary Gierek along with a host of U.S. and Polish officials in the Parliament Building.

The president's security detail received regular updates from Indian intelligence on the status of their investigation, on Zia's whereabouts and the additional steps being taken to ensure the president's safety when Air Force One landed in New Delhi.

Just before 5, the president traveled by motorcade to the Hotel Victoria. The president went to the Grand Ballroom around 5:30 to conduct the 22nd press conference of his administration. The press conference was broadcast live in the United States via satellite and taped for broadcast later that evening in Poland. American and Polish reporters attended the event. Polish reporters used an interpreter to ask questions.

The president discussed U.S.-Soviet relations, the Middle East, religion and internal developments in Poland.

An hour later, the president was back in his private quarters at Wilanow Palace.

The final evening's activities in Warsaw consisted of a state dinner hosted by the first secretary and Mrs. Gierek. After a brief reception and introduction to the guests, dinner was served just before 8. After dinner, a series of toasts were exchanged, followed by a private coffee gathering with the Giereks and the Carters.

At 10:49, the Carters were on their way back to the palace.

At 11:39, the president called the White House signal board operator and left a wake up request for 6 a.m. the following day: Saturday, December 31st, 1977.

T H I R T Y

Sequoia City
The Grand Jury

Seth Freeman, the Sequoia City district attorney, was young and brash with political ambitions far beyond the county. The criminal prosecution of real estate fraud at the very least would assure his re-election. He hoped it would also be his ticket out of town.

Seth and I first met after a Board of Supervisors meeting. It took some time, but we got to know each other fairly well. He provided a lot of background information and off the record material on pending investigations and prosecutions. I stopped by his office at least once a week. It was the perfect symbiotic relationship: He loved publicity and I loved getting the story first.

While Grand Jury proceedings are supposed to be confidential, Seth usually gave me a "heads up" when the Grand Jury was called into special session. He made sure I knew when indictments were to be handed down so I could be in the courtroom and have first crack at reporting on them. I made sure the D.A.'s name was included several times in my story. Freeman was always available for a taped interview following the court action.

A Grand Jury's primary role is governmental oversight. Grand Juries look for inefficiencies, waste, duplication of services or outright fraud in local government operations.

Grand Juries can also hear evidence and interview witnesses prior to issuing a criminal indictment. While an indictment is simply a finding that there is enough evidence to proceed to a trial, public perception of an indictment is often interpreted as a guilty verdict.

During Grand Jury proceedings, witnesses are not allowed to have an attorney present. Refusing to testify in front of a Grand Jury is contempt of court.

Witnesses can be compelled to testify under threat of jail time. If a witness claims the Fifth Amendment right to avoid self-incrimination, the D.A. takes the witness before a Superior Court judge. The judge can grant limited immunity against prosecution in exchange for the witness' testimony.

If a witness still refuses to testify, they can be sent to the county jail. They are housed in an area separate from criminal defendants. They are told "You hold the key to your cell." At some point, if they decide to cooperate, they are brought back to court. If they convince a judge of their change of heart, the Grand Jury is called back into session. If the witness testifies, they are released and free to go home. If they change their mind at the last minute and decide not to testify, they are sent back to jail.

The judge then has to decide if continued jail time will eventually convince the witness to testify. If so, a potential witness can be held for weeks, months, even years. On the other hand, if no amount of jail time is likely to convince the witness to testify, the judge can rule that further incarceration is "punitive" instead of "coercive." The potential witness is released from custody, a setback for the D.A. and any potential prosecution.

Witnesses are sworn to confidentiality and violating that can also lead to a contempt of court citation.

Criminal Grand Jury investigations and indictments are secret until arrests are made. In California, only a Superior Court judge can order the testimony to be released.

A Grand Jury is a great investigative tool for a district attorney looking into potential criminal cases. It is particularly helpful when the individuals under investigation are powerful, politically connected or wealthy.

THIRTY-ONE

Emma's Son

It was a few months before Emma told me she was previously married and had a son named David.

I thought we had gotten fairly close, so I was surprised that she hadn't mentioned this before. She did not seem the least bit troubled that she had kept this part of her life a secret from me.

I found out that her son David was 7 and lived full time with his father. David would occasionally visit on the weekend or during the summer months. Emma was very cautious to introduce David to any of her friends, including me.

"Turns out the judge didn't think a waitress in a bar could also be a fit mother, so my ex has full custody. I have visitation rights." She was a bit angry. "David's father could sleep around, but I was the unfit one."

She was resigned to the situation but far from happy about it.

"I've never introduced any of my boyfriends to David. It's already difficult to explain why Mommy and Daddy aren't together. I don't want to explain who the stranger I'm with is and why it might be a different stranger from the last time he visited. It would be too confusing."

She looked at me, embarrassed, and said, "I don't sleep around, OK. I've only had one serious relationship since David's father and I broke up six years ago."

She looked off and her eyes welled up. "I don't want to hurt my son anymore. I can't protect him from everything, but I can make his time with me routine, predictable and without upset."

"You and Me Against the World"—Helen Reddy

"I'm taking next week off. David's coming to town. I hope you understand, we need to take a break for a while."

MARK'S GREAT AMERICAN NOVEL
Chapter Ten

December 31, 1977
Warsaw, Poland

The Carters concluded their visit to Poland this morning.

The president and first lady took one final tour of the palace, then joined First Secretary Gierek and his wife for the trip to Okechie Airport at 8:20. A final ceremony took place on the tarmac. The president thanked Polish and U.S. Embassy officials for their assistance during the trip. It was followed by another review of troops assembled for the occasion and a warm goodbye to the first secretary and his wife.

The president and Mrs. Carter boarded Air Force One shortly thereafter. "Wheels up" occurred at 9:13 a.m.. The flight to the Imperial Pavilion Mehrabad Airport in Tehran, Iran, would take 4 hours, 13 minutes.

Two hours into the flight, the president held a series of brief meetings with Secretary of State Vance, Assistant for National Secretary Brzezinski, Alfred Atherton of the State Department, Press Secretary Jody Powell and Susan Clough, a personal assistant.

Air Force One touched down in Iran at 4:29 p.m. local time. They were greeted by the U.S. Ambassador to Iran William Sullivan and his wife. The president and first lady were welcomed by Mohammad Reza Pahlavi Aryamehr, the shahanshah of Iran and Farah Pahlayi, the shahbanou of Iran.

Iranian children presented the president and first lady with flowers. The shah introduced members of his official entourage, then escorted the presidential party to a stand for reviewing the assembled troops.

At 4:45, the president and shah exchanged remarks lasting about seven minutes. After greeting members of the U.S. mission in Iran, the president and first lady joined the shah and his wife in their motorcade to Saadabad Palace compound in Tehran.

The palace was constructed in the 19th century and first inhabited by Qajar monarchs and the royal families. The compound includes a total of 18 palaces, with a summer villa and a Fine Arts Museum. Reza Shah lived there in the 1920s. The first floor of The Nation Palace was built in 1932 for his son Mohammad Reza Shah, the Carters' current host.

The complex contains millions of dollars of art and antiquities from the Middle

East, Asia and Europe. The lobby of The Nation Palace contains two enormous silk rugs, one measuring 63 square meters and the other a large silk in three sections. Mohammad Reza Shah moved into The Nation Palace in the 1970s.

Mohammad Reza Shah assumed the title of shah when his father was forced to abdicate the Peacock Throne, which is the centuries old symbol of the Iranian monarchy. His father declared Iran a neutral country during World War II, refusing to allow foreign troops or training on Iranian soil. He also refused to allow supplies to cross Iran's border for shipment to Russia in its fight against Germany. The elder shah was forced from the throne following a massive British and Soviet air, land and sea invasion of Iran in August 1941.

Following the invasion, the British gave the reigning Shah an ultimatum: "Would His Highness kindly abdicate in favour of his son, the heir to the throne? We have a high opinion of him and will ensure his position. But His Highness should not think there is any other solution".

Mohammad Reza Shah took the throne on September 16, 1941. With the way cleared for troop and supply movements through Iran, Winston Churchill later dubbed Iran "The Bridge of Victory" for its contribution to the Allied war effort.

When they arrived at the palace on December 31, 1977, Mohammad Reza Shah and the Carters entered the main hall. Once again, they were greeted by U.S. Ambassador Sullivan, the Iranian minister of state for women's affairs, the Iranian vice minister of the Imperial Court as well as the vice grand master for ceremonies and the Iranian aide de camp.

The president joined the shah in his private office. At 6:19, following a brief photo session, the president and shah adjourned to a conference room for a meeting with U.S. and Iranian officials.

The meeting lasted until 7:15.

At the same time, in New Delhi, security agents were in overdrive now with less than 20 hours until President Carter's arrival in India.

T H I R T Y - T W O

Sawmill Ridge

Sawmill Ridge, at 5345 feet, is the highest peak in the area and towers over the Sequoia River Canyon. Early settlers called it Granddad Mountain as it was the most visible of the tall hills in the area.

Either name was easier to pronounce than the Indian name it held for a millennia. Sawmill Ridge, the modern and accepted name, was also easier to spell. No one was quiet sure how "Sawmill Ridge" got its name. While the ridge and nearby hills were extensively logged in the late 19th and early 20th century, it was over 20 miles from the nearest sawmill.

For the canyon-dwelling Indians, the peak was revered. It was a ceremonial place for weddings and coming of age rituals. Despite tales passed on by early settlers, there was no evidence of human sacrifice on the peak or, for that matter, anywhere else among California Indians.

Cold rains in the valley meant snow on the peak. It was believed that the longer the snow lasted on the peak, the longer the summer growing season would be.

In early September, the handle of the Big Dipper appeared suspended in a perfect arch over the peak. It was the sign that harvest was near and, more importantly, time to prepare for the annual migration downstream and back into the valley.

THIRTY-THREE

Sequoia City

D.A. Freeman formed his Investigative Real Estate Task Force by hiring a mostly young, aggressive staff of attorneys, investigators, secretaries and stenographers.

Most were from out of the area. Many recently graduated from law school or had a law enforcement background. He also hired several seasoned investigators in their 50s. The younger team members were often aggressive and fearless, some would say reckless, in their investigations and stake-outs. The veterans, on the other hand, could assemble and connect threads of evidence that might be overlooked by a novice or lead to other investigations.

Freeman pulled no punches with new employees during the first group meeting.

"This task force is walking through a political mine field. There are some powerful as well as some not very nice people we will be investigating. They have impressive connections in town. You may be followed, verbally or physically intimidated and your family may be threatened."

Freeman never mentioned he ruled out potential employees with a spouse or children when reviewing resumes and conducting in-person interviews.

"I can't stress this enough: Be very careful with conversations in public. Don't leave this office with any of your interview or investigation notes. Don't keep any information in your car or at home. Be sure you lock your desk every night and be sure you know where the key is at all times.

"There is going to be a lot of pressure on everyone in the office. It will be very intense in here as our work progresses. Try to remember we're all on the same side. No one talks to the press, understand? No one. I don't even want you talking to your friends about what goes on in this office. There's no room for superstars here. I guarantee by the time our work is finished, all of you will have a very impressive resume.

"Now, I'm not your mother or your minister, so I'm not going to tell you how to behave outside this office. Let me warn you, though, if you're having a drink after work, be damn sure you know who you are talking to or getting into bed with.

"You have information that will be very valuable to a lot of people outside this office. They will use every trick in the book if they have to."

With a chuckle, he said, "Which means even you ugly guys can get laid if someone thinks you know something."

Nervous laughter helped break the tension for a moment.

On a serious note, he continued. "Folks, we are the 'new sheriff' in town and we're not going to win any popularity contests."

He closed the meeting with a quote from his grandfather: "Starting today, we are going to be as welcome and as popular as small pox."

T H I R T Y - F O U R

AM and FM Broadcasting

Given the foothill terrain around Sequoia City, FM broadcasting was impractical. FM radio signals broadcast on what engineers call line of sight. Basically, if you can't see the transmitting tower, you probably can't receive the signal. So, we had to settle for AM.

I had the radio on all the time. Even slept with it on. I could pick up KNBR in San Francisco, KFBK in Sacramento and one of the stations out of Redding. Given the distance from the stations, reception was often an issue. Most came in great at night. Not so great during the day. It often required moving the radio one direction or the other to pick up a signal.

AM radio waves travel a great distance farther at night. Many stations occupy the same dial position. To reduce nighttime interference with one another, these stations cut their power output at sunset. They return to full power at sunrise. KBSC reduced power from 1,000 watts daytime to 250 watts at sunset.

The Federal Communications Commission restricts AM radio stations in the U.S. to a maximum of 50,000 watts. Many of these 50,000-watt stations occupy "clear channels." These "clear channels" do not interfere with a station at the same dial position because the competing station is normally located a half continent away.

Occasionally I could tune in "Wolfman Jack" on XERF in Mexico. XERF broadcast with 250,000 watts, assuring the "Wolfman" could be heard throughout the Western and Midwestern United States.

T H I R T Y - F I V E

Little Grass Valley
Sunday, December 17, 1978

In California, mountain lookout towers are only occupied during fire season—the dry months, usually mid-May to mid-to-late October. The towers are vacant now, so my campfire won't be spotted. That's good because the wood is still very damp and the fire continues to smoke a lot without much heat.

The towers are California's first line of defense for spotting wild land, brush or forest fires. Once a fire is spotted, a call is placed to the dispatch center. Within minutes, air tankers filled with fire retardant are airborne. The air tankers are to keep the fire from spreading before ground crews arrive on the scene.

Accommodations in the towers range from spartan to somewhat comfortable. Some have showers, some don't. Some have bathroom facilities, some just a pit toilet outside at the bottom of the stairs. Some towers are operated by the U.S. Forest Service while the state provides staffing for others.

Life in a fire tower is a lot like flying: hours of boredom interrupted by moments of sheer terror. It's a wooden or metal tower up to five stories high and it's the tallest object in the area. When a thunderstorm moves into the area, the employee goes on high alert. First, all of the tower windows are closed and sealed tight. Lightning can follow even the slightest wind current, like a draft through a fire tower.

The employee pulls a small platform, about the size of a step stool, into the center of the tower. The platform rests on large glass insulators, the kind that hold high voltage lines on towers. Standing on the platform prevents lightning from passing through the employee should lightning hit the tower.

At least that's what employees are told.

When the windows are closed, the tower becomes very still and heats up quickly. The anxiety of the tower employee adds considerably to the discomfort.

The tower has lightning rods on top. A nearby lightning strike followed almost instantly by a clap of thunder is deafening. And frightening.

The tower employee pinpoints the lightning strike locations using an Osborne Fire Finder and looks for smoke plumes in the area the following morning. The Osborne Fire Finder has been in use since 1915 and requires no electricity. The Fire Finder is a circular rim placed over a topographical map of the area. Using two telescopic sights, an experienced tower employee can make an accurate estimate of distance, elevation and position of a lightning strike and potential fire.

Imagine the routine: Working for the state, you are a part-time, seasonal employee putting in an 84-hour work week—3 ½ days on and 3 ½ days off. You hope that it turns into a full-time job in the future. U.S. Forest Service employees, on the other hand, staff their towers full time throughout the fire season.

Unless there are active fires in the area, radio dispatchers for the state and federal agencies signed off at 6 p.m. Around 8 o'clock, tower employees use the Forest Service radio system to talk to one another. It's the only means of communicating with the outside world. The radio system becomes your closest companion. Isolated tower employees share stories about the wild animals they've seen, the human visitors who climbed to the top of the tower during the day and, on occasion, stories about U.F.O. sightings.

All in all, it can be a pretty lonely life.

Kind of like now, except there is not even any radio reception here. It's just lonely.

I really wasn't prepared for the cold up here. I've been shivering a lot today. I can't seem to get warm.

My grandpa gave me a bottle of 10-year old Jameson's for my college graduation. I remembered to bring it, but forgot to pack a lot of other "necessities" for this trip, like toilet paper.

He told me to save the bottle for a special occasion. This trip seemed as special an occasion as any I guess, so I opened the bottle Friday night after I got camp set up. I wish Grandpa were here to share it with me. He'd know what to do now.

Boy is it ever cold.

MARK'S GREAT AMERICAN NOVEL
Chapter Eleven

December1977

Americans use the word "peon" to describe an individual with little money and few skills. A peon is often among the nameless, faceless, invisible people performing menial work behind the scenes, out of sight, in fields or during overnight hours.

In Sri Lanka, Malaysia and India, "peon" is a frequently used as an actual job description for a servant. In business and government offices, a peon fetches water, runs errands, makes tea, carries files between offices and is expected to stand up when a company boss or official comes into the room.

While western companies were converting many tasks to computers and automation, the huge pool of potential employees slowed the adaptation of labor-saving techniques in India. Banks, for instance, continued to sort and process checks by hand employing hundreds of people for the task.

In the 1970s, thousands of young Indians joined the work force every month at a time when the country already suffered from high unemployment. Many were employed at hotels, as domestic help, railway porters, cycle rickshaw drivers or in the thousands of roadside restaurants (dhabas) that dotted the Indian landscape.

For Zia, feeding and housing the team were a constant financial strain.

He regularly reviewed finances with the group during afternoon planning sessions. None of them had any money. Shortly after arriving in New Dehli, it was clear the expense of individual rooms would be too great a financial burden, so team members agreed to share living quarters. Only Zia, because of his personal daily food, exercise and cleanliness regimen, stayed in a private room.

Individually, members agreed to do what they could to add to the group's meager coffers. Had the plot taken place in Bombay, team members might have found work as a dabbawala. In Hindi, dabbawala literally means "one who carries the box." In this case, the box (dabba) is a cylindrical tin lunch box weighing about 3 pounds. For over a century, dabbawalas have delivered hot homemade lunches to tens of thousands of businessmen in Bombay every day.

The process begins in the morning just after the husband leaves for work. His wife prepares a lunch for him and packs it in a dabba, keeping the food hot. It is then picked up by a dabbawala. The dabba may be transferred as many as six times before it is delivered to an appreciative, hungry businessman.

The dabbawala system employs several thousand people and has evolved over the decades as the demand for the service has increased. Mistakes are rare: less than one in 6 million deliveries.

There was no such a system in Delhi, so other skills and talents were needed. Team member Dipak was barely 20 years old but an adept and very successful pickpocket. Dipak worked in tourist areas near luxury hotels, but was careful not to be seen in the same vicinity more than a couple of hours at a time. Hotel employees and Indian police were constantly on the lookout for scam artists and petty thieves targeting tourists.

Other team members agreed to spend a few hours a day begging in front of the international arrival terminal at Palam airport or at the New Delhi railway station. One member volunteered to work as a street vendor.

With all of the planning required, Zia sensed he was falling behind the personal timetable he had set for himself. In his mind, there was a growing fear that he might never catch up.

T H I R T Y - S I X

Sequoia City

At the apartment, I always locked my doors—front and back. Even during the day when I was home.

I was probably the only person in Sequoia City to lock his car. It was not unusual for even a policeman to leave his patrol car running while he dashed into Melva's for a cup of coffee to go or to deposit a check at the B of A.

Not me. I always locked my car. Always.

At home, even when I was in the bathroom, I locked the door.

And my bedroom door at night.

I just felt better.

Right after I moved in, with the Healys' permission, I installed a couple of dead-bolts to the front and back doors. They thought I lived in the city too long and didn't know what rural life was like, but they didn't object to the new locks.

I just felt safer.

MARK'S GREAT AMERICAN NOVEL
Chapter Twelve

The era of presidential air travel began 40 years after the Wright Brothers flight in Kitty Hawk, North Carolina, and just 16 years after Charles Lindbergh's solo flight across the Atlantic to Paris.

On January 11, 1943, Franklin D. Roosevelt became the first sitting president to travel by air. Midway through the second World War, with German U-Boats still active in the Atlantic, traveling by sea was considered too risky for the president.

Roosevelt planned to meet with Winston Churchill in Casablanca to map out a strategy for the invasion of Sicily and Italy. The president's advisers recommended air transportation, even though most people at the time considered flying dangerous. President Roosevelt was 60 years old at the time. The trip would cover 17,000 miles round trip.

One of Pan Am's "flying boats," the Dixie Clipper, was pressed into service. The Dixie Clipper made history in 1939 making the first scheduled transatlantic passenger flight from New York to Lisbon. The flight occurred just 12 years after Charles Lindberg's solo flight from New York to Paris in The Spirit of St. Louis in May 1927.

Dubbed the flying boats, the Clippers were designed to land and take off on water. They were built by Boeing with a model designation of B314. There were only 12 ever built and all were owned and operated by Pan American. They had a 3,500 mile-range, by far the longest in commercial service at the time. They were known as "The Airborne Palace" as the cabin was one class luxury service. Top speed was 210 mph although normal cruising speed was 188 mph at 11,000 feet. Maximum cruising altitude was just under 20,000 feet.

In normal service, the flying boat had a crew of 11, including cabin stewards. The Clippers could carry up to 68 passengers. The Flying Clippers were the largest planes in scheduled commercial service until the introduction of the 747 jumbo jet on January 21, 1970. The B314 had a wingspan of 152 feet. The wingspan of a 747 is 196 feet.

Planning for President Roosevelt's trip was done under the strictest security conditions. The security for the trip was so tight that the American public was only informed after Roosevelt was back in the White House.

The plan was to make the trip in three segments aboard the Dixie Clipper with the Atlantic Clipper standing by as a back-up. In-flight security was heavy with 35 fighter planes escorting the presidential airplane as it left Miami.

The first leg of the journey was 1,600 miles to the Port of Spain in Trinidad. The next segment was an eight-hour flight, covering 1,200 miles to Brazil. The longest leg of the journey was 2,500 miles across the Atlantic and took 19 hours. The flight landed in British-controlled Gambia. The president then transferred to a camouflaged C-54 passenger plane for the final nine-hour flight into Casablanca.

In 1944, a four-engine Douglas C-54 Skymaster was customized for the president's use. Dubbed by the press "The Sacred Cow," it was used by the president only once before he died. The president made his final trip to peace talks with Stalin and Churchill aboard a U.S. Navy cruiser, the Quincy. The cruiser docked in Malta and the president used "The Sacred Cow" to fly to the meeting in Yalta.

President Truman called his airplane "Independence" in honor of his hometown in Missouri and had the aircraft painted to resemble an eagle, complete with head and feathers.

Believing Truman would lose the 1948 presidential election to Governor Thomas Dewey, the Air Force prepared a new presidential aircraft, dubbed "The Dewdrop." "The Dewdrop" was a Lockheed Constellation featuring a pressurized cabin and four of the most advanced piston engines of their time: the 18-cylinder Wright R-3350 radial engine.

Obviously, "The Dewdrop" never saw service under "President Dewey."

Instead, the plane was used as a backup VIP plane for the U.S. Air Force and administration officials.

As supreme Allied commander during World War II, Dwight Eisenhower dubbed his plane "Columbine I." As president, Eisenhower called the plane used during the first part of his administration "Columbine II."

On one occasion, President Eisenhower's "Columbine II" was used to transport Queen Elizabeth II. A draft of the Eisenhower's "Atoms for Peace" speech was written on board "Columbine II."

Until 1953, the president's plane did not have a unique call sign to distinguish it from other aircraft. That changed when air traffic controllers confused two planes with similar flight numbers in the same airspace over New York City. On that day, President Eisenhower's "Columbine II" was designated Air Force flight 8610. In the same air space, at the same time, was Eastern Airlines flight 8610.

While a midair collision involving the president of the United States was avoided, the official call sign now for any plane carrying the president is "Air Force One."

THIRTY-SEVEN

Little Grass Valley Reservoir
Sunday afternoon
December 17, 1978

Until this weekend, I never realized how frightened I have been every moment of every day of my life.

During the week, I worried I'd be late for work, although it never happened. I worried I might overdraft my checking account, although that never happened either. I worried about food poisoning, running out of gas, being stranded on a lonely highway, getting mugged or beaten up. What if my car breaks down and I don't have enough money to fix it?

The sound of police or fire sirens always set me off.

What would Jim and Joyce think if I was late with my rent check? I never was. I made sure they had the check no later than noon the day before it was due.

I think I even worried that I didn't worry enough.

There was always an edge of anxiety, from the moment I awakened to the moment I went to sleep. My breathing was always a little shallow. I would notice it most if I was walking and talking to someone at the same time. For a long time, I thought I might be having a heart attack, since shortness of breath is a symptom.

I could feel my heart rate go up just talking to people, even Ed or Emma.

I worried that I might have gotten some girl pregnant and never known, but given my "track record" that was pretty unlikely. I worried about the drought and what I could be doing in my apartment to conserve water. I worried about the news of the world and whether we were headed for a nuclear war. Paul Erlich's "The Population Bomb" scared the hell out of me.

Would the doctor's office charge me if I didn't show up for an appointment? I never missed one.

God I've worried a lot. I've never stopped long enough to analyze my feelings and emotions. I have constantly felt "in high gear and on the run" emotionally.

God, I am really screwed up.

And it seems much colder this afternoon.

T H I R T Y - E I G H T

The State Water Project is a massive effort to move water from northernmost parts of California to as far south as San Diego.

A master plan was laid out early in the 1940s to deal with California's supply and demand for water as well as provide reasonable flood control. Electric power generation and recreational opportunities were added benefits.

Oroville Dam, the cornerstone, was dedicated in 1968.

The Auburn Dam project was already on the drawing boards and millions of dollars were spent on infrastructure improvements and road relocations. Later, concerns about the effect of an earthquake on the Auburn Dam's concrete arch design forced the cancellation of the project. Environmental concerns also played a part in the project's cancellation.

The Sequoia River was an untapped bonanza for an ever-growing, and thirsty, California population. It was only a matter of time before water planners in Sacramento and Southern California looked at the possibilities of Sequoia River.

An initial look at the Sequoia was underway when the California Legislature authorized a study of state water resources. Starting in 1951, the first study looked at rainfall totals, normal and flood stage stream flows and statewide water quality. Four years later, a second study estimated current and future water uses. The final study, in 1957, outlined a development plan for harnessing California's water resources.

Final funding legislation for the federal portion of the Sequoia Lake project was approved while President Kennedy was dedicating Whiskeytown Lake near Redding, California. The Whiskeytown dedication took place in November 1963, just weeks before Kennedy was shot to death in Dallas.

Construction on the Sequoia Lake reservoir began the following year as weather permitted. While the dam site was prepared downstream, bulldozers would clear brush and timber 300 feet down from the high-water mark. Clearing reduced the amount of floating debris as the lake level began to fill. This would also help boaters find a clear spot to tie up regardless of the seasonal rise and fall of the lake.

The cleared brush would be burned or buried. Oak, madrone and manzanita could be salvaged and hauled out of the clearing area to be sold as firewood. Any debris that did float would become waterlogged and eventually sink forever. As the lake level dropped during the summer draw down, the driftwood made for great beach campfires.

Recreation was the fourth priority for the Sequoia project, following storage, flood control and power generation.

Surveying for a project the size of Sequoia Lake was a daunting task. While Indian attacks were never a risk historically any time in this region, survey crews faced other dangers. There were rattlesnakes, mountain lions, poison oak, black bears, shifting rocks and rock falls, hornet nests, steep terrain and often a total lack of visible landmarks. In many areas, the brush was so thick, a machete was needed to clear a path. Crews relied solely on their survey instruments and compasses to determine the high water mark, and for that matter, exactly where they were.

Crews consisted of professional engineers and surveyors who supervised part-time state employees and college interns. These part-time crew members resembled a United Nations gathering: American and East Indians, Chinese, Koreans and Japanese, third generation sons of immigrants from Ireland, England and Italy. Most of the college interns planned a career in civil engineering and were attending college at Chico State, Cal State Sacramento or Cal Poly San Luis Obispo.

Crews assembled early in the morning to get instructions for the day's activities. Travel to the survey site was in an Army convoy truck bumping along dusty, narrow roads at speeds far greater than was probably prudent. Some of the roads were so thick with fine dirt that the back flap of the truck had to be closed to keep the choking dust out. The heat, the claustrophobia of the enclosed truck and the inability to see the road ahead led to terrible motion sickness. Getting sick in those circumstances added a new "dimension" to the ride. Most of the crew learned to forgo breakfast before the trips into the hills. On almost any day, the crew believed these trips could qualify as an E-ticket ride in Disneyland.

In addition to their equipment, crews would pack a lunch and several canteens of water. Often the crews had to hike quite a distance to pick up where they left off the day before. During the day, crew members often refilled their canteens in a nearby creek or stream. That practice ended when a dead, decaying deer was discovered in a creek, 20 yards upstream from where crew members had just refilled their canteens.

The crews were to survey and mark the high-water level of the reservoir, an area covering nearly 140 miles of eventual shoreline. With just a 25-foot telescoping survey pole, crews used short-range radios on either side of the river, then drove simple wooden stakes in the ground to pinpoint the high-water mark. The stakes would mark the point where bulldozers would begin clearing brush for the reservoir.

Depending on terrain, the crews could survey and mark as few as two miles to as many as five miles per day using this rudimentary system. The biggest survey challenges the crews faced were in the middle fork. With only animal trails to follow down to the water and huge boulders to traverse in and along the river, it might take crews six hours to get in and get out of a survey area. It was understood that work on these days would run well over the allotted eight-hour time schedule.

Crew chiefs overlooked the days when a survey was finished before lunch or early in the afternoon. The crew was instructed to stay in the field until quitting time. Trying to get payroll clerks in Sacramento to understand or approve eight-hour paychecks for work completed in less time was deemed an exercise in futility—and a waste of time—by the local superintendents in charge. Approval for overtime was just as unlikely.

With temperatures above 100 degrees in July and August, superintendents ignored occasions when an intern "fell" into the river. Those "accidents" happened a lot in the late afternoon.

As difficult as the conditions were, the surveys were amazingly precise. When the lake filled, there was never more than 8 inches difference between the actual lake level and the level marked with the stakes.

California's geography is ideal for large water storage projects. Lots of rain at fairly predictable times of the year. Lots of narrow, deep canyons that are easily plugged by dams to create reservoirs.

In California, there's either too much water or not enough. And usually it's in the wrong place: 70 percent of California's rain falls north of Sacramento while 75 percent of water usage is in Southern California.

California's geography can also contribute to incredible flooding.

There are two kinds of storm systems that roll off the Pacific into California. Cold storms with lots of moisture and heavy snows from the Gulf of Alaska.

Hydrologists and agricultural interests welcome the colder storms. A heavy snowpack helps fill reservoirs as they melt in the spring. This allows the state to meet its contracted water delivery schedules for cities and farms in the summer.

The flip side of the coin is the "Pineapple Express": a series of large storms with enormous amounts of warm rain. The rain can turn snowpack into raging floods in a matter of hours. The "Pineapple Express" storms provided the impetus for the State Water Project and the federal government's Central Valley Project.

At 2.75 million acre feet of storage, Sequoia Lake would be the third-largest water storage facility in California.

Just after Sequoia Lake construction was completed, the New Melones Dam was under construction. New Melones would be the fourth-largest water storage facility in California.

MARK'S GREAT AMERICAN NOVEL
Chapter Thirteen

Tehran, Iran
December 31, 1977
8:17 p.m.

After meeting with the shah and American and Iranian officials, President Carter went to his suite and spoke by telephone with Special Assistant for Appointments Timothy Kraft.

An hour later, the president and first lady returned to their motorcade for the brief trip to Niavaran Palace and a state-sponsored dinner. They were accompanied by the Iranian Aide De Camp Gen. M. Khosrowdad. Surrounded by 50 acres of woods, Niavaran Palace was the summer residence of the Shah and his family.

The dinner was hosted by the shah and his wife. At 8:40, the presidential party greeted dinner guests in the palace reception room and then were escorted by the shah and his wife to the banquet room at 9:08. There was a photo session just before dinner, which was served at 9:14.

Dinner was followed by an exchange of toasts between the shah and the president.

At 10:30, King Hussein I of the Hashemite Kingdom of Jordan arrived. Following the evening's entertainment at the Imperial Theatre, the king met with the president and the shah for 15 minutes. The meeting included another brief photo session.

Just before midnight, the president's group gathered again with the dinner guests to join a New Year's Eve party.

T H I R T Y - N I N E

Sequoia City

Living near a large reservoir, you quickly become acquainted with water statistics and terminology.

At the radio station, I ended my newscasts with the weather forecast and the latest data from the Sequoia Lake project. I reported the level of the reservoir, total acre feet in storage, the lake surface temperatures, water inflows into the lake and the flow of releases downstream from the project.

The U.S. Army Corps of Engineers underwrites a portion of major California state water projects. The Corps' contribution reserves a portion of lake capacity for flood storage during the winter and spring runoff months. The flood storage area keeps reservoir levels well below the crest of a dam and provides a cushion in case hot weather or heavy rains trigger the sudden melting of mountain snowpack. Project releases downstream can be adjusted, hourly if necessary, to keep the reservoir level below the flood storage level. During peak inflow periods, project releases are increased gradually to equalize what's known as "hydrostatic pressure" on levees downstream. Increasing releases too quickly will overwhelm the levees.

The Corps of Engineers regulates the filling of reservoirs until the end of April. After May 1, the threat of heavy rains or quick snowmelt declines significantly and reservoirs are allowed to fill, usually peaking in mid-June.

In the 1800s, water measurements were in "miner's inches." Gold miners used it to measure the water flow in a sluice box. A miner's inch was the amount of water flowing over a 12-inch wide, 1-inch high board during a 24-hour period. A miner's inch flow is about 1.5 cubic feet per minute or just over 16,100 gallons in a 24-hour period.

As larger quantities of water were needed for irrigation and other water intensive industries, the miner's inch was dropped in favor of cubic feet per second. In Arizona, California, Montana and Oregon, it takes 40 miner's inches to equal one cubic foot per second. In other states, it can range from 38.4 to 50 miner's inches to equal a cubic foot per second. Oddly, the measurement is not exact or standard throughout the country and there's no explanation why a cubic foot is measured differently in different states.

The accepted standard cubic foot of water is 7.48 gallons and weighs about 62 pounds. A full bathtub of water holds about 5 cubic feet of water. Average daily water usage in the United States is between 80 and 100 gallons per person or as much as 13 cubic feet of water.

Cubic feet per second simply measures the velocity and volume of water at a given point. Average water flows from Shasta Dam in Northern California are between 3,200 and 5,000 cubic feet per second. In the summer, releases are cranked up higher than 10,000 cfs for agricultural users downstream.

By comparison, the Niagara Rivers dumps 85,000 cfs over Niagara Falls but only ranks 11th in cfs water volume worldwide. Inga Falls on the Congo River in Africa is No.1 with flows of up to 1,500,000 cfs. Two waterfalls now buried by hydroelectric projects on the Columbia River, Celilo Falls and Kettle Falls, would have ranked sixth and seventh worldwide in cfs.

Water storage is measured in acre feet. An acre foot of water is enough to cover one acre of ground with one foot of water. In raw numbers, 1,000 cfs equals a little more than an acre foot a minute.

Running the math out, 1,000 cfs is over 82 acre feet per hour and nearly 2,000 acre feet per day.

California reservoirs hold an impressive amount of water. Lake Shasta, part of the federal government's Central Valley Project, holds 4.5 million acre feet. That's enough to cover more than 7,000 square miles with one foot of water. Lake Shasta is the largest reservoir in California.

Lake Oroville, California's second-largest reservoir, is part of the State Water Project. At capacity, Lake Oroville holds about 3.5 million acre feet or enough to cover nearly 5,500 square miles with a foot of water.

Sequoia Lake at capacity would cover almost 4,700 square miles with a foot of water, an area the size of Los Angeles County.

As impressive as the storage numbers are, historic flood flows in California are astonishing.

Weather experts dubbed the California flood of 1955 the "1,000-year Storm." The 1955 storm held that distinction for just nine years.

In 1964, rain began to fall on December 19. Then, between December 20 and 26, a flood of biblical proportions occurred north of San Francisco. It is estimated that the amount of water that poured into the Pacific Ocean was 10.4 million acre feet—enough water to fill Lake Shasta twice, Lake Oroville three times or Folsom Lake nearly 10 times. In six days.

At Oroville, the half-completed earth-filled dam held back the enormous flood flows of the Feather River. Upstream from the dam was a funnel-shaped intake for diverting river water through a tunnel and around the construction area. Known as a "glory hole" it produced a gigantic whirlpool as flood waters continued to rise. Engineers at the construction site were concerned if the rain and runoff continued, the unfinished dam itself would be in jeopardy.

The 1964 flood occurred with a heavy snowpack in the mountains followed by a "Pineapple Express." In meteorological terms, the Pineapple Express is an "atmospheric river." The river transports huge amounts of water vapor in a trail several thousand miles long and a few hundred miles wide. An atmospheric river can contain up to 15 times the average amount of water flowing out of the Mississippi into the Gulf of Mexico. The atmospheric river is also accompanied by strong winds. The Pineapple Express can account for up to half of California's annual rainfall. It's also estimated that 80 percent of California's most damaging floods resulted from an atmospheric river. When a Pineapple Express makes landfall and stalls near the mountains of the west, extreme amounts of rainfall occur.

In 1964, the Pineapple Express and the melting snow sent torrents of water toward the ocean. The flood waters were met by a record high tide on the Pacific Coast. The combination dammed the rivers and backed up water over hundreds of square miles.

On the coast, flood flows at one point were calculated at more than 800,000 cfs—a level usually associated with the flood stages of the Mississippi or the Columbia rivers. For perspective, 43,600 cfs equals an acre foot of water per second. At 800,000 cfs, that was enough water to cover more than 18 acres with a foot of water every second.

An estimated 100 million board feet of processed lumber was lost as floods ripped through mills on the north coast. Five thousand head of cattle were lost.

The 1955 flood demolished one California state highway bridge. In 1964, 16 state bridges were destroyed or damaged beyond repair.

Three massive storms slammed into the West Coast over a six-week period, finally ending January 31, 1965. In some locations, at its peak, rainfall figures reached 15 inches in 24 hours.

The storm affected an area the size of France, more than 200,000 square miles in Northern California, Idaho, Nevada, Oregon and Washington.

The flooding resulted in 47 deaths, left thousands homeless and caused $540 million in damages.

"And it never failed that during the dry years the people forgot about the rich years and during the wet years they lost all memory of the dry years. It was always that way."
—John Steinbeck, "EAST OF EDEN" 1962

F O R T Y

The 1964 Atmospheric River in the forests above Sequoia City

The rainfall was staggering. Even longtime residents couldn't remember a period of heavier rain.

Normally, Sequoia City gets about 38 inches of rain per year. At this elevation, close to 3,500 feet, rainfall amounts more than double as the clouds lift over the Sierra and Cascade ranges. The rainfall here in the last 72 hours totaled more than 20 inches. Within a week, rainfall would be nearly double that total.

Just before dark on Wednesday afternoon, December 23, a fresh-cut load of logs was stacked on the narrow gauge train for delivery and processing at the mill 22 miles downstream. Train crews were anxious to get as many loads as possible to the mill before taking time off for Christmas. Once loaded, the train was parked on a siding until the following morning. "One more load per day" was the chatter among the crew in the weeks before Christmas.

The engine crew wanted to get as early a start as possible on the 24th, so they stayed the night in the temporary mill offices, which had six bunk beds in the rear.

To the crew's dismay, the locomotive took longer to get up a head of steam, so the expected departure was delayed 45 minutes. As the train moved downhill at around 6 miles per hour, the pounding rain could be heard over the squealing brakes of the locomotive and cars.

A careful look out either side of the locomotive cab revealed a few initial survey markers for the high-water mark of Sequoia Lake. From this point on, the area would be inundated by the reservoir at peak capacity. Reservoir construction would be the death knell for the railroad. The railroad and the mill here in the upper reaches of the lake would cease operations within six years. Much of their history would soon be buried by the waters of Sequoia Lake.

As the train rounded the last downhill curve a mile or so from Sequoia City, the engineer saw the trestle had been washed away. Even at the reduced speed this morning, there was no way to stop the train in time. The track incline, coupled with the reduced braking capabilities on wet rails and the enormous weight of the log load made an emergency stop impossible. As a last-ditch effort, the engineer threw the locomotive gears into reverse. If, by some stroke of luck or momentary suspension of the laws of physics the train stopped in time, damage to the engine would have been significant.

The engineer and fireman were confronted with an easy choice. They could take their chances of surviving a 200-foot plunge to the bottom of a raging creek ravine or jump from the slow-moving train. With a quick look at each other, the engineer and the fireman bailed out either side of the cab. They had less than 40 yards to spare just before the engine crossed onto the bridge abutment. The wrenching sounds of the machinery tearing itself apart overwhelmed all other sounds as the crew rolled away from the tracks.

The engine and nine trailing cars then plunged to the bottom of the ravine. The engineer later said he was surprised how little noise the crash made. There was no explosion, no cascading sounds of logs spilling into the abyss. One loud crash and that was it. Then silence. Except for the sound of the rain and the rushing water below.

While the crew was safe, they were faced with the obvious question: how to get back to their homes on the other side of the ravine.

Farther to the east, at a much higher elevation, snow fell in huge quantities very quickly on the 23nd. For the truck driver trying to complete his delivery schedule and get home early for Christmas, a decision to take a fair weather shortcut through the upper foothills proved fatal. The mostly packed gravel road quickly became impassable.

Marooned at 5,000 feet, the driver apparently set out on foot to hike to safety. His body was never found.

The truck was loaded with liquor for deliveries to bars and stores throughout the foothills. The deliveries were expected before New Year's Eve. Instead, the truck was stranded for weeks in snow drifts several feet deep.

Searchers eventually found the truck in late February.

It was empty. The back doors of the truck had been crudely pried open. There was no liquor on board. Nothing.

Nearby, in the few remaining snow drifts, there were snowshoe tracks. Lots of them. And a few empty bottles. The rest of the load was missing.

The truck had been looted.

FORTY-ONE

"Whiskey's for drinking, water's for fighting over"
—Mark Twain

Coloma, California
Sutter's Mill, 1848

When the shout went out "gold" it could just as easily have been "water." Water in California is the real gold rush. And it's always "on."

John Sutter found those first flakes of gold in the American River at Coloma, east of Sacramento. Sutter found some of the highest quality gold: at least 23 karat. His discovery triggered the California Gold Rush. Within two years, San Francisco's population swelled from 1,000 to 25,000. By 1855, 300,000 people came to the "Golden State" infected with Gold Fever. California contains the richest gold deposits in the lower 48 states and is among the top 10 most productive gold regions in the world.

Since that day in January 1848, water and gold have always intersected in California.

Initially, water was used to pan gold from river sand. Later, powerful hydraulic jets helped wash away entire hillsides in the search for gold. Hydraulic mining left huge scars in the California landscape still visible today.

Water provided the base for huge, self-propelled, floating gold dredges in the rivers of Northern California.

The dredges scooped up millions of tons of sand, rock and gravel from stream and river beds in search of nuggets. The dredged materials were dumped onto a conveyor belt and sifted to remove the gold. Once processed, the sand, rock and gravel was either dumped back into the river or along the banks into large rock piles called dredger tailings. When they ran out of stream beds, the dredges created their own waterways: carving into the river banks, sometimes moving miles into the surrounding countryside with water leading the way. Behind the dredgers, stagnant pools of water—dredger ponds—were left.

Mosquitoes loved the dredger ponds. As a result, malaria was endemic in Northern California until the late 1940s. The disease can be treated in 48 hours once diagnosed, but recurrent cases are not unusual. Immune systems are no match for malaria. It may take years of reinfection and treatment before an immunity develops.

One observer said malaria was so prevalent at the time, there was no need for air conditioning since everyone had the chills even during the hottest weather.

The dredger ponds only flushed when the rivers ran at flood stage. A century later, the dredger tailings were used in massive construction projects like Oroville Dam, Sequoia Dam and New Melones.

Water was used to move logs from the harvest area in the mountains to the sawmills through a series of flumes. Water held the logs in mill ponds before they were processed. Water fired the steam boilers at the lumber mills and in the locomotives that hauled the finished product to market.

The Sequoia River area was only a minor player during the California Gold Rush.

All of Northern California's creeks, streams and rivers were targeted by prospectors. The Sequoia, however, did not yield the quick riches of other Northern California waterways, so prospectors moved on in less than two years. Decades later, water helped clear the bedrock for the Sequoia Lake dam. For weeks, high-pressure water monitors scoured every inch of the area that would be the eventual foundation of the dam. These water jets were far more powerful than fire suppression pumps and their enormous pressure required as many as six men to direct and control each of the units. Engineers inspecting the work discovered the area around the dam's foundation was a natural "catch basin" for black sand and gold nuggets.

During construction of the Sequoia project, workers were strictly forbidden to leave the area with any of the wash material. Violating the rule led to immediate dismissal. The wash material was diverted and transported off-site to another location. Despite the threat of losing their job, more than one employee's lunch box went home several times heavier than when it arrived on the job site. Heavy with black sand and the hope of finding a gold nugget or two.

The California Gold Rush really never ended. Neither did "gold fever."

Months later, even the wash material dump site showed signs of drilling from dedicated "gold diggers."

F O R T Y - T W O

Sequoia City

The Sierra and Cascade ranges are dotted with thousands of gold mines. Some were very successful and are still being mined today. Most were not and were simply abandoned.

On official U.S. Forest Service maps, they carry names like "Calliope", "Bucks Mountain," "Fool's Gold," "The Bee's Knees," "Stay to the End," "The Ritz" or even "Black Bart's." The names often reflected a miner's hope for buried treasure. The mines were also named for towns and cities like "The New York" or "The Washington Cache." Nearby creeks or the names of the miners who staked the claim were often used as well.

Gold mining is extremely hard work. If you are digging, you may have to move as much as a ton of material to recover 1 ounce of gold. But strike a vein of gold or silver, often found in quartz deposits, and you've hit the "mother lode," a term first coined by California miners in the early 1860s.

To a novice spelunker, an abandoned mine offers the mystery and allure of "striking it rich." An inexperienced explorer entering an abandoned mine alone may never come out. Like pilots, mine explorers need to file a "flight plan" to let someone know where they are headed and when they expect to return. Otherwise, unless their off-road vehicle is found days, months or years later, the person is simply listed as "lost in the mountains" on a missing persons report.

The hazards inside an old mine shaft are significant. Some are obvious and some are not.

If the weather turns hot before California bears shed their winter coat, they will seek shelter in an abandoned mine. Rattlesnakes love the cool temperatures in the mine. Wood floors put in a hundred years ago to cover a shaft 10 to 40 feet deep are brittle and will shatter under any weight.

Ground water also accumulates in the shaft and is usually toxic, a mix of naturally occurring minerals and chemicals left over from the mining operations. As the decades pass, this toxic brew fills in the deep vertical shafts. An unsuspecting explorer walking through ankle-deep water will suddenly plunge into one of these shafts. If they surface at all, they usually have inhaled the water, exposing their sinus, lungs and any open wounds to virulent strains of bacteria.

A deep horizontal mine is called an adit—a derivative of the Latin word for entrance. Adits can stretch more than a mile into a hill or mountain. Oxygen levels diminish the deeper you go. It is possible to suffocate deep inside an old mine.

When the gold ran out, miners simply abandoned the tools of their trade, including picks, shovels and ore carts. Dynamite, which deteriorates over time and becomes very unstable and explosive, can also be found in old mines.

There is a constant threat of cave-ins. Miners were more interested in the quickest ways to get ore out of the mine, not engineering the safety or durability of the mine shaft or roof.

The "Keep Out" or "No Trespassing" signs at the entrance are not designed to just to discourage "claim jumpers."

FORTY-THREE

The Motherlode

Gold miners are a lot like fishermen and golfers: You never get a straight answer when you ask them how their career/hobby/vocation is going.

Fishermen always talk about the one that got away. Talk to enough fishermen, and after a while, their description of the "one that got away" starts to sound like the same fish. Over and over. Like the Loch Ness monster: Everyone says they've seen it, but nobody catches it.

Golfers always talk about how close they came to a hole-in-one or how their swing had improved and their handicap was going down. My golf handicap is golf.

When fishermen have a good day, like golfers, they can't wait to tell everyone and anyone.

Gold miners never have a good day—at least not when talking in a casual conversation. They've never seen a large nugget, their panning efforts are tedious and unproductive. In short, they never seem to have any luck. They would often lament the hard work and wonder aloud why they were still doing it.

They might find "a couple of flakes or two," now and then. If they knew you or liked you or trusted you, they might show you a vial filled with water and some small gold nuggets. But that was it. Nothing more.

They always had a wad of cash. Big wads with big bills. They never trusted banks. Ever.

Serious gold miners would leave town a lot during the winter months. They often returned driving a brand new car or truck. Sometimes they would be returning from a long, seemingly expensive vacation.

These were explained away by "an inheritance" they received or cash they received from a parent or sibling who had done really well in the stock market or a prepaid family reunion on board a cruise ship. Sometimes it was because they had a friend in the car business who could get them a really good deal.

But they never had any luck finding gold.

Ever.

The Sierra are littered with abandoned ghost towns. These towns sprang up wherever there was a whisper of a gold find. Towns were often located next to a creek or river where the gold collected in sand bars or under rocks.

Just as quickly as they sprang up, the towns were abandoned when the gold was gone. Most pioneer ghost towns have since been picked over by treasure or scavenger hunters. The job of the treasure hunters became easier after the invention of the portable metal detector. It was not unusual to sweep through the ruins of a 100-year old collapsed building and find an old belt buckle, tin can, rusted coffee pot or a bag of nails. It was also possible to find old coins that had dropped through the cracks in the floor.

For a $100 annual fee, any U.S. citizen can claim a 20-acre parcel to work exclusively for one year. The claim allows you to mine for precious metals or minerals on U.S. Forest Service land. There are restrictions on construction of buildings, digging depths and water quality, but no restrictions on the amount of material that can be harvested from a claim.

Gold miners are very protective of their claims. You never want to surprise a miner working his claim. You'd never joke about being with the IRS or the county assessor's office. Much like dealing with a grizzly bear, if you stumble on a working miner, it's best to simply back up and hope he didn't see you.

In the past, some claims, near a river, ended up being summer camping spots for families. The Forest Service doesn't allow semi-permanent camping on claims.

Rangers look for evidence of mining or mining equipment to determine if the camp is a legitimate mining operation or simply a way to avoid paying overnight camping fees in designated Forest Service campgrounds. Systems like water spring boxes are one indicator. Such systems funnel water from a spring into a large collection tank or box for drinking or for keeping food cool and safe from raccoons and bears.

When a claim produces little or no gold, miners often put their claim on the market. Before a prospective buyer arrives, the claim owner will "salt the property": hiding gold in pockets under rocks or scattering some gold flakes around. This gets an unsophisticated buyer very excited.

When the "stash" is discovered, the negotiations begin. The current claim holder could sell the claim for as little as the $100 he has invested. More often than not, depending on the enthusiasm of the buyer, the seller "reluctantly lets go of the claim" for several hundred, even several thousand dollars.

The seller just "mined" the buyer.

The excuses for selling are the same: family commitments, job change, not enough time to work the claim, a sick family member needing round-the-clock help or moving out of the area.

The seller takes cash on the spot and moves on to the next claim several miles away with renewed hopes of striking it rich.

FORTY-FOUR

The Big Story

Reporters are a funny lot. We make jokes about car accidents, murders, you name it. We speculate and share insights on the local news and personalities.

The one thing we never share are details of the "big story" we are working on. Every reporter knows when he's on to a "big story." Maybe it's information passed on by a law enforcement officer who tells you "you ought to look into this" and, of course, "this is off the record."

Every reporter "knows" they are on the verge of a story that will bring down corrupt politicians or expose waste in a government program or solve a murder that has confounded police for years. Your pulse quickens with the thought.

Bob Woodward and Carl Bernstein right now are everyone's heroes in the news business. They tracked down leads, developed sources and brought down the presidency of Richard Nixon. Through their investigation of a burglary at the Watergate hotel, Woodward and Bernstein discovered the break-in was orchestrated at the highest levels of the Nixon administration. Congressional investigations uncovered illegal shenanigans leading all the way to the Oval Office.

On August 8, 1974, Nixon resigned the presidency. All because of two reporters.

Even though Ed Thatcher and I were great friends, there was still a natural rivalry between newspaper and radio reporters. As well as we knew each other, we would never share even a hint of stories we were working on. We didn't want to get "scooped" by a competitor.

In November of last year, I knew Ed was working on something "Big." I just didn't know what.

I was no different. I had a "Big" story idea. And when it broke, I was sure I could find room for the Pulitzer medal somewhere in my apartment. And I wondered how long it would be after my big story broke before "60 Minutes" would want to hire me.

There is a saying in journalism that reporters always find the story they are looking for. Psychologists call it hypothesis bias: You accept everything that confirms your train of thought and dismiss everything that does not.

That's often the case with "The Big Story."

MARK'S GREAT AMERICAN NOVEL
Chapter Fourteen

Early evening
Santacruz Airport, Bombay, India
January 1, 1978

Zia hurried through the airport.

He continually looked at his watch. To a casual observer in the terminal, he simply looked like a man late for a plane. He had arrived by plane from New Delhi a couple of hours earlier. Now it was on to his connection: an Air India flight to Dubai. He would occasionally look around, but not enough to draw attention. He just appeared to be a man in a hurry.

While the U.S. and Dubai enjoyed cordial diplomatic relations, Zia's plan was to catch a connecting flight in Dubai to a country more hospitable to his cause. The U.S. had meddled too long in the affairs of the Middle East, he thought.

Just two months earlier, in November, Anwar Sadat addressed the Israeli Parliament. It was obvious to Zia and others like him that the heavy hand of the Americans were orchestrating events behind the scenes.

"The plan was probably doomed from the start" Zia muttered under his breath. Too many amateurs. Too many people knowing too many details. Even the wrong guns. He stepped up his pace through the terminal. It was Sarajevo all over again, he thought, letting his mind wander. But at least that group of amateurs pulled it off.

The president of the United States, Jimmy Carter, had arrived earlier in the day for a three-day visit.

The message we planned to send, Zia remembered, would be heard around the world for decades to come.

Honestly, Zia thought, kill an American president here in India? Hurrying through the airport now, it sounded ludicrous. It hadn't sounded so crazy for the last few months. His team consisted of fervent believers who knew their time had come.

Zia never knew it was his father who uncovered the plot. In one uncharacteristic lapse, Zia left his journal on his bureau while he visited a school friend home on holiday. Leafing through the pages, his father found specific details referring to the plot and the planning. At first, his father was amused, thinking it was some sort of class assignment. The more he read, the less amusing the writing became.

Knowing Zia would be in a panic without his journal, his father committed to memory as much as he could, then decided to visit the local police station. The police alerted Indian security forces and then the U.S. Secret Service.

FORTY-FIVE

Silent Killers
May, 1978

There are a lot of "silent killers" identified by medical science.

There's high blood pressure: the silent killer.

There's carbon monoxide poisoning: the silent killer.

Colon cancer, breast cancer, ovarian cancer: the silent killers.

In the foothills above Sequoia City, hypothermia is also a silent killer.

Hypothermia symptoms show up when the body temperature drops just a few degrees. The body throws off more heat than it generates. Exposure to wind and snow is the most obvious risk with hypothermia, particularly if a person is wet from rain.

Hypothermia can occur in older people exposed to air conditioning over a period of hours. Children are also susceptible.

Hypothermia begins when the body temperature drops less than 4 degrees to just under 95. A victim often shivers. The skin is cold to the touch. When the body temperature drops below 90 the situation is critical and life threatening. A great deal of heat is also lost if a person is not wearing a hat.

In winter, hypothermia often shows up in cross country skiers. Families who visit foothill areas so "their kids can play in the snow" also risk exposure if extra care is not taken. Boy Scouts on a "snow cave" weekend face the chance of both frostbite and hypothermia.

It's not unusual for individuals with hypothermia to become disoriented, confused, dizzy. They hallucinate. Despite the cold, they will often remove their clothing trying to "cool off."

You have arrived just in Death's waiting room.

Less obvious is hypothermia in the summer. With the outdoor temperatures near 100, it seems incongruous. The difference between the air temperature and the temperature of the water, however, can be more than 60 degrees. As a result, whitewater rafters—paddlers—often overlook the risks of hypothermia in the cold waters of the Sequoia River.

The whitewater rapids, stretching more than 25 miles above the reservoir, are considered among the best in the world.

During early spring, the river runs at its highest levels of the year, fed by snowmelt. There are lots of seasonal sand bars that allow you to pull your kayak out of the river to make repairs, have lunch or simply catch your breath.

Experienced paddlers take care and are aware of the hazards. Less experienced paddlers will combine an afternoon in their kayak, a picnic lunch on a sand bar and a few beers. Alcohol, cold water and inexperience are deadly.

Of the 10 people who die from drowning in the U.S. every day, 80 percent are male. Among adolescents and adults, 75 percent of drownings involve alcohol.

The two paddlers on the Sequoia River were hardly 20. A search and rescue helicopter was needed to bring their bodies out of the canyon.

I was at the hospital when their bodies were brought in. I'm not sure why I went. I brought the camera I used for the occasional pictures the Sacramento Bee would print from our area.

It was quite a process getting the black and white film to The Bee. I'd call in a story and if I had a picture, I would put the unexposed film in a can, mark it clearly and then get it to the Greyhound Bus station by 2:30 in the afternoon. Most days it would reach Sacramento by 8:30 p.m. Someone from the Bee would be at the bus station to pick it up.

The paper would get the film developed in their darkroom. The final decision about whether the picture was used was made by the overnight editor of the Bee. I never knew whether it got used until the next time I talked to the Bee editor.

The paper published several editions daily. The earliest printed edition left Sacramento between 8 and 9 p.m. The early edition would be shipped to the northernmost reaches of the state, ensuring delivery to subscribers before 6 the following morning. I envisioned the Greyhound carrying my undeveloped film heading south, passing the truck with the early edition of the Bee heading north.

Cameron caught my eye and angrily barked, "No pictures." Just as quickly, he mellowed and said, "You know, the family" and his voice trailed off. I swung the camera around behind me. It wasn't a picture I wanted anyway.

The helicopter crew brought the first body out.

The young man looked so peaceful. No terror. No fear. Not quite like he was sleeping, but not wide-eyed either. Limp. The other victim had tried to come to his friend's rescue. His body was badly bruised. He didn't look peaceful. Their friends said they had finished lunch, had a couple of beers, and came through a patch of particularly difficult rapids. The first young man was not wearing a wetsuit at the time. Inexplicably, he took off his life jacket saying he was hot and jumped out of his kayak into the water. He tried to swim to shore from the middle of the river.

The powerful river current dragged him underwater and pinned his body next to a boulder for about 20 minutes. His friend suffered a similar fate.

If there been a hospital or ambulance crew nearby when the young men were pulled from the river, they might have been revived. In cold water, the "mammalian diving reflex" takes over. The reflex explains how people who apparently have drowned can be revived, sometimes even after being pronounced dead on the scene.

In water below 70 degrees, the heart rate slows, breathing stops and blood vessels constrict. Oxygen stored in the blood and muscles is released. The cold shunts blood and oxygen from the body's extremities and directs it to the heart and brain. On

"Star Trek", this is the equivalent of the captain ordering the crew to "shut down all but essential life support systems." The colder the water, the more blood and oxygen is shunted to the vital organs.

Medical professionals refer to the "Golden Hour," where a person receiving medical treatment in the first hour after a traumatic injury has the highest likelihood of survival.

But today, on a beautiful, warm afternoon on the upper reaches of the Sequoia River, there was no medical assistance close by. No diving reflex. No "Golden Hour."

Two strong, healthy and vibrant young men died.

Members of their group had to kayak the rest of the way down the river to get help.

Two young lives lost. Two lives snuffed out of their promise and hope. Their dreams, careers, future, children and grandchildren. On a warm afternoon in Northern California on an isolated stretch of river: Gone. I was reminded of the Irish lament: "Johnny we hardly knew ye."

I was pretty shaken. They weren't much younger than me.

I looked over at Cameron. Almost anticipating my question, he quietly said, "No, some things you never really get used to."

FORTY-SIX

"How Long (Has This Been Going On?)"—Ace

Ed and I were having a beer at the Rip Roarin'. I tried to catch a glimpse of Emma, but then remembered she had taken the day off.

When I think about it now, Ed's question was an innocent one. Harmless really.

He wasn't trying to surprise me or shock me or make me feel bad. But the question really caught me off guard.

"When did Emma and Gerry start seeing each other again?"

I tried to look nonchalant. I couldn't. I probably looked incredulous. "Huh?"

"Oh, hey…I thought you knew. They apparently had a thing going for a long time. It's been on again, off again. I saw them parked down by the river late yesterday. From what I could tell, they were very much on again."

Ed was suddenly aware he'd stepped on a verbal land mine. There was an uncomfortably long pause in the conversation. "I'm sorry man. You haven't said much about her recently. I thought you two had broken up. I thought she was back with Gerry."

I couldn't pretend it didn't matter. I had the same feeling when a serious relationship broke down in college. Out of breath. Out of the room I was in. It was strange. It seemed like this was happening to someone else.

"She never said anything. I don't know." I babbled a bit and said I needed to go home. Ed said he would buy the beers. I could tell he was embarrassed with the conversation.

"Man, I'm really sorry."

"Yeah. Uh, no, it's OK," and I left.

At the apartment, I wondered what I should do next. I was angry. I was confused, hurt and dazed. Fearfully alone again. I tried to make sense of a situation that seemed to make no sense.

Emma and Gerry? Gerry was almost three times my age. What were they doing down by the river? Ed said they appeared to be very much "on" again. I wondered how "on." Where did I fit in her life? Did I fit in at all?

I called her.

"Hey, I was just getting ready to call you," she said. "What are you doing tonight? I thought we might get together for a couple of beers and hang out for a while."

"Sure, sounds good," I said in a less than convincing voice. "That would be great."

I suggested we meet somewhere other than the Rip Roarin'. We agreed on The Cork and Bottle Lounge. It was a bit classier than the Rip Roarin' and the other well frequented bar in town, The Knothole. The Cork and Bottle was a great place for a quiet romantic conversation. Or a serious one.

We ordered our drinks.

"What's up with you and Gerry?" I asked, getting straight to the point.

"What do you mean 'What's up'? Gerry and I are really good friends. He's my boss. Why do you ask?"

"Ed said he saw you and Gerry down at the river yesterday. He said you guys seemed pretty hot and heavy." I was a bit nauseated at the thought and the image.

"Is that true?"

I couldn't tell her mood. After a bit, "Yes, Ed saw me yesterday. And Gerry." Then she became angry and defiant. "What's the big deal? I told you I've had one serious relationship since my divorce. It was Gerry. I thought you knew."

"I didn't." Then, after a pause, "What about us? I thought we had something going. Do we?"

Our drinks came.

She cut me off. "Mark, it's complicated."

"And just what the hell is complicated, Emma?" The volume of my voice was high enough to attract the attention of other customers in the lounge.

"Keep your voice down, please. Look, I never said you couldn't see anyone else." She seemed unsure as to what to say next. "It's not like you and I were going to get married." She looked at me after a moment and said, "Were we?"

I thought I was going to be sick. I hadn't walked our relationship "down the aisle" yet, but it certainly didn't seem out of the realm of possibility.

She quickly changed and became dispassionate and very matter of fact. "Well, I'm not about to go down that road again. Gerry's wife doesn't seem to mind. Why should you?"

"I, huh. God, I'll say this is complicated. We never talked about other people."

"I know, but it's not like there are a lot of other people."

I remembered when she first told me about her son. "I don't want to explain who the stranger I'm with is and why it might be a different stranger from the last time he visited. It would be too confusing."

She interrupted my train of thought and went on. "Listen, Gerry and I are good friends. You and I are good friends. OK? Can you just leave it at that? Think of us as a work in progress. Let's see where it goes."

She was direct and a bit harsh. It was like I was talking to someone I didn't know.

Then, softening a bit, she said, "Hey, Mark, let's talk about this another time."

She patted my arm, left most of her drink on the table, got up and left.

I was being dismissed.

I watched her go out the door and wondered what just happened. Science fiction writers might call a moment like this "a bend in the space/time continuum." Others might refer to it as "an out-of-body" experience.

In aviation, it's called a "death spiral." It usually happens at night or in poor weather. The pilot, usually inexperienced, loses visual awareness or experiences "spatial disorientation." The brain, even the inner ear, without a point of reference, cannot pick up clues as to the plane's attitude. The pilot often ignores his altitude and attitude gauges, preferring instead to trust his "instincts." Without a visual horizon, a pilot often inadvertently puts his plane into a spin. The spin becomes tighter and tighter and is ultimately unrecoverable. It cannot be corrected in time to prevent a crash.

The conversation with Emma felt like a "death spiral." My head was spinning and I couldn't get my bearings. What the hell just happened? What is happening?

I was fighting for altitude and losing. Fast. Somehow I envisioned us as more than just "good friends."

FORTY-SEVEN

"Angel of the Morning"—Merilee Rush

For me, college was a heady experience.

Idealism is the undeclared major for every college student. Lots of intensity and enthusiasm for life and learning. It's the first time away from home for many of us.

We loved to debate, argue, contemplate and philosophize on the issues of the day: Vietnam, race riots in cities across the country, poverty, the pros and cons of the space program.

It was easy to conclude that we had the answers to the all world's problems. Now if only someone would ask the questions.

I always regretted not getting laid more in college. In four years, there were only two women. Two. Total.

There was Christine. She would be the first woman I had sex with. She had a neurotic affection/attraction for me in junior college. I never reciprocated, but was always polite. We never dated. We attended a few class parties, but never as a couple. We hugged a couple of times but never even kissed. I thought it was a casual friendship. She didn't. Looking back later, it occurred to me that she had the hots for me. She seemed to hang on my every word and laughed at even the goofiest comments I would make.

I went off to a four-year university about 300 miles from home. I was surprised one Friday afternoon a couple of months later when Christine showed up on campus, unannounced.

"You came to see me?" I was stunned.

And incredibly turned on. I was surprised how quickly that happened. And how very uncomfortable it was in a tight pair of jeans.

"Where are you staying" I asked.

She had a room downtown at The University Villa Motel. Room #15.

The room was clean and smelled fresh. The door had barely closed and we had our clothes off.

During the weekend, we had a couple of pizzas delivered to the room. There was a Pepsi machine two doors down, too. And we took a couple of long, hot showers.

Sunday night we walked a couple of blocks to the Arctic Circle and had dinner.

On Monday morning, either she had satisfied her curiosity about me or she wasn't satisfied at all. Whatever the case, after an awkward goodbye, she left and I never heard from her again.

Whenever I drove by the University Villa Motel, I would get really horny thinking about that weekend in Room #15.

And I thought about it often.

Those fantasies and memories ended graduation weekend. My mother came for the ceremonies and stayed at the University Villa Motel. Yes, in Room #15. I knew if I didn't stop fantasizing about having sex in that room and the weekend with Christine, I would end up like a character in Greek mythology.

It was just too weird after that.

FORTY-EIGHT

Little Grass Valley Reservoir
Sunday morning
December 17, 1978

"There's no Place like Home for the Holidays"—Perry Como

My journal entries from yesterday are a bit jumbled and confusing. My thoughts wandered off and never quite made it back on track. I think I might be drinking too much, although there's not much else to do here.

It is really cold again this morning.

I don't have the right gear for camping in December. The tent and sleeping bag are perfect for summer camping, but all wrong for this time of year.

The damn air mattress went flat again overnight. The flat mattress didn't provide much insulation, even inside the tent, so I woke up sore and cold.

It's miserable here.

I wonder what Mom's doing today.

This is normally the day we'd get the popcorn balls and fudge made, the cookies baked and the bourbon balls ready. Then we'd decorate the tree Grandpa and I picked out from one of the tree lots that appeared after Thanksgiving. It would always take us at least 45 minutes to find the "right tree" for the house.

One time we picked out a tree in the pouring rain and didn't realize it was pretty flat on one side. It became known as the "wall tree"—one that could be pushed close to the wall without crushing any branches. It did give us more room in the living room but it also gave Mom and Grandma fodder for jokes for years. Every time we went to pick out a tree after that, Mom and Grandma, in unison—like they had practiced the line together—would say, "No wall trees this year guys." After that, Grandpa would ask the tree lot guy for any branches that were trimmed off.

He told me if we ever picked out another "wall tree," he'd drill holes in the tree trunk and stick the loose branches in them. I was never sure if he was joking or irritated.

Grandpa put the electric train he received as a boy under the tree. It ran almost nonstop during that week before Christmas.

Mom's parents had an open house with an invitation for friends and neighbors to drop by any time after 5 o'clock the week before Christmas. There were cocktails, eggnog and lots of laughter.

Inevitably, one of the guests would bring a tin of fruitcake as a hostess gift. Grandpa called fruitcake "a baked boat anchor."

And there would always be Christmas music playing on the radio. Nat King Cole. Judy Garland. Johnny Mathis. Frank Sinatra. Every year, the music added to the sights, smells and warmth of the house.

For a lot of reasons, this year would be different.

MARK'S GREAT AMERICAN NOVEL
Chapter Fifteen

Bombay, India
January 1, 1978
Early Evening
Santacruz Airport

Zia was stunned at how thorough the security check was at the boarding gate.

He was patted down from his neck to his feet. The guard became acquainted with every part of Zia's body. Zia was embarrassed and very uncomfortable. He had heard about "strip searches" when prisoners enter jail and was not sure a strip search could be any more thorough, or personal, than the airport security check.

Arriving in the New Delhi by train a few weeks ago was an entirely different story. The New Delhi Railway station is the busiest and largest in India. The station handles more than 300 trains and over a quarter of a million passengers daily. If you had a train ticket, no one gave you a second look except for an occasional short, perfunctory check of passports. And passport checks at the railway station were very rare.

The security at the airport loading gate was in sharp contrast to the main ticket lobby area. There the ticket agent asked no questions when Zia bought his one-way ticket to Dubai with cash and checked no luggage.

Not so boarding the aircraft. Guards with rifles stood throughout the airport concourse. The boarding area had an armed guard watching over the scene while his partner frisked passengers before they were allowed on the plane.

Zia wondered if this was standard procedure or if the heightened security was the result of the day's events in Delhi. He would be glad to get on board. Maybe then he could start to relax and sort through, detail by detail, what went wrong.

FORTY-NINE

Night Class in Sequoia City

I spent a lot of time trying to work through the mystery of my relationship with Emma. Try as I might to look at the situation from as many angles as possible, it remained a mystery.

I told Ed we would have to meet at The Knothole for a while. I really wasn't ready to see Emma again at the Rip Roarin'.

We lamented the dismal state of our social lives.

I told him I was going to take a night class in writing. I told him I had a book I was working on and it needed some help. I was stuck. I never fully appreciated "writer's block" until I started the book. I could sit for hours, blankly looking out the window of my apartment for inspiration. None came. I would go back and re-read parts of the manuscript, hoping an idea or thought would jump off the page and start me back on the road again. No such luck.

I remember reading about Peanuts cartoonist Charles Schulz. He apparently would not leave his studio until a comic strip was done. Sometimes it would happen in a matter of minutes. Other times he would work late into the night before turning out a finished strip.

Professional writers recommend "writing something every day."

Right now I have my main character in New Delhi at the airport. I had Fodor's India Travel Guide, but getting a feel for the streets and back alleys of New Delhi is difficult. Walking my characters through the neighborhoods and districts was proving a challenge.

I thought a night class on writing might also be a way to get a new circle of friends.

From a writing standpoint, the class was not helpful. When I discussed the concept and ideas for my book, class members thought I should add some science fiction, life on another planet or a galactic hero to the mix. "Star Wars" was released the previous year, so everyone wanted to write the next installment.

There were also suggestions to include mass murder or demonic possession, suggestions inspired, I'm sure, by recent horror movies "Carrie" and "The Omen." Someone suggested dealing with the threat of extinction of life on earth. I knew there was no way to generate the suspense of Michael Crichton's "Andromeda Strain."

In my head, I quickly dismissed the suggestions from the class.

It wasn't a total loss, though. That's where I met Sarah. "With an 'H'," she said with a flourish.

I honestly didn't know any other way of spelling it.

Introducing myself, I said, "I'm Mark. With an 'M'." I don't know if I said it with a flourish, but Sarah laughed.

People would call our relationship a rebound: trying to get over a bitter break up by finding someone new. In Sarah's case, her fiance called off their engagement a few weeks earlier.

Rebound relationships are bittersweet: elements of loneliness, a strong desire to be attractive to someone with a twinge of revenge thrown in for good measure.

Sarah and I were great physical distractions for one another. It didn't take much to get her into bed and she was incredibly energetic once we got there. She loved to experiment.

Sarah (with an "H") was fun to be with. She said my voice was sexy.

Both of us knew it was temporary. But we enjoyed it while it lasted.

My writing challenges remained, however. The typewriter stayed silent.

After Sarah (with an "H") and I broke up, I found the flier from Greg Olman's Trail Ride business in a stack of papers at the apartment. I decided to call him and plan one of the trips.

I needed another distraction.

"...after two days in the desert sun, my skin began to turn red ...after three days in the desert fun, I was looking at a river bed..."

—America, "A HORSE WITH NO NAME"

F I F T Y

The Trail Ride
A Saturday in August, 1978

On the previous night, there had been a massive lightning storm. Fire tower crews reported more than 700 lightning strikes up and down the spine of the Sierra and Cascades over the course of a couple of hours.

Nearly half of those were in the watershed above the Sequoia Lake reservoir. Fire lookout towers were busy pinpointing small puffs of smoke located near the lightning strike locations. Firefighters would call this a siege.

Summer lightning storms occur at the worst possible time in California. The long hot summers are accompanied by little or no rain. Drought years are worse.

Depending on the rain and snow earlier in the year, grasses thrive and flourish. Then the hot weather turns the plush green to golden brown. Manzanita and madrone grow quickly during heavy rainfall years, storing up high amounts of combustible oils. Both plants make great firewood and throw off tremendous amounts of heat. They burn hot and fast. A boon for homeowners heating with wood. A headache for firefighters in a wildfire.

Earlier in the week, I called Greg and booked a reservation to ride to the boundary of the Wild and Scenic River section on the middle Sequoia. The boundary was 18 miles due west of the Pacific Crest Trail.

The Pacific Coast Trail follows the crest elevations of the Sierra and Cascade mountains from Mexico to the Canadian border. The trail is open to equestrians and hikers. The trail covers more than 2,600 miles and ranges in elevations from sea level in the Pacific Northwest to more than 13,000 feet in the southern Sierra. The midway point on the trail is Chester, California, where the Sierra and Cascade mountain ranges meet. By horse, Chester would be 38 miles due east from where we are headed this morning.

The Pacific Crest Trail was designated a National Scenic Trail in 1968. The National Scenic Trail system covers nearly 19,000 miles of hiking trails in the U.S.

The construction of the Pacific Coast Trail was a cooperative venture between the federal government and volunteers. It would take decades to complete.

The designation of a Wild and Scenic River was a controversial one for residents of Sequoia City. Most folks thought it was another huge government land grab—an effort and expense to benefit a handful of whitewater rafters who use that stretch of the river.

The Wild and Scenic Rivers Act was passed by Congress in 1968 and signed into law by President Lyndon Johnson. The goal of the law was "to preserve certain rivers with outstanding natural, cultural and recreational values in a free-flowing condition for the enjoyment of present and future generations."

Only one-quarter of 1 percent of America's rivers are protected under the Wild and Scenic Rivers system.

The Wild and Scenic Rivers designation can be made by Congress or the Secretary of the Interior. In June 1975, Rogers Morton, Secretary of the Interior for Presidents Nixon and Ford, designated 28 miles of the middle fork of the Sequoia River a Wild and Scenic River.

Greg and I started out just after first light. The trip from Sequoia City was over 20 miles round trip, so a friend of Greg's offered to drive us and our horses to one of the trailhead parking lots. It was just over halfway to the boundary line. The plan was to ride in from the trailhead, then back to Sequoia City before sunset. It would be a very long day, but our plan would shave over 6 miles off the trip and get us back to town before dark.

The horse I rode was fairly old and not very strong. Greg's friend said it reminded him of the coffee at Melva's. It was an ideal mount for a greenhorn like me.

The trail was dusty and narrow and the temperature by 11 was about 100.

It was scary when my horse slipped on loose shale several hundred feet above the canyon floor and fought to regain his footing.

Our conversations were pretty banal. The weather. The lightning storm. Occasionally, Greg would point out an old mine or Indian campsite. I always suspected he had an IQ two notches above a houseplant. Nothing he said today convinced me I was wrong.

He said we were making good time but had to find a way down to the river as the horses needed water. It took close to an hour to navigate a trail to the river. Greg was very quiet as we gingerly worked our way through the bed of cobblestones to the water.

It was then that Greg pulled a gun and pointed it at me.

"What are you doing?" At first I thought he was kidding around.

He flashed a goofy, menacing grin and was pretty sure of himself. He obviously wasn't kidding.

"What the hell are you doing, Greg?" I asked again. The way he squirmed in the saddle made me think he was actually turned on.

"I don't like you. A lot of people don't like you. You ask too many questions. Weren't you just a little curious when I jumped at the chance to take you on this trip today? Did you think I was just sitting around waiting for your call? Look around, Mark. There isn't a soul around for miles. You think anyone will find your sorry dead ass up here?"

Jesus, he's going to kill me.

He squirmed some more and rearranged himself again in the saddle. He really was enjoying himself.

He went on. "Let me ask you: What the hell difference does it make to anyone where Timberline gets their workers or how they get here? And what do you and Seth Freeman talk about behind closed doors all the time? I know Seth keeps you up to date. Are you talking about Gerry and Bobby's past business dealings? Is the Grand Jury back in session? Bobby's dead for God's sake. What the hell difference does any of that matter now? Wanna tell me Mark? You make people mighty unhappy and uncomfortable, asshole. You want to tell me what's going on? What you're working on?"

My throat was so dry I couldn't talk. I could barely catch my breath.

"And while we're at it, Gerry doesn't like seeing you with Emma. Neither do I."

It hardly mattered at this point that I wasn't seeing Emma anymore.

"You college guys think you're so smart, don't you? Your buddy's going to be taking a trail ride soon, too. He's asking a lot of questions around the sheriff's office."

He might as well have been speaking a foreign language at this point. I didn't have a clue what he was talking about.

"It will be a lot easier if you just tell me what I want to know right now, Mark. The outcome will be the same. Your life's over today, pal. You are not going to be riding out of here."

I'm not hearing any music in my head. There are no sounds, no melodies, not a single note. For the first time in my life I am experiencing a deafening silence in my brain.

My God this isn't happening.

"Get off that horse and answer me hotshot. Answer my questions, Mark. I'll make this quick. You won't feel anything. I've done it before. Let's just get this over with buddy. There's nowhere to run."

It was the first time Greg said something I actually believed. This is unreal. What the hell is going on?

I thought I was going to pass out. I started to say something when our horses became agitated, sensing danger.

They were spooked. Ears twitching in every direction, snorting and tails swishing rapidly back and forth.

Snakes or a mountain lion, I thought.

A moment later, there was a rumble, low at first and getting louder. It was the sound of approaching aircraft.

CDF air tankers.

The California Department of Forestry is responsible for fire protection and wildfire suppression on 31,000,000 acres in the state. The department also contracts with cities and counties for fire services throughout the state. CDF operates more year-round fire stations than the cities of New York, Los Angeles and Chicago combined.

Every spring, CDF forecasts the outlook for fire season based on the amount of rain, growth of grass and brush, the rate of drying, humidity levels, weather forecasts and a variety of other factors. In the news business, when the CDF forecast is released, we privately refer to it as the Agency's annual "this will be the worst fire season ever" forecast. The forecast also comes out in the weeks before budget negotiations begin with the state Legislature.

Wildlfires are unpredictable and in California the combination of high elevations, steep canyons, dry interior valleys, deep reservoirs and the Pacific Ocean create unusual weather and burn patterns.

Most fires burn from lower to higher elevations, like fire in a chimney. There are places where the wind will suddenly switch directions and carry the fires from higher to lower elevations, contrary to expectations.

In Europe, the condition is called a foehn. In the northwest, Northern California and the Great Plains, it's a Chinook. In California, it's the Santa Ana.

Chinook is the Indian word for "snow eater." It brings a significant drop in humidity accompanied by a sharp increase in temperature. In Spearfish, South Dakota, in January 1943, the temperature was minus 4 degrees. Two minutes later, on the heels of a Chinook, the temperature stood at plus 47 degrees.

Perhaps the best known foehn is the Satana's (Satan's) wind in Southern California. Years ago, a reporter called it a "Santa Ana" wind and the name stuck. The hot, dry, gusty wind blowing from the desert interior creates compression heating. As the wind picks up speed, it sucks the humidity out of the air and raises the risk of wildfire to extreme levels. When Santa Ana winds are forecast, additional state fire crews are moved to Southern California as a contingency .

In the Santa Barbara area, it's the "Sun Downer" effect. A fire will burn up hill all day. As the sun sets, with the Pacific Ocean to the west, the hills surrounding the fire rapidly start to cool. This cooling effect will pull the fire downhill.

Near Clear Lake, California, Mount Konocti triggers another weather pattern. Its 2,300-foot elevation combined with hot inland temperatures, the cold water of Clear Lake and the cool ocean breezes off the Pacific often push the wind in unpredictable directions.

Then there is the Sequoia Surge here in the canyon, a phenomenon that became more pronounced after the reservoir filled. Following last night's storm, a small low-pressure system began to form several hundred miles to the west in the Pacific Ocean. The low's short-lived existence was enough to begin pulling air down the canyon and out into the valley. As a result, the Surge is very active this morning.

Without careful planning, situational awareness and weather observations, fire crews can be trapped when the wind reverses directions.

On August 5, 1949, in Montana, 15 smoke-jumpers from Missoula dropped into an area a half mile from a lightning-sparked fire. At the time, meteorologists believed winds on the Missouri River only moved upstream in the afternoon. When the wind changed direction and moved downstream, the fire exploded, burning 3,000 acres— almost 5 square miles—in less than 10 minutes. Thirteen firefighters died trying to outrun the flames at Mann Gulch.

On July 9, 1953, in the Mendocino National Forest in California, an arson fire was nearly contained as crews worked to complete a firebreak. Containment doesn't mean the fire is out. Within the containment area, there are spots that can still burn very hot. Once the fire is 100 percent contained, crews work to extinguish the remaining hot spots, bringing the fire under control. At its peak, 100 firefighters were on the line of the fire dubbed The Rattlesnake Fire. That evening, when the wind died down and the air became quiet, part of the crew sat down to eat dinner.

Suddenly, the wind picked up from the opposite direction, blowing close to 20 miles per hour. Fifteen firefighters died trying to scramble out of the fire's way to safety.

The Rattlesnake Fire prompted officials to focus on additional firefighter training and rely more heavily on helicopters and aerial tankers to attack fires early.

Air tanker pilots have two missions: arrive on the fire scene within 20 minutes and, if possible, keep the fire to 10 acres by dropping water and retardant. Fire flying is tricky: slow air speeds, heavy aircraft, strong and unpredictable winds as well as close proximity to the ground.

Fighting fires from the air is a ballet. High above the fire is one tactical aircraft—a traffic control plane—coordinating the air tanker drops with crews on the ground. The air tankers follow a circular pattern dropping their retardant as close to the fire as possible.

CDF tankers carry up to 800 gallons of retardant. Releasing over 5,000 pounds of retardant will cause the aircraft to rise a couple of hundred feet in a few seconds.

To offset the sudden weight loss, pilots dive toward the spot where the retardant will be dropped. Otherwise, a plane flying at a level altitude can climb so sharply, stall, then rapidly lose altitude and speed. Combined with the low elevation, a pilot may not be able to prevent a crash.

Helicopters can carry up to 360 gallons of water. The tanker retardant and water drops help cool the area, slowing the fire's progress until ground crews can move in.

Greg and I are far down in the canyon. Now I'm seeing bits of ash falling in the area and just as suddenly, I feel a swift increase in heat: The fire is blazing downhill through the canyon toward us, pushed by the Sequoia Surge.

Behind us, Grumman S-2 air tankers stationed in Redding roar up the narrow canyon toward the fire. The tanker noise echoing off the canyon walls is incredible. The wind is picking up speed quickly as is the heat from the fast-moving fire. The combination is stunning.

My horse shuddered, nervously moving sideways a few steps, kicking up enough water to splash on my boots. When the planes came into view, flying close to 200 miles an hour about 500 feet above the riverbed, Greg's horse suddenly reared up, catching him off guard. With the gun still pointed at me, he was thrown from his horse.

The gun fired. A bullet screamed past my head. Greg's horse ran off, bucking and kicking.

When he fell, it would have been impossible for Greg's head to avoid hitting large stones in the river bed. His head slammed into several of them. He's not moving and his body is twisted in a weird position. His eyes are wide open and he is looking straight up. River water is flowing over his mouth and nose.

A fraction of a second later, from under his head, there is a large expanding pool of blood flowing downstream.

Now there is a cacophony screaming in my head. It is like the last night at my father's house in Illinois. It is excruciating. Sounds but no music.

It's crazy what I thought as the bullet whistled by my head. Hearing the gun fire meant the shot missed me, since a bullet travels several times faster than the speed of sound. Otherwise, I would have been dead before I heard the shot. What a weird thought. The sound of a bullet that close was nonetheless terrifying. It piggybacked on an equally chilling thought: a piece of lead traveling several thousand feet per second intended for my brain. Intended to end my life.

My mind is spinning and my swirling emotions right now surprise me. I'm angry at myself.

I should have known better. Greg was a creep the day I met him. What was I thinking? Why did I trust him? He can go to hell. If he is alive, he can find his own way back on foot. As quickly as that thought occurred to me, another one struck me. I know better. Greg's not alive.

Greg kill me? In retrospect, that was ludicrous. He was an idiot. I'm surprised there was a bullet in the chamber. He could barely chew gum and walk straight at the same time.

After what I saw today, he certainly wouldn't make it on the rodeo circuit either.

"You won't be riding out of here today either Greg," I said out loud.

My thoughts and emotions are changing rapid fire. God, if things had gone his way, I'd have just been another lost hiker/rider/miner/explorer lost in the hills.

What a son of a bitch.

I can hear him back in town: "We got separated on the trail, then his horse came back without him. I searched the area calling his name, but no answer. Then it started getting dark…" blah, blah, blah.

If they searched for me at all in the next few days, he would probably direct them somewhere other than our location.

Bastard.

I'm dizzy. Nauseated. And shaking as if it were 15 degrees with a wind chill.

Smoke started to burn my nostrils. My horse had ignored the air tanker noise and the gunshot, but the smoke in the air made him very restless. He didn't need any encouragement when I turned him back downstream. For me, it was just a matter of hanging on.

We stayed in the river bed until we were well clear of the fire danger.

About a mile or so downriver, I felt the wind shift from downhill to uphill. The fire would slow down, burn back on itself and eventually burn out with multiple drops of retardant from the aerial onslaught. The air attack would be assisted by hand crews, engines and bulldozers on the ground.

I got off my horse. Actually, I nearly fell off. The past 90 minutes were a blur.

The horse drank.

I threw up. Deep, retching, painful. I'm not sure I had ever been that sick. Even after beer keg parties in the dorm at college.

I also broke into a drenching sweat. Even though I am standing in the river, it feels like the soles of my feet are sweating.

I can't believe this. What's going on?

I threw up again. I hadn't eaten much today but that didn't stop several rounds of painful dry heaves, followed by quick gasps to try and catch my breath.

I tried to let my brain process what just happened. I put my head in the river several times. The shock of cold water helped. I gagged again thinking about Greg's blood, no matter how minute, mixed with that same river water.

I kept looking upstream, expecting Greg to show up at any moment. I knew that wasn't possible. His horse was long gone and he was dead. I kept looking anyway.

This all seems so unreal. Again I am struck by the things my mind is focusing on.

As a reporter, you find yourself with an uncomfortable even disquieting interest in crime scenes, plane crashes and car accidents. I've seen mangled bodies in car wrecks. Once I was escorted by a Highway Patrolman to the scene of a fatal log truck accident where the driver, still inside the crushed cab, was pinned under several tons of fresh-cut timber. I had even been to the murder scene of a transient found stabbed to death next to the railroad tracks. I pored over commercial plane crash investigations, reading cockpit recording transcripts and imagining the last moments before impact.

But I'd never seen anyone actually die before. Greg is certainly dead, but I couldn't rouse a single emotion.

I really don't know how long it was before I got back on my horse.

Today was only the third time in my life I've been on a horse. The first time was at a county fair where the horses walk in a circle, tied to a pole in the center of a corral. There was a ramp and a fair employee to help you on and off.

Then there was the trail ride when I first got to town. There had been help there, too. This morning, Greg's friend helped me get on my horse at the parking lot.

Trying to get on a horse without help is not as easy as it looks in the movies. If you don't hold the reins just right, the horse starts moving in a circle, making it impossible to get back in the saddle. After several attempts and a significant amount of cursing, I finally managed to get on and start making our way back up to the trailhead.

Back to Sequoia City.

FIFTY-ONE

Sequoia City

It was hours before I made it back to town. I drank all of the water I carried with me. I tried to eat part of the sandwich I packed, but choked and gagged on the first bite.

I was dazed and not paying attention to the trail or the direction we were headed. Fortunately, the horse was "barn sour" and didn't need directions back to the stable. Like a four-legged homing pigeon, the horse knew how to find his way to a dependable supply of water and food. Sometimes a "barn sour" horse will bolt for home without warning. Others, like mine, will just turn and amble in the direction of the barn.

It was almost 7 when I got back to the stable. It gave me time to sort some things out in my head.

One of the guys at stable said, "Are you all right? You look awful." I no doubt looked like hell. "I could use some water" I whispered. I probably sounded like Peter O'Toole in "Lawrence of Arabia" after a daring rescue in the desert.

One of them handed me a canteen. The water was cool and refreshing. I drank so fast a good portion ran onto my shirt. When the cold water hit my empty stomach, it caused a spasm and I thought I was going to throw up again.

Greg's horse was already there. Catching my breath, I motioned to his horse and asked, "When did that son of a bitch get back?"

Knowing full well he hadn't.

I went on. "Where is he? We got separated on the trail. He left me out there to find my way back. If it was some kind of joke, it wasn't funny. I just let my horse bring me back. So, where is he? I'd like to punch his lights out."

Someone said the horse came back alone a couple of hours earlier.

I thought I should let someone official know what happened, so I called the sheriff's office from a pay phone near the barn. I gave a minimum of details, leaving out the part where Greg tried to kill me.

A well-known defense attorney told me he counsels witnesses to answer questions in the simplest form possible. "If you are on the witness stand and an attorney asks, 'Do you know what day of the week it is?' You answer 'yes,' but you don't volunteer the actual day of the week. It sounds simplistic, but the more you talk the more likely you are to say something you shouldn't. Salesmen will tell you the more you talk, the more likely you are to lose a sale. It's the same in court. Don't volunteer anything. Short answers throw off the rhythm of an opposing attorney. Shorter answers lead to more questions than the attorney planned to ask. It unnerves prosecutors and plaintiff attorneys."

That defense attorney won a lot of his cases. It was said he could get a sodomy charge reduced to "following too close."

I answered the deputy's questions quickly and simply and that was it. In reality, I have no idea where Greg and I were in the canyon. We were supposed to be headed toward the Wild and Scenic boundary line, but all I had to go on was Greg's word. I guess if I was actually interested, I could have pinpointed the fire's location and worked out our location from there.

I wasn't really that interested.

When I hung up, I thought, Happy trails, Greg. You dumb bastard.

As I headed to my car, I asked one of the guys, "I thought I heard air tankers a couple of hours ago. Where was the fire"?

A modest search party was organized the next day. The searchers knew there was little chance of finding someone lost in the canyon. Especially if they didn't know where to look or if the person was injured, disoriented or caught in a fast-moving fire.

It didn't help that few people in town wanted to spend any time looking for Greg.

Greg was as welcome as the Hong Kong flu.

What a statement about a person's time on earth: just a few questions, a small search party, notifying next of kin and then an even smaller turnout for a memorial service No one was going to miss him much.

No one, perhaps, except Gerry.

"...The things you lean on, the things that don't last, well it's just now and then my line gets cast into these time passages..."

FIFTY-TWO

Back in my Apartment

The apartment was very warm when I got home around 8:20. I set the air conditioner to "colder" and realized now I was actually hungry.

Of all the things I worry about, I never worry that leftover food might spoil in the refrigerator. Like most guys, my test was simple: Regardless of age, if it doesn't have green or black mold growing on it, it's probably OK to eat. I always rationalized saying, "I have an immune system. I am supposed to make it work."

So, it was no big deal that the only thing staring back at me from the top shelf of the refrigerator was a thigh and leg from a 10-day-old package of supermarket fried chicken. Fortunately there were also a couple of beers in the there and a half-eaten bag of potato chips in the cupboard. Turns out that was plenty.

A cool bath accompanied by a cold Michelob helped me relax. My thoughts were still racing. I remembered Winston Churchill's comment: "Nothing in life is so exhilarating as to be shot at without result."

Just before 10, I laid down and was quickly asleep.

I slept, as Mark Twain said, "like dead people."

When I woke up, the sun was already above the windows on the east side of the apartment. I hurt all over, like I had fallen down a flight of stairs.

My God, I thought, I've been asleep for a long time. It took a fraction of a second to realize Emma was next to me. She was looking at me and gently stroking my hair. She was so beautiful. Warm. Naked.

"Softly"—Gordon Lightfoot

The air conditioner hummed in the background. "I let myself in the back way" as she continued to stroke my hair. "I heard what happened," she whispered.

Then, softly, she added, "I really do care about you, Mark."

Maybe it was the fire or the adrenaline. Maybe it was a bullet whizzing by my head. Perhaps it was as simple as the incredibly strong feelings I still had for Emma and as simple as her lying next to me again.

In any case, I was certainly wide awake now as she slid her fingers gently, sensually, through the hair on my chest. Then her fingers moved beneath the covers.

The first time that morning, we were together quickly, almost furiously. It was as physical, powerful and passionate as I had ever experienced. Intoxicating. The intensity was so overwhelming I thought I might pass out just before I climaxed. It felt like my brain would explode. I hoped Jim and Joyce went to church this morning, since I was sure even the neighbors two doors down could have heard us.

Cameron once told me people often have rousing, passionate, even rowdy sex after a funeral or a near-death experience. Something about wanting to feel alive and reassured.

A few minutes later, the second time, we were much more tender and loving, but for me it seemed just as powerful and passionate.

We laid there for several minutes, her head on my chest, not saying a word. Her breathing was soft and low. It was so peaceful.

"Will you, uh, can you, stay? Please. I've missed you so much." I immediately knew how that sounded to her.

She took a deep breath and said, "Listen, I'm not sure where we—you and me—are right now. I really do care, but let's take things a step at a time, okay?"

> *"You ask me if I love you and I choke on my reply. I'd rather hurt you honestly than mislead you with a lie. And who am I to judge you on what you say or do? I'm only just beginning to see the real you..."*

A few moments of somewhat awkward silence, she patted my chest and said, "You stay here. I'm going to get us some coffee." She slid out of bed and walked into the kitchen. My God, she is beautiful.

She turned the Mr. Coffee on and then came back to bed and turned me on again.

She was so lovely. It was beautiful. Even exquisite. I can't believe how alive I felt Incredibly strong and confident. Those were new feelings for me.

We made love a couple of more times that morning and again in the afternoon. When she dozed off, I was struck by the fact that I loved her. I had never felt this way before. But it was more than just a "feeling."

"My Sweet Lady"—John Denver

It was plain and simple. And so obvious to me now. I love her.

Lying here, I notice how brilliant the sunshine streams into my apartment. I honestly never paid attention to the everyday sights, scents and sounds around me.

But how do I broach the subject with her? She made her feelings pretty clear a couple of hours ago.

Ed told me it's possible to scare a woman off if you tell her you love her. She may not be ready to hear it. "She may not feel the same way. She might cut and run. Guys aren't the only ones looking for someone to have sex with you know.

She might just be looking for a good time and not a life relationship. You could get crushed by the truth."

That four-letter word "love" certainly represents a huge risk for me. And maybe us.

"...and sometimes when we touch, the honesty's too much, and I have to close my eyes and hide. I wanna hold you till I die, till we both break down and cry, I want to hold you till the fear in me subsides..."

So when do I tell her? When do I say, "I love you Emma?" How do I say that to someone for the first time in my life? How do I even say it out loud for the first time in my life?

"Can't Find the Time to Tell You"—Rose Colored Glass

After I left Illinois, Emma and Cameron would be the only people other than my mom and grandpa to see me cry. Oh, wait, there would be one other person.

"...at times I'd like to break through and hold you endlessly..."

It was quite a weekend. I really had missed her. Her gentle touch and caress. The smell of her hair. The softness of her skin. The incredible way it feels when we make love. So physically synchronized and in tune and in touch.

"Long Ago and Far Away"—Jo Stafford

At this moment, feeling the way I do, I know whatever drove us or kept us apart can be fixed. She is absolutely perfect for me. In every sense of the word.

I gently wake her up with a kiss and we make love again.

"It's Too Late to Turn Back Now"
—Cornelius Brothers and Sister Rose

FIFTY-THREE

3:30 the next morning

I woke up an hour and a half before the alarm went off, energized with my mind in high gear. I was quickly filled with ideas for moving the plot along in my book.

I hammered on the keys. I didn't want to lose the inspiration or the ideas before I had them down on paper. I tried not to disturb Emma, but the typewriter makes a lot of noise.

She stirred a bit. "What are you doing?"

"I had some ideas for my book and wanted to get them down on paper while they were still fresh in my mind."

"Oh," she said. Then she rolled over and went back to sleep. I can't remember if I had even told her I was writing a book.

Sometime in the middle of the night, she had turned off the air conditioner and opened all the windows.

A cool breeze was flowing through the apartment.

And the words kept coming. I didn't stop to correct typos or grammar. I just kept typing.

Before leaving for work, I slid back into bed, gently woke her up and we made love again. I laid there for a few minutes until she drifted off to sleep again. I woke her up to tell her goodbye and told her I would be home after my noon newscast.

I still made it to work on time.

FIFTY-FOUR

I left the studio right after my 12:45 newcast.

Emma had Sundays and Mondays off. When I opened the door to my apartment, I don't think I'd ever been more turned on in my life. And while I didn't have a lot of experience, I did have a few prior occasions to compare to my current state of excitement and anticipation.

Emma and I quickly stripped off our clothes and made love on the sofa.

My God it was incredibly hot and physical.

Emma had done some shopping that morning, so she made a quick lunch then we went to the bedroom and made love again. I dozed off for a few minutes, sleeping very peacefully.

When I woke up, she was resting on one elbow and looking at me. "I think you have a lot of shame and guilt you're dealing with." She had taken a psychology class in junior college, but had to drop out after one semester. She said still enjoyed reading psychology books and Psychology Today from time to time.

"I have noticed you sleep with both arms folded across your chest. It's almost like you're hugging yourself. You've built up quite a wall, I think, Mark." She paused a moment and put her hand on my chest. "Any chance I can get over that wall?"

It was a simply an observation. A statement. Not a criticism.

That's not how I took it. "Don't make fun of me please." I said sharply. I could feel tears welling up.

"Hey, hon, I'm not making fun of you, honest. Didn't you ever notice it before?

Maybe not enough tender physical contact in your life? It's a very protective, defensive gesture."

She wasn't grilling me.

"Do you ever wonder about that babe?"

Her questions were not as pointed as my response.

"No, I don't."

Then I got very quiet. I took a deep breath and quickly turned away and got out of bed.

"Hey, babe, I really didn't mean anything. I'm just curious that's all. I'm sorry, Mark, wait. Don't go." She tried to resort to humor to lighten the situation. "Don't you know it's my job to hug you?"

Without saying another word, I went into the bathroom, washed my face, got dressed and muttered that I needed to get back to work.

"Babe, don't go. I am sorry, really. I won't mention it again," I heard as I closed the door and went back to the station.

I was surprised how sad her statement made me. Driving down the street, I felt an overwhelming urge to cry. I bit my lower lip, took a deep breath and drove back to the station.

MARK'S GREAT AMERICAN NOVEL
Chapter Sixteen

New Delhi, India
Early December, 1977

Zia studied every news clipping he could get his hands on concerning President Carter's upcoming trip.

He spent long hours on the streets of Delhi, walking, then re-walking the planned presidential route from Palam Airport to the Indian Presidential Palace Rashtrapati Bhavan, a distance of 12 kilometers (8 miles).

Zia would walk one side of the boulevards and streets, looking for vantage points. Then he would walk back on the other side, doing the same thing. Tall buildings, balconies, trees. Day after day. Studying the traffic patterns, the changing sunlight and shadows, looking for a place to hide until the right moment when the presidential motorcade would approach.

It was during one of these survey trips that Zia realized the pistols the group had secured would be woefully inadequate. In order to be successful, the team would have to get through the crowd, past a very tight security perimeter and get close enough to shoot the president. It was terribly late in the game to discover a flaw that massive.

While he intently focused on the final planning, Zia didn't realize he was being followed. Indian security agents had him under surveillance the day he stepped off the train in New Delhi. Initially, three agents were assigned to him. One or two followed him during the day. The remaining agent or agents were following leads, trying to determine if there were other individuals involved and how many.

On more than one occasion, Zia's room was carefully searched. Photos of his journal along with any recent entries were taken and added to the growing file developed by the Indian and, now, U.S. security team. Anything the agents moved during their search was meticulously replaced in the exact same spot. Revealing their presence at this point would be counterproductive since the extent of the plot was still unknown.

The U.S. Secret Service acts quickly, efficiently and discreetly to prevent harm to the president.

The Secret Service investigates hundreds of threats against the president every year. A few are dismissed quickly as threats from a disgruntled taxpayer, a mentally disturbed individual or unemployed worker. A letter fired off to the president in the heat of the moment without considering the ramifications often results in a follow-up visit from local or state police. In some instances, an FBI agent will tag along.

The Secret Service uses a threat assessment system similar to the weather service process of predicting severe weather. The weather service Tornado Watch, for instance, looks at developing conditions over a wide area, as much as 25,000 square miles.

The Secret Service examines every threat. Those moved to a Watch List early on are threats worth investigating more closely. The Watch List elevates the level of surveillance to determine if someone poses a credible threat to the president. Agents investigate the behavior of a suspect: Does the person travel a lot? Do they travel domestically or overseas? Do they have a police record of any kind, no matter how insignificant? Do they live close to where the president will be speaking? Do they have any radical political viewpoints, acquaintances or involvement with any radical group? Are they employed? Are they married and, if so, do they have a family? Are they visible, known or active in their community or a local church? Or are they single and classic loners? Are they registered to vote? Have they written any "Letters to the Editor" that overtly threaten the commander in chief?

The outcome of those inquiries determines whether an individual is dropped off the active Watch List or elevated to the Warning List. For the Weather Service, a Tornado Warning is based on a specific conditions. There is no specific criteria for moving names to the Warning List at the Secret Service. Individuals become a priority for investigative personnel and resources based on the experience, the input and even the gut instincts of a field agent. The sophisticated use of wiretaps and search warrants are quickly brought into play for names on the Warning List in the weeks prior to a presidential appearance.

In some instances in an effort to derail a pending plot, the Secret Service will reveal to a suspect that they are being watched. Unannounced, two or more agents will visit the suspect in person. These visits may take place when the individual leaves or arrives home, at their place of employment or even in a grocery store parking lot. The surprise visit vividly illustrates the extent of the service's investigation capabilities. This may dissuade the person from proceeding and, having sufficiently unnerved the suspect, lead the Secret Service to others who are involved.

Often, the service will let an investigation proceed undercover for a few days or weeks to determine the severity or scope of the threat. This helps flush out and identify any co-conspirators as well as provide information on the timing of any plot.

This was the case with Zia.

He made the Watch List after his father found his journal and called local police. A follow-up interview was conducted by Indian security forces. That led to an investigation of Zia's whereabouts, college writings and companions and quickly promoted him to the Warning List.

As a result of living, believing and acting as if he was more clever and intelligent than anyone, Zia was oblivious to the agents following him as he moved about New Delhi.

The agents rotated duties throughout the week, reducing the chance of discovery. New Delhi streets are filled with thousands of people at all hours of the day and night, which made their job easier.

Zia knew those same crowds would provide excellent cover for the assassination. In spite of the crowds, Zia knew security would be very tight along the route of the presidential motorcade.

Certainly tighter than the day Archduke Ferdinand and his wife were shot to death. Ferdinand was the heir to the Austrian empire and was shot to death during the second attempt on his life that day in Sarajevo.

On the morning of June 28, the archduke and his wife were riding in a seven-car procession heading to a ceremony at city hall. Two of the assassins froze, missing the opportunity to shoot the archduke as his motorcade passed in front of them. Another assassin threw a hand grenade at their car but it bounced off the fender and exploded under the car directly behind the archduke's. Twenty bystanders were injured. The archduke and his wife, unfazed and unhurt, proceeded as though nothing had happened. The remaining assassins, including Princip, also failed to react when the motorcade passed by.

Incredibly the archduke decided to return from the ceremonial event using the same route. Ignoring suggestions that he leave Sarajevo as quickly as possible, he chose to visit a member of his entourage who was injured in the earlier assassination attempt. The archduke's driver took a wrong turn on the way to the hospital, putting his passengers directly in front of Princip. As the car attempted to turn around, Princip jumped into the archduke's car while it was stopped and began firing. At his trial, Princip insisted his eyes had been closed when he fired the shots that killed the archduke and his wife.

Zia knew gaining a high vantage point along Carter's route, without being detained or detected, would be impossible. More planning and different guns, preferably automatic weapons, were going to be needed, but time was too short. It was obvious that procuring new weapons at this point was out of the question.

New Delhi was excited about the upcoming presidential visit.

President Dwight Eisenhower was the first U.S. President to visit India in December 1959. Eisenhower visited New Delhi and Agra, the site of the Taj Majal. He also addressed the Indian parliament and conducted high-level meetings with Indian President Prasad and Prime Minister Nehru.

Nearly two decades would pass before another U.S. president would visit the Indian subcontinent: the 39th president of the United States, Jimmy Carter.

FIFTY-FIVE

Little Grass Valley Reservoir
Sunday just after noon
December 17, 1978

I'm pretty depressed today.

It's probably the combination of camping, the cold and the alcohol, although my life in general is depressing enough on its own.

I've been thinking a lot about Ed today. What a great guy. He was always so confident and seemed to know something about everything. He could change electrical outlets without shutting the power off or getting shocked. He was great with woodworking. He could do a lot of the mechanical stuff on his car like tune-ups and brake jobs. Whenever we camped, he could pitch a tent and tie knots in ropes in what seemed like record time. He would also tie up our food in nearby trees, out of the reach of bears.

He knew what to look for on trail hikes: deer crossings, edible berries, wildflower seeds and even animal scat. Then there was poison oak: "leaves of three, leave them be" is the traditional advice. Early in the spring, before the leaves sprouted, Ed pointed out the new shoots of poison oak—innocuous and easily overlooked. He said, "Step carefully around those or you will have a historic case of poison oak to regale your grandchildren with."

Ed challenged the "lost hiker" wisdom that moss only grows on the north side of a tree. He pointed out several contradictions along creek beds, in trees growing in gullies or a hollow.

"Relying on the conventional wisdom can make a bad situation worse," he said. "If you think you are lost, look around for your footprints. If you think you know how to get back, leave some markings on the trail in case you are wrong and have to retrace your steps. Kind of like Hansel and Gretel leaving bread crumbs in the woods." He smiled. "Of course, the best advice is not to get lost in the first place."

He was pretty easy going and fun to be around. He could see humor or irony in every situation. At city council meetings, I knew better than to look at him when discussions got heated at the council table. He would cross his eyes or pretend like he was getting ready to throw up or something equally silly.

He's been gone for nearly four months now. Even though we were best friends, I haven't thought about him much until today. And why now when I'm all alone?

I guess I really haven't wanted to think about him.
I wish he'd had the chance to meet my grandpa.

MARK'S GREAT AMERICAN NOVEL
Chapter Seventeen

New Delhi, India
Early December, 1977

In recent days, Zia sensed a wavering in the dedication and commitment of fellow team member Dipak.

Dipak, in Sanskrit meaning "inflaming, exciting," started coming late to the team meetings. When he returned from his pickpocket outings, he had new, sometimes flamboyant excuses for the meager contributions he made to the team's finances. And his outings kept him away longer each time. There seemed to be an inverse relationship to the time spent away from the group and the amount of money he collected.

During team meetings, Dipak added little to the discussions and offered no input on the planning. He seemed distracted with a vacant stare.

Zia knew caution by team members was necessary. Observing him closely, however, it was obvious Dipak was not just having second thoughts. He appeared to be in full blown revolt about his involvement.

Johar agreed Dipak was a concern. And a risk.

Zia said he would deal with the situation.

When the team dispersed after one of the late afternoon strategy sessions, Zia took Dipak aside. He could not look Zia in the eye. He was nervous and evasive. He gave Zia vague assurances of his commitment. Unconvincingly, he said he was proud to be part of the plan. His body language said otherwise.

After a few minutes of conversation, Zia excused himself and went to his room.

He found his pistol and checked to make sure the magazine was full. There was already a bullet in the chamber. He tucked it carefully into his trousers and covered it with his shirt.

When he returned to the team room, Zia suggested Dipak take a walk with him—to clear their heads and talk some more. They walked for nearly a half mile. Zia said very little. Dipak, on the other hand, talked incessantly, like a school boy on holiday, filling every second with commentary. He appeared terribly uncomfortable with any silence between them. He talked about how much he loved New Dehli: the sights, the sounds, the food, the people. He talked about growing up in his village, his family and the cousins he hoped to see again soon.

Despite his talking, the tension between them was palpable. When he wasn't talking, Dipak's eyes darted in every direction, as if he were looking for an escape route—ready to bolt in any direction.

Walking down the crowded sidewalks, Zia let his mind wander, imagining Dipak getting a few steps ahead. He imagined pulling his pistol and firing point blank into the base of Dipak's skull. Obviously, that wouldn't happen on a busy sidewalk, but the image helped distract him as they walked.

Traffic in New Dehli is chaotic. Buses, taxis, rickshaws, private cars, loose cattle and even elephants add to the cacophony of sights and sounds. At times it is actually quite mesmerizing. Like pages of the National Geographic coming alive in front of you.

At an intersection, Zia and Dipak were the first to gather at the corner waiting for the traffic light to change. Zia gauged the speed of an oncoming taxi, then deftly put his foot in front of Dipak and shoved him into the taxi's path. In the split second as Dipak started to fall, Zia turned and pushed his way back through the crowd.

It happened quickly. Dipak barely uttered a sound before he fell head first into the speeding taxi. He was killed instantly. His body was thrown 15 feet, falling limply into the street.

The taxi slammed to a halt. Several women screamed. Passersby rushed to Dipak's body although it was clear there were no signs of life.

A block and a half away, Zia stopped and turned back toward the accident scene.

No one was looking his way. Zia was surprised his breathing had quickly returned to normal and he had barely broken a sweat. A moment later, he was unable to fight the overwhelming urge and became powerfully aroused.

At the hotel, Zia would simply tell the team Dipak wanted to do some extra pickpocket work to build up the team's dwindling finances. He expected to be back at the hotel by nightfall.

When Dipak didn't return that evening, speculation ran rampant among team members. One member thought Dipak must have been arrested while "working" near one of the hotels. Someone wondered aloud if Dipak had been snatched by security authorities and if their plot had been discovered.

Zia steered the conversation by fueling a different track of speculation. He fabricated parts of their conversation. "We talked for a long time. Dipak seemed unusually nervous. He told me he didn't want to go to jail if the plot failed. He talked a lot about his family and where he grew up and how much he missed all of that. He wasn't even sure stealing to finance the plot was the right thing to do. He was really struggling with his involvement. I wouldn't be surprised if he just ran for home."

As Zia hoped, the talk then evolved to believing Dipak had developed second thoughts and simply fled Delhi. The team's concerns then quickly turned to anger.

Zia closed the discussion by encouraging team members to remain vigilant and report anything suspicious. He assured them Dipak was a minor player in the plot and his absence would not derail the plan. Zia also said he would try to find out more about Dipak's disappearance.

Johar did not engage in any of the conversation. He knew that Dipak had not run away. And he also knew Dipak was never coming back.

FIFTY-SIX

I'm not sure about my self-image.

I read "I'm OK, You're OK." Ed kidded me once, saying, "I read the book, too. It turns out I'm OK, You're Not. In fact, you're nuts."

I am always trying to figure out who I am. Maybe even what I am. I wonder if other guys harbor these kinds of insecurities. Most of them appear so confident.

In grade school, teachers, parents, even friends said I was cute. I was able to play the "cute" angle until I was about 9.

In high school, people told me I was good looking. In college, I heard it from men and women. And the guys who said it were "all American"—you know, straight not queer.

I don't see myself as good looking. My smile is crooked. Even in college, when Carole or Christine said I was sexy, it never seemed to ring true.

I remember when I was a freshman in high school, my mother told me once—and only once—how much I looked like my father.

I never saw myself the same way after that.

I never liked what I saw in the mirror.

MARK'S GREAT AMERICAN NOVEL
Chapter Eighteen

New Delhi, India
Mid December, 1977

It was on one of his walks reviewing the presidential motorcade route that Zia developed powerful, nagging second thoughts about the entire plan.

Ten days before the president's arrival, he began to question everything: from the equipment they had secured to the participants on the team. He had already addressed one problem on the team. He suspected others might be questioning the plan as well.

Personally, there had always been some doubts, of course, but he had pushed them out of his mind resolving to think about them later. He was a master chess player at school and could anticipate, with great excitement or anxiety an opponent's upcoming moves—sometimes as many as a dozen moves ahead of time.

His ability to anticipate now lacked any of that kind of excitement, creating only enormous anxiety instead.

The first troubling development was the realization that the revolvers the group acquired would be woefully inadequate for the job. In the drama and frenzy of planning, Zia overlooked and misjudged this critical element. When a team member announced he had secured a half dozen revolvers, Zia mentally checked that item off his list and moved on to other planning issues.

Zia thought he had approached the assassination plot methodically, like a pilot using a pre-flight checklist. A preflight checklist gives a pilot the opportunity to review hazards, plan for possible delays, check fuel levels and availability, review equipment issues, communication frequencies, runway lengths and even ground transportation at the destination. A checklist allows the pilot to concentrate on flying the plane once airborne and reduces the chance of being distracted by trying to gather such mundane information in flight.

Now too late, Zia realized he should have come to Delhi months ago, walking the streets and boulevards. He would have known earlier what was needed. Not only was there no time to get rifles or automatic weapons, there was no time to practice firing them.

Even after dealing with Dipak, Zia's doubts multiplied about the group. He started to seriously wonder about the members he and Johar had recruited. Zia looked around the room studying each of the individuals involved. Everyone was within three years of age of one another. But age wasn't the issue today. It was the level of maturity that struck Zia.

Did they really have any idea what they were getting into? Did they understand the risks? Did they understand the shame, embarrassment, even torture they could be subjecting their friends and family to if they were discovered or if the plot failed?

Everyone in the group shared a passion to change the world and make a statement "for the ages." Their youthful enthusiasm was contagious and fed on itself during their meals or long sessions over tea late into the evenings.

The FAA warns pilots about preflight "attitude hazards" like impulsiveness, overconfidence, emotions, a sense of invulnerability or even fatigue. There is also the hazard of believing there are no second chances or there is no time to waste or no time to regroup. For pilots it's called "get-there-itis". Zia ignored the "attitude hazards" bubbling up within him and decided to push forward.

Did any of the team members really envision potential consequences? The enormity of their undertaking? Was this simply youthful idealism? A lark? What was their actual level of commitment?

In Zia's mind, only Johar met all of the criteria for moving forward. The others, he feared, were simply naive, probably incapable of seeing the end game.

These new doubts now competed with the others swirling in his brain. Zia found anxiety a new and highly uncomfortable feeling. And the feeling seemed to be growing out of control: at first by the hour, then by the minute.

Zia's disciplined life never included a prayer life. Any semblance of spirituality evaporated when his siblings died. At the university, he studied the beliefs of Jainism, Muslim, Hindu even Confucianism, but followed no particular religious tenets.

While walking the streets of Delhi, Zia was intrigued by the regular calls to prayer at the Jama Masjid, known as the "Friday" or "Congregational Mosque." Although curious, he never considered attending a service.

The Mosque is the largest and most famous in India. The courtyard measures 246 feet by 217 feet and can accommodate 25,000 worshipers. Construction began in 1650 and was completed six years later. India's most prolific and well-known Moghul architect and builder, Shah Jahan, laid the foundation stone for the Mosque. Jahan was also responsible for the construction of the Red Fort in New Delhi as well as the Taj Mahal in Agra. The cost, not including donated building materials and the inlaid precious stones, was estimated at 1,000,000 Indian rupees.

Construction of the Jama Masjid required 6,000 laborers, craftsmen, artisans, calligraphers and chiselers. The work was supervised by some of the best-known engineers and architects in the world.

Like many young zealots, Zia let his personal beliefs and prejudices co-opt any interpretation of history's sacred writings. Convinced he had the only correct understanding, he selected beliefs that supported and confirmed his political thinking.

Hypothesis bias is not dependent on language, culture or circumstances.

It is universal.

"There are all kinds of love in this world, but never the same love twice"
—F. Scott Fitzgerald, "THE GREAT GATSBY"

FIFTY-SEVEN

The other woman in college was Carole. I thought she would be the love of my life. We were pretty hot for a few months. We'd party, dance, talk long into the night about our dreams, plans, the future. And, of course, there was lots of sex.

I had three roommates in my dorm room at the time. Our dorm room was three rooms divided by two walls. There were two bunk beds in the middle room along with a bathroom and a shower. Our desks, drawers and small closets were on either side of the bedroom. Two of us on either side.

Privacy wasn't really an issue for Carole and me. We were really hot for each other. On more than one occasion, a roommate came home at a particularly "inopportune moment." They were more embarrassed than we were and would quickly exit. We weren't too particular where we did it. And we did it a lot.

I loved going to the movie theater. Carole had a special way of making the evening memorable once the lights went down and the movie started. For the life of me, though, I can't recall the title or the plot of a single film we saw together. Not a single one.

As things cooled, we realized we had less in common than we thought. We drifted away.

"It's Too Late"—Carole King

I'd see her on campus once in a while. We would say "hi,", but that was about it.

"If You Could Read My Mind"—Gordon Lighfoot

I never got used to her being with another guy. Part of me wanted to believe there was still a chance we would get back together. Seeing her with someone else only emphasized that the world and Carole had moved on.

"Don't Expect Me to be Your Friend"—Lobo

I tried to pretend our break-up was no big deal. But it was. For weeks, I walked around feeling like I had been punched in the stomach. And kicked in the groin. I would wait until I was in the shower to cry, so my roommates wouldn't hear.

I was pretty blue.

"Never Gonna Fall in Love Again"—Eric Carmen

At that age, perspective is tough to come by. Thoughts of killing myself crossed my mind with an attitude of "I'll show her."

Then it occurred to me: In two months, probably less, I would be just a memory. And if there was a college class reunion five years from now, the conversation might go something like, "Do you remember the name of the guy who killed himself?" Or worse yet, "A guy killed himself while we were in college?"

So, I stopped thinking about Carol. And killing myself.

In any case, there were just two women. For God's sake. Two! In four years!

Hell, there are high school sophomores doing better than that every weekend. Sometimes better than that immediately after school.

FIFTY-EIGHT

When mom called me at the station that morning, her news was unexpected. Out of the blue.

"Your grandfather had a heart attack last night." Her voice tightened. "He passed away this morning."

Years ago, I remember playing in the ocean. I was probably about 9 or 10. My mother told me never to turn my back on the ocean. Forgetting that advice for an instant proved terrifying when, with no warning, a large wave knocked me down and rolled me over and over in the sand. The last moment before I went underwater I saw my mother and heard her scream.

By then it was too late. The weight of the water knocked me down and held me there. I couldn't stand up or even figure out where I was or what was happening. I remember instinctively gasping for breath—underwater—filling my lungs with salt water. I remember the terror, the burning in my eyes, throat and lungs.

Grandpa came out of nowhere and pulled me out of the water and onto the shore.

All of that had taken a matter of seconds. It took 15 minutes, though, before I stopped coughing and crying. It took mom at least that long to stop crying, too. Grandpa wrapped a towel around me. Sitting between Mom and me, he held us both tight, not saying a word. I remember how safe I felt.

Now that same feeling of helplessness, before Grandpa came to the rescue, was back. Only this time there was no towel, no rescue and no Grandpa.

"I didn't know anything about it," and then, "Nobody told me," not really knowing what I was saying. "I…" my voice trailed off.

"He didn't suffer," mom broke in. "Your grandmother called the ambulance last night around 11:30. He wasn't breathing when the emergency crew arrived and he never regained consciousness." Mom went on without pausing. "We're going to have the funeral Friday morning at St. Isadore's. Grandma wants you to be one of the pallbearers."

After a moment, she said, "I'm sorry. I know how much you loved him." Then, in a matter-of-fact tone, trying to control her own emotions, she said: "You can stay here at the house Thursday night. I'll see you then."

Her voice cracked as she said, "I love you" and then "Goodbye" before hanging up.

I finished preparing my newscast. After all, "The show must go on." Then I left and drove down to a spot by the river, parked and cried for a very long time.

Alone.

I remember feeling homesick at Boy Scout camp when I was 10. It was the first time I'd been away from home along with everything and everyone I knew. I felt isolated. I cried a lot. Of course, the other scouts called me a sissy and a girl. I heard comments like, "Maybe you should be across the lake at the Girl Scout camp."

So, I faked a stomach ache, called home and Grandpa picked me up a couple of days early. Grandpa probably knew I wasn't sick but didn't say anything right away. I was very quiet on the two-hour drive home. Finally he asked, "Do you want to tell me what's really going on, Mark?" I confided about how and why I was teased. I remember what he told me: "Mark, behind the exterior of every strong, confident man is a scared little boy who doesn't know what to do next. The world is still a very scary place for them. The difference, Mark, is they wait until they are alone to show it."

So, I resolved to never cry around someone else ever again. It was a resolution I kept for most of the rest of my life.

MARK'S GREAT AMERICAN NOVEL
Chapter Nineteen

New Delhi, India
December, 1977

Intelligence agencies are often reluctant to share information or surveillance with each other. Agencies responsible for intelligence gathering are protective of their methods and the results of any investigations. The idea of a complete sharing of proprietary intelligence with other departments runs counter to decades of practice by most agencies.

The coordination of presidential security intelligence is different. Agents assigned to the protection of the president or other dignitaries are focused solely on the safety and security of the individual they are assigned to protect. There is a free flow of information and this cooperation extends to working with security agencies all over the world. Withholding any security-related information, even the slightest detail can be embarrassing in the best of situations. In the worst situation, it can result in the death of a president, a V.I.P. or innocent bystanders.

During the month, the increasing scope of Zia's plot added to the growing anxiety of security officials. The surveillance of Zia and other group members expanded quickly.

Extensive meetings and a thorough review of the information agents had gathered prompted Indian security officials to form a rapid response strike team on December 18. The Secret Service was advised of the development, but the final decision to use a strike team would be a made by Indian authorities. The team consisted of eight elite Indian army members. They were skilled in quick, surgical tactics aimed at removing imminent threats with a minimum of collateral damage.

The strike team leader was 28-year-old Ajit Misra, whose Sanskrit name translates "victorious, invincible, unconquerable, honorable".

The use of the strike team would be a last-resort option before Air Force One touched down in New Delhi.

The final decision to use the strike team would be Ajit's alone.

Secret Service protocol keeps the existence or number of threats confidential. They are not shared with the president and or his staff. Only in cases of an extreme or imminent threat is the president informed and his itinerary changed accordingly.

FIFTY-NINE

My apartment
Sequoia City

"I hated my father," I said after she asked, "Do think you will ever want to talk about it?"

My insides had been churning since the day Emma mentioned my sleeping as if I were hugging myself. I've felt a pounding in my head like a migraine headache. I've felt very weighed down. My thinking has been muddled and sluggish.

I remember reading, "Feelings buried alive never die." I was about to exhume a lot of feelings I thought were dead and buried a long time ago.

We were sitting at the kitchen table. Emma was holding my hand, but I couldn't look at her.

"My father beat me every day." It almost sounded like an apology.

It felt as if time had stopped. I don't recall hearing a single sound: not in my head, not in the room nor outside on the street.

My lip was quivering and I felt a shudder. Then I started crying. Deep sobbing between huge gulps of air. "He beat me every day, Emma. Every single day. I never did anything to him. I did whatever he told me to do and he still beat me."

I cried for a long time, then became very angry. Emma winced when I tightened my grip on her hand while slamming my free fist onto the table. "I hated the son of a bitch, Emma. You are not supposed to hate anyone. But I hated him. He was my father and I hated him." I let go of her hand.

I was surprised how easy the next statement came out. "I'm glad he's dead, Emma. I really am. I've never told anyone that before, but I am really, really glad he is dead. I hope he rots in hell for all eternity."

Emma stayed silent, then took my hand again. She squeezed my hand ever so slightly—a nonverbal way of saying, "it's OK."

"I beat him up the last time I saw him. I think I could have killed him." I started crying again. Almost wailing. The Irish and the Scots call it keening: grieving over the dead.

But I wasn't grieving my dead father. I was grieving a little boy who never felt safe, invincible or carefree. A little boy who was always afraid.

A few moments passed. Then in the softest voice I'd ever heard, she said, "I think you waited a very long time to tell anyone that story." She sounded so tender and

210

understanding. "Thank you…for trusting me."

I was suddenly aware, though, how silly I must have looked to her. I tried to regain my composure. I must have looked wretched and pitiful. My God, I'm a grown man who has made love to her dozens of times and here I am crying like an 8-year-old.

I feel guilty and ashamed about my outburst.

A minute or two passed before I finally looked up. I managed a weak smile. Embarrassed, I said, "I'm sorry," in a half whisper. "I don't know what happened."

Emma's next words caught me off guard. In fact, at first I wasn't sure I heard her right. I couldn't imagine she could possibly feel that way.

"It's OK, Mark. Really, it's OK." There was a pause, followed by a quick breath. "Mark, I haven't said this to anyone in a very long time. I'm not sure I ever truly knew what it meant until now."

There was another pause, longer this time. She took a very deep breath and said "Mark, I…I love you."

We sat silently for a few more minutes. I slowly became aware of the sound of the clock, the air conditioner and a car passing on the street. My head hurt, but I didn't feel weighed down as much.

She took both of my hands in hers and kissed them. "Come on. Let's make love."

As she got up and led me to the bedroom, I was suddenly very turned on. I couldn't wait to make love, too.

I read about "make-up sex" where a couple makes passionate love after settling a heated argument. We hadn't had an argument, but I can't imagine "make-up sex" being any less intense than our time together that day.

We spent the rest of the afternoon and evening in bed. Our lovemaking was as passionate, exciting, sensual and physical as the weekend after the trail ride.

> "…and sometimes when we touch, the honesty's too much, and
> I have to close my eyes and hide. I wanna hold you till I die, till
> we both break down and cry, I want to I want to hold you till
> the fear in me subsides…"

Sex was very different between us after that day. After all this time, I finally understood what it meant to "make love."

S I X T Y

Sequoia City
3 weeks after the trail ride

Gerry was never the same after Greg disappeared. At least around me.

"You must have had quite a time up there. It must have been something," Gerry said the first time I saw him downtown.

"Yeah. I thought he ditched me as a joke." Gerry and I both knew that Greg had no sense of humor, was incapable of telling a funny story, remembering a punchline or pulling off a practical joke.

"I was lost and alone." I paused for effect. I was surprised how easy it was to lie to Gerry. I am surprisingly good at lying. "I waited for him for a long time and kept calling his name. I didn't want to be in the canyon after dark, so I finally started back and called his name all the way back to the stables. I really thought he was goofing with me."

It was like I was reporting the events as a bystander, not a participant.

Whenever I ran in to Gerry, he continued with comments that were not quite questions and not quite statements. He was fishing. And I imagine Emma dropping him for me was a real shock to his ego. Gerry was used to getting whatever, and whenever, he wanted.

"Ever been in a situation like that before? Guy disappears and he's never heard from again? Must have been something. Are you sleeping OK?"

Sure, I thought, I have people trying to kill me all the time and leaving me for dead in the wilderness, you jackass.

"Yeah, I'm sleeping OK, I guess." Actually, I thought, you have no idea how well I'm sleeping.

Jackass.

Before Greg died, I was never comfortable around Gerry. Now our relationship felt more like the dance between a mongoose and a cobra. The cobra is sneaky and cunning while the mongoose is fearless and agile. The mongoose usually wins but only after a fierce battle with the snake.

It was easy to figure out which of the two of us was the snake. It was hard to imagine myself as the mongoose.

"The guys at the stable said your horse smelled like smoke when you got back. How close were you to the fire?"

Gerry never waited for an answer to any of his questions and pressed on. "You guys had a lot of time to talk on the trail. What did you talk about? You guys have any common interests? "

"We talked gold mining, Indian camp sites, hunting lore, sports, even women we were sleeping with." He turned a bit red. I knew that would get under his skin but I went on, pretending not to notice his irritation. "You know, guy stuff."

"Did you talk about your work at all? You know, how you develop stories? How you talk to people, what do you news guys call it, 'off the record'?"

It was a curious line of questioning that seemed more pointed all the time. Every time I saw him, he was more persistent. Like circling his prey: waiting for the right moment to pounce.

"No particular reason," he said when I asked him why he was so interested. "Just curious. Greg and I knew each other a long time, so you know, I wondered what you talked about all that time you were out on the trail. That's all. Must have been something."

Yeah, it was something all right. What a frigging jackass. I wondered whose gun Greg had the afternoon he tried to kill me. I also wondered what Gerry missed more: Greg or the gun.

Smirking, Gerry said "You and Emma have really hit it off again. She's leaving your place pretty early in the morning these days, huh? Most be nice."

Knowing how much it would irritate him, I said, "It is really nice, Gerry. It's incredible, actually. We're not getting much sleep, I can tell you that."

His face reddened. I knew it made him angry.

In the next instant, I was ticked, too.

"And how the hell would you know what time Emma leaves in the morning, Gerry?"

"Oh, you hear things around. You know. Small town. Big mouths. Tough to keep secrets around here." After a pause, "The canyons won't keep their secrets forever either, you know," he said menacingly. "Someday we'll have all the answers."

The canyons, I thought, would keep their secrets long enough.

Jackass.

MARK'S GREAT AMERICAN NOVEL
Chapter Twenty

Bombay, India
Santacruz Airport
Early evening
January 1, 1978

Zia settled into a seat somewhere in the 46th row. Moments after buckling his seat belt, the stewardess asked him to move to another row to accommodate a family traveling together.

He chose a vacant window seat and opened the air vents. For the first time, he realized how much he had been sweating. After takeoff, he would take time to freshen up in the lavatory at the rear of the aircraft.

His mind detailed the last few hours over and over in his head. He ignored the safety instructions being repeated in three languages. He thought this would be a good moment in his life to drink alcohol for the first time. Something else he would do when the plane was airborne. He would also ask for a cigarette pack from the stewardess.

The 747 was incredibly large. Zia had only seen one from the ground. This was the first 747 Air India had acquired. Purchased in 1971, it was named the "Emperor Ashoka" and advertised as "Your Palace in the Air."

Zia agreed. It certainly seemed like a palace compared to the small traveler's hotel he and the others had been staying in for the last few weeks. Located eight blocks from the five-star hotel district in downtown New Delhi, "The Lotus Leaf" was clean and cheap. There was a hot plate for heating water and light cooking. The room faced north and was sheltered from the afternoon sun. There was an instant water heater for washing and bathing. There were no dividing walls in the room, so the toilet was next to the wash basin and just a few feet from the bed.

No room service, no maid service, no amenities, no phone.

Zia loved the tandoori chicken and rice served at a restaurant a few doors down from the hotel. Washed down with a Thumbs Up cola, it was the perfect evening meal.

Breakfast was scrambled eggs cooked on the hot plate. Lunch would be with the rest of the team poring over maps, escape routes, and traffic bottlenecks as well as cleaning and re-cleaning their weapons. The weapons might as well have been toy pistols, he thought now.

There was a pitch of excitement in all of them. Zia and Johar were the oldest at age 21, bringing the average age of the team members to 19. Their meetings were electric. So much passion. So much energy. Try as they might, most team members could rarely sleep longer than four hours at a time during the weeks of planning.

They're all sleeping now, Zia thought. Sleeping forever. Or in prison.

SIXTY-ONE

Sequoia City
The Grand Jury Indictments

Looking back, the first sign legal troubles happened over two and a half months before Bobby's drowning and came boiling over just after 6 on a Monday evening in mid-March.

The phone rang in Gerry's office. One of Gerry's occasional girlfriends, Gail, worked at a title company in Sequoia City.

She was in a panic: half crying, half hysterical.

Gail said: "A couple of us in the office were served with Grand Jury subpoenas from the D.A.'s land fraud unit this morning. What's this all about? You told us, Gerry...no, you promised us, no one would ever ask about the work we did for you and Bobby. You said no one would question us about notarizing all those deeds. I could lose my job. I could go to jail. You promised, Gerry. What am I supposed to do?"

Gerry didn't know, but he switched gears and did what he did best: He minimized the issue and Gail's concerns. Verbally patting her on the head, Gerry told her there was nothing to worry about.

"Listen, I've got a meeting to go to right now. Why don't I bring over a bottle of wine later and we can talk some more. About 9? And Gail, don't worry about anything."

He quickly got off the phone, then made another call.

"Jordan, we need to talk. Now".

Bobby couldn't remember the last time someone called him Jordan. Nor could he remember ever hearing Gerry's voice as tense as now.

"Where? The office."

"No place public. Can I meet you on the ship? I can be there in 45 minutes"

"Sure, what's up?"

Gerry had already hung up. Bobby finished the conversation, to himself, saying "OK, see you then."

Gerry knew the meeting would have to be over in less than three hours. The shuttle service to and from the marina ended at 9:30. He planned to spend the night with Gail and not on the ship with Bobby.

Gerry knew a Grand Jury investigation into their land dealings would quickly uncover the scope of the deception and criminal fraud involved.

Either or both of them would go to jail. He assumed Bobby would come to the same conclusion.

Gerry grabbed a bottle of Lancers. He was turned on just thinking about Gail, excited at the thought of being in bed with her again in a couple of hours. He hadn't seen her in a while. She lived alone and was always happy to have him spend the night. He was more than happy to oblige.

He locked the office door, headed downstairs and drove to the lake.

On the way, he was already minimizing the impending legal difficulties gathering on the horizon and planning a way out. Gerry was able to compartmentalize his thoughts, fears and desires very quickly.

It may or may not have occurred to Gerry that he was on his way to proving the adage about honor among thieves.

SIXTY-TWO

The following morning

Gerry was awake at 5. Just before getting out of bed, he thought about waking up Gail. He wanted to get it on again, but decided against it. He had things to accomplish today. Besides making love once the sun was up would require him to linger. And talk.

Not today, he thought.

While getting dressed, he reflected how well the evening had gone. On the ship, he and Bobby discussed the D.A. investigation and laid out some initial strategies. Bobby agreed to talk to his lawyer, Glenn Robert ("the guy with two first names" as he was known in town). He would ask Glenn to research land laws and also try to discover how much the D.A. knew about Bobby and Gerry's activities.

Gerry, on the other hand, remained evasive about his plans, privately deciding to meet with lawyers in Sacramento. Over the years he had become acquainted with legislative lobbyists and attorneys working in and around the Capitol. He had a couple of names to call and set up interviews.

Gerry was a deal maker and knew there was a deal to be made here.

Then there was Gail. Gerry didn't drink even one glass of wine during their time together last night. He preferred to stay in control but made sure Gail's glass was never empty. He listened carefully to Gail, echoing back her concerns and fears in a quiet voice. Sometimes you might even have detected just a hint of sensuality in his responses.

Gerry was only marginally interested in conversation. He was in full seduction mode.

Occasionally, he asked a few general, non-threatening questions. His curiosity was about the subpoenas was innocuous and non-threatening. No need to spoil his plans to get her into bed. Did she or her co-workers know anything about the investigation? How was her boss reacting to the developments of the day?

He could sound compassionate and empathetic. He sat close to her, leaning in as she talked. He held her hands lightly in his. Gerry discovered decades ago this method was the quickest way to a woman's heart. And her bed. Gail, on the other hand, thought Gerry was someone who cared and understood her feelings. For her, sex with Gerry would be a natural evolution to the evening.

Saying goodbye in Gail's apartment, he gave a modified version of his usual, noncommittal "I had fun last night. Can't wait to get together again soon."

In the car, Gerry was pleased that, in spite of his age, he and Gail had sex three times overnight. She always wanted to make the most of their time together in bed and didn't mind experimenting. He was more than happy—and, fortunately in this case, willing and able—to exceed her expectations.

As he drove away from the apartment house, he felt a stirring. "Maybe I should have tried for a fourth time this morning."

He looked at himself in the rear-view mirror and smiled.

Great evening all the way around, he thought. He was fairly self-impressed.

"Wow" was the only other word that came to mind.

S I X T Y - T H R E E

Thursday, April 27, 1978
The Rip Roarin' Office

Gerry Apte lived his life "planning for the worst and hoping for the best."

In business dealings, he lived according to airplane safety instructions: "In the event of an emergency, put your oxygen mask on first before assisting others. The nearest exit may be behind you and, in the event of an evacuation, leave all your personal belongings behind."

Jill Parker was the bookkeeper at the Rip Roarin' and one of Gerry's part-time lovers. Jill never minded Gerry's lack of exclusivity. She was content with their professional and occasionally casual physical relationship. Jill was also the bookkeeper for the Sequoia Land Development Corporation.

At the bar, she kept two sets of books: one for Gerry and one for the IRS. The IRS journals showed more expenses and less income for tax reporting purposes. This was easy since The Rip Roarin' was a largely cash business. Jill used a stationery catalog to order identically numbered receipt books from two out-of-town printers: one in Redding and one in Portland. During the week, the bartender and the waitress each had a receipt book. On Thursday, Friday and Saturday nights, the bartenders shared one book, the waitresses the other.

The cash register at the Rip Roarin' was left open at all times. It's a trick used by businesses to hide the actual amount of cash coming in. Bartenders and waitresses issued bar and meal tab receipts and could make change but never rang up individual transactions.

The next day, Jill would balance the amount of cash taken in with one of the two receipt books. For tax purposes, she kept a file with those receipts along with the daily deposit slip from the B of A.

She removed and destroyed the duplicate numbered receipts in the other receipt book and put the remaining money in a bank bag left in a safe in Gerry's office. The morning after that, the bank bag would be empty and back on Jill's desk.

Every Tuesday morning, like clockwork, the bag would be returned with three crisp 100 dollar bills in it. Gerry told Jill these bills were "wigglers": bills that wiggled their way out of the cash register and into her pocket.

In the 1920s, Charles Ponzi established an investment company promising returns of 50 percent return in 45 days. As improbable as it sounds today, Ponzi said he was investing in the guaranteed value of international postage stamps. Ponzi told investors the stamps had fixed values, whereas international currencies following World War I did not.

There were no securities, regulatory or consumer watchdog organizations in place at the time.

Ponzi never invested the money. He simply used money from new investors to pay the return promised to earlier investors.

Word spread quickly of the investment's potential and new investors flocked to Ponzi's firm. Newspapers touted his net worth, keen investment insights and uncanny ability to make money. Ponzi encouraged investors not to take distributions, instead letting their earnings compound at the phenomenal, promised rates of return. As a result, Ponzi rarely had to pay any funds out. Of course, there were always enough funds to pay Charles Ponzi a healthy advisory fee for his expertise.

Investors received regular statements of the investment performance boasting unmatched returns. Investors were then encouraged to add money to their portfolio. He would often close one investment portfolio, and encourage investors, old and new, to buy into a new portfolio.

Ponzi's PR man brought the house of cards down by providing the Boston Post with incriminating evidence that Ponzi was broke. The revelations triggered a series of investigative articles exposing the operation as a fraud. The Post's detective work also uncovered a criminal conviction involving Ponzi in Canada and a pending FBI investigation.

The Boston Post was awarded the 1921 Pulitzer Prize Gold Medal for Meritorious Public Service following its reports on the scheme. It was one of the earliest Pulitzers awarded for investigative reporting.

After his fraud conviction, Ponzi summed up his business plan this way: "My business was simple. It was the old game of robbing Peter to pay Paul."

Ponzi was a one-man operation. Pyramid schemes or chain letters, on the other hand, start with one person, who then sells the concept to other investors. These investors then sell the concept to additional investors, keeping some of the money for themselves and while also sending funds to the person who recruited them into the plan. Money moves "up" the pyramid. The earlier you get into a pyramid scheme, the more likely it is you will get your money back plus a healthy return.

Pyramid schemes eventually collapse under their own weight: There is not enough money in circulation or people on earth to perpetuate the earnings of a pyramid scheme. The "eighth wonder of the world: compound interest" explains why. If you had just one penny, then doubled it on the first day of the month and continued doubling it every day for 30 days, you would have $10,737,418.24 at the end of the month. Math wins: you eventually run out of investors and money to keep building the pyramid.

The Sequoia Land Development Corporation was neither a Ponzi nor a pyramid scheme in the classic sense. It was a fraud nonetheless. While never promising spectacular returns, the corporation did tap into the powerful human emotion of greed: the desire to "get in on the ground floor" of a "sure thing" investment.

The corporation more closely resembled a con man's "shell game." Money and property deeds moved in so many directions that it was impossible to keep track of them.

Without a sharp eye.

Jill Parker, on Gerry's recommendation, also served as bookkeeper for the Sequoia Land Development Corporation. Drawing on her experience at the Rip Roarin', she developed and managed two sets of books for the corporation.

The second set skimmed money from the corporation, sheltering many of the financial transactions from Bobby and any potential criminal investigations. These funds found their way into Gerry's accounts.

The Sequoia Land Development Corporation followed the advertising adage:

"Sell the sizzle, not the steak." Obviously, no one would be interested in buying land that couldn't be developed. So that critical part of the disclosures was left out of the corporation's advertising.

The Rip Roarin' and the Sequoia Land Development Corporation had adjacent mailboxes at the post office. Jill picked up the mail around 11 every morning and sorted the mail from both boxes on a large table in the lobby. Once or twice a week, any payments mailed to the corporation containing checks made out to "cash" or where the payee was left blank were funneled into the Rip Roarin' bank bag. Some envelopes contained cash with an account number scribbled on a note. Those funds, too, made their way to the Rip Roarin' bank bag, not the corporation's.

With more than 300 payments coming in every month and new property sales occurring all the time, it was easy to hide the true cash flow of the Sequoia Land Development Corporation. Jill kept an excellent set of fraudulent records to show Bobby anytime he asked. There were also careful notations of payments that hadn't been received. These were often the cash payments diverted to the Rip Roarin' bank bag. Like the classic shell game, payments were shuffled in different directions to different property accounts every month. The following month, the ledger might show one or two payments on those parcels, so no one loan looked perpetually in arrears.

When a property owner actually did stop making payments, Gerry would send an Official-looking "demand note" to pay in full or sign over the property back to the corporation. Most owners simply canceled their contract and deeded the property back to the corporation. Bobby was unaware of the process and was never told when these reclaimed properties were later resold. The set of books Bobby saw would reflect these properties as "vacant," "for sale" or "in foreclosure." While Jill had no formal training in bookkeeping or accounting, her deception was meticulous.

The property sales at Sequoia Land Development resembled term life insurance policies or time share sales in resort areas.

Term life insurance policies are profitable because policies are rarely kept to maturity or they expire without a claim. Agents like term policies because commissions usually equal one year's premiums. Over time, policies are either canceled by the policyholder or by the company for non-payment of premiums. The premiums that have been paid up to that time funnel directly to an insurance company's bottom line.

In resort areas, large condominium developments are converted into time shares. A 300-apartment/condominium complex can be divided into weekly "shares" for sale. The sales presentations are held in locations bordering tropical beaches or other impressive surroundings. Vacationers are told they can "own a piece of Paradise" or "plan their annual vacation carefree in their own private corner of the world."

A 300-condominium apartment complex represents 15,600 "weeks for sale." (300 apartments X 52 weeks = 15,600 weeks). The sales price doesn't include annual "maintenance fees" on the properties. Over time, fees or the inability to vacation in "Paradise" as often as hoped prompts many share owners to walk away from their investment. They will quit claim their "weeks" back to the developer. These "weeks" can then be sold again. Time share owners may also try to sell their weeks on a thinly traded and mostly illiquid secondary market.

Time share salespeople appear to have a job for life.

In Sequoia City, the turnover of properties was significant. When the owners stopped sending payments, Jill kept the demand notes and returned deeds with her second set of books.

Gerry siphoned off the skimmed cash for rental properties, new cars, out-of-town apartments, houses, trips and stock market investments. After Jan.1, 1975, when the federal government lifted restrictions on the ownership of gold by U.S. citizens, Gerry started buying bullion and gold coins.

Gerry registered most of these assets in joint tenancy using his wife's maiden name and Social Security number. Her name and personal information was listed first on any title or account making discovery of these assets nearly impossible without a thorough and expensive forensic accounting investigation. His wife was happy to sign whatever documents he sent to her, no questions asked.

For assets he didn't even want his wife to know about, Gerry opened a large post office box in Redding and had statements and other official mailings sent there.

"Jesus, Gerry, what the hell have you done."

Bobby couldn't believe what he was hearing.

"What do you mean you cut a deal? With who? With what?" Bobby was visibly shaken and his face was flush. He was close to a boiling point.

Over the years, Gerry observed a person's anger and outrage is like standing on a beach, watching a huge wave develop. First, the water recedes as the wave starts to build momentum. Next there is the anticipation as the wave develops height.

Then at the point of maximum energy, it crashes on the beach with lots of sound, fury and froth. The water runs up the beach until all of its energy is exhausted and it can go no further.

Eventually it recedes. Architectural designs contend with the opposing forces of tension and compression. Gerry did too.

While someone's anger "wave" is building or crashing, the key is to remain a silent spectator and simply wait. Don't respond. While it may take longer to play out than a breaking wave, a person's anger will eventually run its course after the initial crash and froth. When their anger is spent, people can deal more reasonably with what comes next. They won't be happy, but the majority of the anger has diminished and the conversation can continue.

"Jordan, the world is crashing down around us," Gerry said. "Can't you see that? I took steps to protect myself and my interests. I assumed you were doing the same."

Gerry could have minimized the 1906 San Francisco earthquake.

Bobby was speechless.

"What the hell are you paying Glenn Robert for anyway? Isn't he supposed to keep your ass out of trouble?"

Gerry didn't wait for a response. "Jordan, I turned over the records of the corporation to the D.A. There are going to be some pretty stiff fines and you and I could face jail time. At the very least, we're looking at a long probation. Either way, you and I will be barred from any real estate transactions for 10 years."

Bobby went pale. In a matter of moments he had gone from disbelief to rage to near physical collapse. He was grateful to be sitting down.

Gerry went on, with all of the emotion of reciting a grocery shopping list. "Some of the folks at the title companies will probably do some jail time too. And those companies will also be paying dearly for their part in all of this."

"Jordan, our corporation's bank accounts are frozen. Sooner or later, the funds will be forfeited to the county to cover the cost of the real estate fraud unit in the D.A.'s office."

Gerry chuckled and said, "It's kind of like choosing the rope for your hanging and having to pay for it, too."

Bobby was far from amused.

Still reeling, Bobby took a mental step back and said, "What do you mean 'frozen'? You mean, we're broke? I'm broke? Jesus, Gerry, I have huge financial commitments. You son of a bitch. I have loans, builders, advertising, marketing. The housing development is only partially finished. I am up to my ears in debt, Gerry. I've deposited every dime of my money and all of the investors' money in the corporation's bank accounts. The D.A. can't have those accounts frozen. That's not his money."

"It is now, Jordan. Please don't tell me you've developed a conscience and suddenly decided to become a model citizen. It's not like we were Boy Scouts helping an old woman across the street."

The silence in the room was piercing.

Gerry said, "Bobby, you can't be broke for God's sake. Tell me you put some money aside somewhere."

As an afterthought, Gerry halfheartedly added, "I'm sure we can work something out with Seth Freeman. He seems like a reasonable guy."

Despite his effort to sound concerned, Gerry was not convincing.

MARK'S GREAT AMERICAN NOVEL
Chapter Twenty-One

Niavaran Palace
Tehran, Iran
Sunday, January 1, 1978
12:50 a.m.

The evening's festivities, including the State Dinner and the New Year's Eve celebration, concluded just before 1 a.m.

The president and first lady returned by motorcade to Saadabad Palace. At 1:22, the president called his daughter, Amy, then left a message with the White House signal board operator requesting a wake-up call at 7.

Just before 8 a.m., the president went to the palace entrance to meet King Hussein of Jordan. This was followed by a "meet and greet" session with the president, the king and members of the press, which lasted until 8:18.

The president and the king adjourned to a conference room for a meeting with U.S. and Jordanian officials. During the meeting, members of the press were escorted in and out of the conference room for photo opportunities. The meeting lasted just over 30 minutes.

The president said goodbye to the king at the palace entrance at 8:50. The first lady and the president were then escorted by the shah and his wife to their motorcade. During the 27-minute ride to the airport, the president participated in a question-and-answer session with members of the press.

Meanwhile, on the ground in New Dehli, security officials were checking and rechecking the airport perimeter in preparation for the arrival of Air Force One. Army troops, in uniform, camouflage or street clothes, walked the streets and alleys on either side of the airport to ensure a clear, secure approach to the airfield for the president's plane.

The Secret Service and Indian Aviation officials had previously determined the runway the president's plane would use. That plan, like all others, was subject to change in the event of a last-minute threat, crisis or a change in the weather.

In Iran, the presidential motorcade arrived at the Mehrabad Airport at 9:23 a.m. The president, the shah and their wives entered the Imperial Pavilion at the airport. The presidential party and the shah then took a short walk to a reviewing stand. On the way, the president greeted members of the U.S. community in Iran and their families.

A final review of the troops marked the end of the presidential visit to Iran. The president and first lady boarded Air Force One at 9:45, local time. Two minutes later, Air Force One lifted off from Mehrabad Airport for the two-hour, 51 minute flight to New Delhi.

En route, the president held brief meetings with Press Secretary Jody Powell, chief speechwriter James Fallows, personal assistant Susan Clough and Assistant for National Security Affairs Zbigniew Brzezinski.

On the ground in New Delhi, miles from Palam Airport, Zia was more than halfway through his mental countdown to the destiny he knew would change history.

SIXTY-FOUR

Highway 31 Railroad Overcrossing
18 miles from Sequoia City
Thursday, August 31, 1978

The area was part of the new railroad and highway alignments necessary as the waters of Sequoia Lake inundated the old rights of way.

It was just after 10 a.m. The engineer was looking at the air brake gauges when something caught his attention. Something out of place—not quite right—out the cab window. Then he saw it: a body crumpled on the tracks under the 70-foot-tall highway bridge.

A body on the railroad tracks at this location was easy to explain: suicide.

Trains were limited to 30 miles per hour through this section of track, but it was still too fast to stop the 40-car manifest before it ran over the victim.

Cameron Evans was called and, as deputy county coroner, assumed control of the scene.

The victim was a young male. Cameron immediately knew the identity of the victim. They'd had coffee a couple of times.

Respectfully and carefully, Cameron placed the remains in a body bag. He talked to the locomotive engineer and brakeman, took some measurements and a few photos.

Then, with the help of two sheriff's deputies and a great deal of effort climbing a steep embankment, he moved the remains up to the highway where his hearse was parked. When the hearse door was closed, Cameron looked down one more time at the railroad tracks, then at the highway bridge.

On his way back to town, he made up his mind to call me.

"Mark, you need to come over right now. It's important."

"Sure. Why, what's up?"

There was a very long pause.

"Cameron, are you still there?"

"Ed Thatcher is dead."

I stopped for a moment and took in a huge breath. The room was spinning and I was dizzy. I think I was close to passing out. For a moment, it felt like the wind had been knocked out of me.

"What are you talking about? Ed? What do you mean he's dead? Are you sure?

He was just here the other night. He can't be dead. Cameron, are you sure?"

"I'm sure, Mark. This isn't a joke" Cameron said. "You need to come over. Please." His voice was soothing and comforting. He sounded just like a funeral director.

Then, with a bit more urgency, "Please, Mark, come over here now and meet me in back."

Fortunately, it was just a short distance to the funeral home although I don't remember driving there. I was so distracted I nearly ran into the hearse parked under the covered entrance. When I left later that afternoon, I realized I could not have parked any closer to it if I had tried.

Cameron was waiting by the back entrance. We went inside, into the chapel and sat in the front row.

There was no music in my head now. No song titles, no lyrics, melodies. Only a high-pitched ring screaming in my head.

"What happened? Are you sure it's Ed? Where did it happen? How did he die?" It was like a presidential news conference where I asked questions in rapid fire succession but didn't for an answer.

Cameron was matter of fact when he said, "At first I thought he had committed suicide."

"Not Ed. Jesus. No, he couldn't...he...he wouldn't. I would have known. He would have said something."

My voice trailed off. I stammered trying to put the information into some kind of order. Some kind of perspective. In my mind, the information seemed like a square peg attempting to go into a round hole. Until now, I never fully appreciated Grandma's comment: "You could have knocked me over with a feather."

Cameron explained how he found Ed's body and where it was located.

"Mark, I know this is tough." He paused a moment. "You don't look well. Let me get you a glass of water."

Distracted, I said, "Yeah, that would be great. Please," I said as my voice trailed off. I was still trying to absorb the news and get my bearings. Again a terrible feeling of losing altitude or being pummeled in heavy turbulence.

Cameron left for a moment.

It was like watching a movie where everything was moving in slow motion. It was bizarre. Surreal. I was very, very warm. And sweating.

Cameron came back with a large glass of water and picked up where he left off.

"Mark, I started to look around a bit more and began to question my initial impression about how Ed died. The highway bridge crossing the tracks is nearly 20 miles from town. Ed's vehicle was nowhere to be found. So how did he get there?"

"When I got back here, I decided to take a closer look."

Cameron left out some of the gruesome details about the condition of Ed's body but told me enough to grasp what happened. "There were bruises inconsistent with jumping or falling off the bridge. Bruises that wouldn't happen getting hit by a train."

Although Cameron paused it was not for effect.

"I'm sorry. I know he was your friend." He paused again. "A very good friend. Mark, I know. There's no easy way to say this." He took a deep breath and looked at me, "Somebody really worked him over before he died."

I gulped the water down. I think I drained the glass in one breath.

I wasn't sure I understood what Cameron just said. "What do you mean 'worked him over'?'"

"I found cigarette burns on his chest, groin and legs. He had welts on his back and chest as if he had been beaten with a belt or hose. The bottoms of his feet also appeared to have been beaten with a stick or a cane. They were terribly bruised and his hands had been bound."

"Bound? What do you mean bound?" As if all of the other details were minor in nature and of no consequence.

"His hands had been tied pretty tight, Mark. His wrists were bloody."

And, almost as if he didn't want to say it, Cameron went on. "I believe Ed was strangled. Mark, and died hours before he was thrown off the overpass."

There was a long silence.

The room was spinning. I started to gag. I wondered if anyone had ever thrown up in this room.

I tried breathing deeply, but all I could manage were short, quick breaths. I remembered my Boy Scout training: If you feel faint, put your head down, between your knees. Something about redistributing the blood. I followed that advice now.

"Jesus, Ed, what the hell were you up to?" I said out loud addressed to no one.

For a long time, Cameron said nothing. Then, he put his hand on my shoulder. I had never been around compassionate or caring men. I actually recoiled briefly at his touch. It was a very odd reaction to a gentle, understanding gesture.

His hand stayed on my shoulder.

A moment later he said softly, "I am so sorry, Mark." He paused another moment. "You can stay here as long as you want this afternoon. There aren't any services today. I'll leave you alone. If you want to talk some more, I'll be in my office."

I hadn't cried since my grandfather died a few months ago.

I cried now. I found a box of tissues and grabbed a handful.

Then, on the way home sometime after 4, I drove to the river, pulled off the road and cried again for very long time. I kept trying to regain my composure, but every time I thought about Ed and the way he died, I'd break down again and cry.

Uncontrollably. The images of him being tortured kept rolling over and over in my head.

"Jesus, Ed, what the hell were you up to?" I kept repeating the question over and over in my head.

The Sequoia City news cycle continued.

SIXTY-FIVE

"She's Gone"—Hall and Oates

I was completely exhausted when I finally got home just before 6. I trudged up the back stairs and was actually out of breath when I sat down on the sofa.

Emma knew Ed, mostly through me. I really needed to talk to her tonight. I wanted to hear her voice. I wanted to be the one to tell her. I wanted to hold her tonight. I need the reassurance of making love tonight.

I called Emma's house. No answer.

That was happening all the time lately. I never ran into her at the Rip Roarin' or at the grocery store or, for that matter, anywhere else in town. She was never home. I could never reach her by phone.

She had nearly become a phantom. A fantasy. I don't know why we weren't together or seeing each other anymore. I couldn't seem to find any way to communicate with her.

I probably shared too much of my "personal issues" with her and scared her off. She was taking pity on me that afternoon in bed. She was trying to let me down gently. What woman wants an emotional wreck for a partner? It wasn't make-up sex that day. It was break-up sex.

If we're ever together again, I'll go back to being a regular guy and keep my emotions to myself.

Naturally, then my thoughts drift to the bedroom. I probably disappointed her in bed, too.

For the first time since college, I cried myself to sleep. A writer might call this time in my life a "loss of innocence." It was more than that. It was yet another loss of someone I knew. And cared about. And, I think, even loved as a friend.

It was a hell of a lot more than just a loss of innocence.

S I X T Y - S I X

September 8, 1978

Because of the holiday and the schedule at the cemetery, Ed's services were held over a week later on the Friday after Labor Day.

Before the graveside service, there was a memorial held at Cameron's Funeral Home.

Ed's folks, David and Betty, had arrived in town the previous Sunday night. David and Betty looked numb with shock and disbelief. David was stoic and misty eyed, staring out to nowhere in particular. Betty sobbed throughout the entire service.

Until the sheriff's office completed its investigation, the cause of Ed's death was listed as "accidental." It saved unnecessary speculation about the way he died and spared his family the gruesome details. His parents decided not to have a viewing the night before, preferring a closed-casket service.

Ed's funeral was well attended by local elected officials, friends and co-workers from the newspaper. The funeral home was filled to overflowing. A lot of people in attendance simply knew Ed from his bylines in the paper.

After the memorial, a procession drove to the Pioneer Cemetery. I was a pallbearer. I wore a suit and tie for the first time since the day I arrived in Sequoia City. Emotionally, I was nearly comatose.

The Pioneer Cemetery had been in constant use since the 1880s.

For a while, locals called it Boot Hill—the place where people who "died with their boots on" were buried. During the early years in Sequoia City, Catholics, Jews, Negroes, Chinese, and other non-white Americans had to be buried elsewhere.

The cemetery was terraced for the burial plot areas. The paths leading down to the terraces were steep, rocky and, depending on the weather or the watering schedules, very slick.

It rained fairly heavy the night before, but the sun was out and the air was fresh and cool. Joyce Healy would call the air today "delicious."

Ordinarily, I enjoyed this kind of weather. Not today. Nonetheless, at the cemetery, I know Ed would have appreciated the two or three times we lost our footing and slipped on the path leading down to the plot area. I had a vision of us dropping the casket and watching it slide down to the bottom of the hill. It was honestly tough at times not to smile with that image in my head.

Whenever there is a murder or death under suspicious circumstances, plain clothes police officers attend the funeral and graveside services. Sometimes they are in the crowd of mourners. Uniformed officers will stand a couple of hundred feet away to see if there is anyone watching the proceedings from another vantage point. They are on the lookout for someone who is out of place or stays to the back of the crowd, pacing back and forth, often looking down—as if they have something to hide. I saw the deputies. I didn't see anyone out of place.

I saw Gerry Apte for the first time in several weeks. Then I saw Emma standing next to Gerry—talking and laughing. So that's why I hadn't heard from her, I thought. And why she wouldn't return my calls.

I gave her a quick nod and a small smile. On again, off again Emma. Apparently off again with me and on again with Gerry. I don't get it. We had been pretty hot and, I thought, falling in love. She even told me she loved me.

Emma came over to me just before the minister started and asked how I was doing.

"OK, I guess." I was cool. I resisted the urge to ask her to come by my apartment later, even though I was turned on by just hearing her voice again.

She said she was in and out of town a lot. "I'm dealing with some major stuff right now, Mark," she said, "and I'm trying to get my head straight. There's just a lot going on. I really need to talk to you after the service."

"OK."

Fine, I thought.

If she's going to tell me she is back with Gerry, I'm in no mood to hear it. Certainly not today. Not now. I'm beginning to think she might be crazy.

During the service I thought back to the day a few weeks ago when Ed needed to borrow my car.

His car was making its almost monthly visit to the mechanic's shop. I kidded with him that his car always seemed to need repairs around the time the mechanic's rent was due.

He bought a 1974 Chevy Vega. The car had an ignition/seat belt interlock system.

The system was introduced on 1974 model cars and prevented a car from starting unless occupants in the front seat had their seat belts fastened. It was supposed to be a "safety enhancement."

It was irritating enough when it worked. It was off the charts maddening when the system didn't work and no matter what you did the car wouldn't start. So, the auto club was frequently called to tow Ed's car to the garage. I think Ed was one of the auto club's best customers. Finally, one of the tow truck drivers showed Ed how to pop the hood and jump start the car using a screwdriver across the ignition points.

In any case, his car was in the garage and he needed to borrow mine. We agreed when he was finished, he would park the car outside my apartment and leave the car keys under the back door mat.

I laid down for a nap.

About 45 minutes later, I heard a rattle at the back door. I thought it was Ed. I figured he forgot "the plan" about where to leave the car keys. So I got up, a little pissed off, and went to the back of the house.

I opened the first of the two doors between the apartment and the sun porch.

"Jesus, Ed, I told you where to leave the damn car keys."

The rattling at the back door stopped.

When I opened the second door and went out onto the porch, I'm not sure who was more startled: the guy trying to break in or me. In an instant, he took off running—down the stairs, out the back gate and down the street. He never looked back.

I walked down the stairs and opened the back door. It was obvious he was trying to work the door open. Lots of scratches around the lock. Then signs he tried to pry the door open.

In Sequoia City, you pretty much knew everyone. The police could pick up a suspect and solve a crime within an hour of it being reported. Kind of like Claude Rains in "Casablanca" ordering his officers to "round up the usual suspects."

When I called the police, the dispatcher said officer Marv Daniels would be over to take down the information.

Marv was one of the occasional morning coffee group members and knocked at the Healys' front door. The Healys were out of town visiting their daughter.

I told Marv I'd never seen the guy and the description I gave didn't match any of the "usual suspects."

"Probably a transient and the house looked like an easy mark. There are no cars out front, so he probably figured no one was home. You might keep an eye out around town, but I doubt we'll see him again. He's probably long gone."

"He was pretty well dressed for a transient, Marv. He didn't look like he just fell off an eastbound freight train."

"Well, keep an eye out and let me know if you see him again."

Marv left and I locked the door behind him. The next time at the Ace Hardware store, I bought some additional locks.

Ed's graveside service was short and a reception was held afterwards at the local Veterans Hall. I guessed there were more than 125 people in all.

I didn't mingle much and avoided coming in contact with Emma again even though she wasn't hanging around Gerry. I didn't have a chance to say much to Ed's parents. Everyone was still in shock and very emotional. I could barely introduce myself. Ed's mother said, "Oh, yes, Ed said you were good friends and did some climbing and hiking together. You work at the radio station, I think, right?"

"Yes, I do," in a voice just above a whisper.

"It's been a terrible day. Thank you for coming."

I choked up and said, "Yes it has been really tough" and, "you're welcome."

I don't think I even said "I'm sorry." I couldn't muster the courage to say anything else.

MARK'S GREAT AMERICAN NOVEL
Chapter Twenty-Two

New Delhi, India
Just after noon, January 1, 1978

Zia packed his meager belongings into a hap sack. During his reconnaissance of the motorcade route over the past few weeks, he wore the traditional Hindu garment, the dhoti, allowing him to blend in with the Delhi crowds. He would wear it again later today for the assassination. He doubted there would be time to change into more casual clothes when the mission was complete.

Zia was the unofficial treasurer and put the group's emergency cash into his wallet. At their final meeting today at 1:15, he would distribute cash to team members. As a precaution, each member would choose their own way out of Delhi without discussing their plans with the rest of the group. Then, in the event of capture or discovery, there would be no information to share with authorities on the whereabouts or plans of fellow team members.

The team developed two general plans of escape. One called for the group to meet at a small train station outside Delhi five hours after the assassination. If the plot failed, however, the other plan called for everyone to scatter and leave the city as fast as possible. While unspoken during their planning meetings, everyone knew there was a possibility that some or all of the team members would be killed. If they survived, it was also possible that they would never meet or be able to return home to India again.

The group memorized airline, bus and train timetables. They agreed taxis would only be used as a last resort, since traffic jams and large crowds could slow down an escape and put members at risk of discovery and arrest.

Zia decided to have his last lunch in Delhi at his favorite restaurant. He needed time to mentally review the plan alone. A final checklist, if you will, before takeoff. Everyone else was in the process of packing up and far too excited to eat.

President Carter's motorcade would leave Palam Airport at 2:50. Members of Zia's group would be stationed along the motorcade route providing multiple opportunities to shoot the president. The trip from the airport to the president of India's official residence, Rashtrapati Bhavan, would take just under an hour.

Zia's misgivings over the past few weeks dissipated as the moment neared. Even if one of the members had a change of heart at the last moment, the plan could still succeed. He paid his tab and left.

As he exited, Zia noticed a young Indian military officer standing near a parked Army vehicle and briefly made eye contact with him. Zia didn't immediately recognize the sounds he was hearing. Truck backfire? Firecrackers? Then it struck him: gunfire. It took an instant to pinpoint the location of the shots. It was clear. The gunfire was coming from inside the hotel.

Oh God! It's the team!

Zia heard screams followed by more shots inside the hotel.

The military officer he had seen a moment earlier was obviously in charge and now moving quickly toward the hotel entrance.

Standing motionless 150 feet away, Zia watched as Johar ran into the street and was shot in the back trying to flee. With the deadly intent of the bullets clear, Johar looked to Zia like a frightened, dying animal.

Pedestrians scattered in every direction. Additional police sirens could be heard in the distance—lots of them.

Slowly, instinctively, almost mechanically, Zia turned around and walked in the other direction. Zia found himself breathing quick, short breaths. He felt dizzy and disoriented. With police cars screaming past him, it was several blocks before he got his bearings. He leaned against a building with one hand and took several deep breaths. The sweat of his hand against the cool cement of the building helped him focus on a plan to get out of New Delhi.

The "last resort" escape plan, using a taxicab, right now was the only option to get out of the city center. The events of the last few minutes also underscored the need for a quick departure from New Delhi and India.

Zia found a cab and told the driver to take him to the Palam airport's domestic terminal. Zia froze when the driver turned the cab around and headed in the direction of the hotel. With the sound of blood pounding in his ears, Zia fought the urge to bail out of the cab and run. Then, two blocks from the hotel, a police roadblock detoured traffic away from the area. As the cab passed, Zia tried to catch a glimpse of the hotel, but his view was blocked by dozens of parked police cars with their lights flashing.

Once at the airport, he used the emergency cash to book a ticket on the next flight to Bombay. When he completed the purchase, he took a deep breath, realizing this was the same cash he'd planned to distribute to the team just an hour earlier.

Once airborne en route to Bombay, lulled by the vibration of the plane and the drone of the engines, Zia dozed fitfully.

Within the hour, just after 2 o'clock, Air Force One touched down safely in New Dehli.

On the ground, the president and first lady were welcomed in a ceremony marking their arrival in India. There were speeches by President Carter and Neelan Sanjiva Reddy, the president of India, followed by a review of the troops assembled on the tarmac. The presidential party was also greeted by the diplomatic corps of India and the American Embassy.

With more than 90 minutes left in his flight, Zia stirred and looked at his watch. It was 2:50.

At that moment in New Delhi, he knew, President Carter's motorcade would be leaving Palam Airport for what would now be an uneventful 50-minute trip to Rashtrapati Bhavan.

Rashtrapati Bhavan, formerly known as the Viceroy's House, is the home of the Indian president. The president of India is the leader of the largest democracy in the world.

The Rashtrapati Bhavan complex is massive in scope, covering 320 acres—about a half square mile. The main buildings encompass 200,000 square feet. Outside, there are gardens, stables and residences for staff and security.

Rashtrapati Bhavan may well be the largest public official residence in the world.

Zia nodded off again as the flight wore on.

When he landed in Bombay, Zia recalled the airline timetables he'd memorized and decided to book a flight out of India that evening. Inside the terminal, he made his way to the Air India ticket counter and reserved a seat on a flight to Dubai.

Air India Flight 855.

SIXTY-SEVEN

I spent every waking moment developing the story lines for my book.

A friend at the Sacramento Bee sent me copies of all of the news clippings available on President Carter's visit to India. I also asked for copies of the paper from a few days before and after the president's visit.

I sat down with a local travel agent and discussed Air India flight schedules and connecting flights between Bombay and destinations around the world.

I sent away for travel information from the India Tourism Bureau.

I touched bases with the people I knew at Associated Press and United Press International. They sent me copies of the news stories about the president's visit and other events from that time in New Delhi and Bombay. These were far more detailed sources of information than printed editions of the Bee could provide. UPI and AP had access to complete reporting on the visit and were not limited to the space on printed pages.

I think I was wearing out my welcome with these folks, because as soon as I sat down and typed out a couple of pages, more questions would come to mind. I spent hours poring over whatever material I could get my hands on to fill in details and add color to the story. I tried to use the microfilm reader at the library, but it always made me dizzy and nauseous.

I mailed off requests and money orders to the Chicago Tribune, The Washington Post and New York Times circulation departments. I asked for copies of their papers from late December 1977 through early January 1978.

The mailman was very curious about the packages coming from these out-of-town newspapers. I think it added to my credibility. At least with him.

SIXTY-EIGHT

Sequoia City
September 22, 1978
Two weeks after Ed's Funeral

When the deputy called and identified himself, I figured it was a news tip.

I wasn't prepared for the news.

"A hiker found Ed's car in the hills off one of the 4-wheel trails. It was near an old mine shaft. The car was badly burned and the license plates had been thrown into the brush." After a pause, he said, "and, there were two bodies at the bottom of the mine shaft."

I felt sick inside. I couldn't believe this was starting all over again.

Another pause and the deputy asked, "Can you come down to the office and help the officer working on the case? The sheriff brought a detective in from Redding. He'd like to talk to you. You knew Ed best. You might be able to fill in some of the blanks."

That's the thing, of course. Guys don't really know one another, no matter how good friends we are. We're pretty private. And lonely. We don't let anybody in. We can't afford to let anyone really know who we are. We try hard not to show any emotions. Most of us wouldn't dream of sharing our deepest thoughts, sexual fears, questions or fantasies. We would never talk in detail about our hopes, dreams or career plans. We're sure, at some point, that information will be used against us or ridiculed. Sharing our deeply held beliefs with other guys is usually met with sarcasm. Guys tend to verbally gang up on one another, like the time I was homesick at scout camp. Probably the reason men die of heart attacks more often than women is we keep everything inside. Bottled up. And, we are usually careful with the women we love. Even if we love them for a lifetime.

I remember overhearing Blanche, a widow friend of Joyce's. Blanche had been married for 58 years. She said she loved her husband and he loved her but, despite their years together, she felt she never really knew him.

At the time I thought that was strange.

Ed and I spent hours and days totaling weeks together. But I didn't really know much about him. We'd talk about news, sports and sex. We were experts on the first two.

I knew who his favorite sports teams were and when he got laid the first time. (At a drive-in theater, of course.) I knew who he wanted to get into bed with at the paper. I only knew his mom and dad's first names after I'd met them at the funeral.

Until the funeral, I didn't even know he was an only child.

I really didn't know much. I was not going to be much help, but I went to talk to the detective anyway.

On the way to the sheriff's office, I was suddenly very angry. Angry at Ed. Angry at the way he died. Angry that I was having to relive the event all over again.

By the time I got out of my car, I was nearly at a boiling point.

The detective introduced himself as Casey Wells. He had been a police officer in Redding for more than 20 years. His jaw jutted out. He reminded me of a pug dog.

He got right to the point. "The two bodies in the mine shaft were members of a Southern California motorcycle gang—The Motorcycle Masters. Their motorcycles were tossed in on top of them," he said. "Pretty messy scene.

"There was evidence of a large campfire nearby. Lots of motorcycle tire tracks and the grass was crushed all around. Must have been a fairly large gathering."

I'm sure I had a blank look on my face, so he continued.

"You know the gangs use the forests as a distribution point for their drugs. Easy to move about undetected. Also easy to take care of members who have become a problem. There may or may not be a perfect crime, but murders up in those hills come pretty close.

"Any idea what Ed was doing up there?" He paused and continued: "You guys aren't dealing drugs, are you?"

His question was sharp and pointed. He was obviously trying to shock me into an admission of some kind. Catch someone off guard and they often respond without thinking. Great tactic. Attorneys use the method in court.

My answer was quick and just as pointed: "What? No! We weren't dealing drugs."

I felt rage welling up in me. Who is this jerk? What a dumb ass question, I thought.

Before thinking, I blurted out, "Where the hell would you get a dumb ass idea like that?"

I looked at him like he was a third grader.

He flipped through some papers and said, "Some guy named Gerry mentioned he thought you and Ed smoked a lot of dope. He figures you can't be making much money at your jobs. Pretty easy to see the opportunity to make a fast buck or two in drugs."

I sat there silent with a mental feeling of disgust. Casey looked at me, menacingly. "Don't try playing me for a fool, Mark. How dumb do you think I am?"

Without thinking, I said, "I really don't know."

Jackass.

The other officers in the room stifled a chuckle. Casey looked around sharply and the officers quickly started shuffling papers or picking up the phone to make a call.

What a dumb ass. Asking dumb ass questions. Just like reporters, I thought, cops always find the story they are looking for.

"You think this is funny, Mark? A joke?"

"You asked me a question and I answered it." I nearly spat the next words. "Is there anything else you need to know, officer?" I said "officer" like a cuss word.

"Are we finished here?"

Casey continued to stare at me, hoping I guess, that I would "crack." Detectives are trained to stay silent after asking questions. Sometimes the silence encourages a witness to talk more than they should. In sales, for instance, the rule is, "He who speaks first at the close, loses."

Smoking a joint once in a while, I thought, was a far cry from hanging out with drug dealers, pot growers and motorcycle gangs. I kept quiet.

"Can you tell me what he might have been doing up there?"

I thought a moment, trying to calm down.

"Well, he loved to rock climb, maybe he…" My thought trailed off, interrupted by another. Like a lightning bolt out of a clear blue sky: "Oh my God! Wait! That was the story he was working on! Jesus. He said he was on to something big for the paper, but never said what. Jesus…oh Jesus…Jesus."

"Then can you tell me how his car got up there?"

In an instant I knew that too. I read once that to re-establish your bearings in a threatening or confusing situation, you should physically take a step backwards. Apparently that allows your mind to reset its perspective and reassess your surroundings and situation. At this moment, sitting down, I had no way to reset my perspective. It was like slipping on ice as you lose your balance and realize that the world is spinning out of control. I felt like a cartoon character with my arms flailing around wildly. Nothing you do will keep you from a hard landing.

"Oh God!" I tried to find the right words. "It was a game. We used to goof around on the weekend. Oh, God, it was just a stupid game." I nearly lost control and fought hard not to cry. Tears filled my eyes anyway. "God, God, God. It was just a game. Jesus, Ed, what the hell were you thinking?" I pounded my fist on the desk. "It was just a damn game, Ed!"

The detective was silent again. And now very intent.

After a moment, he quietly asked, "What was a game, Mark?"

I looked blankly out the station window, trying to focus and seeing nothing in particular. "We used to follow someone in our car at night, without our headlights on. Honest to God, it was just a game. It was easy on moonlit nights, but we got pretty good following in the dark on the other nights as well. If the car ahead braked, we would use our emergency brake to slow down, since it wouldn't set off our brake lights. We'd follow someone for a mile or two, then turn on the headlights, appearing to come out of nowhere, no doubt startling the driver. We would always get a good laugh."

I choked a bit. "Oh my God, it was just a game."

My voice trailed off. I was lost. I felt my throat tightening like I was going to throw up. I looked around for a waste basket.

The detective had a perplexed look on his face. He probably wondered why we weren't out drinking or chasing women like other guys our age. Saying this out loud did sound a little weird. High school freshman like. I must have sounded like Peter Pan who never wanted to grow up.

"He must have followed a gang member up one of the dirt roads without being noticed. Until it was too late."

My voice trailed off. "God, it was just a game." I was aware tears were now running down my face. I quickly wiped my face on the sleeve of my short sleeve shirt.

*"Don't know why you should feel that there's something to
learn, it's just a game that you play..."*

It seemed like another minute or two before Casey, flipping through the report pages in front of him, said, "OK then, I don't have any more questions." He rambled on about something although I can't tell you what. He told me he might want to talk to me again and asked for a phone number. I gave him the radio station's number. He asked for my home number as well.

He slid his card across the desk and told me if I thought of anything else, he'd appreciate a call.

"Right," I thought "when dogs sing opera and read Shakespeare."

I was sure his next words would be, "Don't leave town, I may have some more Questions," but he said nothing.

I stood up to leave. He reached out to shake my hand.

His hands were as sweaty as mine.

I thought that was weird.

S I X T Y - N I N E

That evening
Sequoia City

When the phone rang, I hoped it was Emma.

It wasn't. I hadn't seen or heard from her since Ed's service.

"Mark, this is Casey Wells."

What the hell does he want?

"Any chance we can talk for a few minutes, just you and me, off the record? I'd like to bring you up to speed on some things. There's a lot more going on than you know."

I wasn't sure if the call was legitimate or an opportunity to get me into a less intimidating setting and grill me some more. Detectives like to get someone they consider to be a "person of interest" in a comfortable setting and talk to them casually. Often in this situation, a suspect will volunteer critical information before realizing it.

"Where do you want to meet? Melva's?"

"No, we need to meet someplace private."

"I can come down to the station again."

"No, not there. Can I come by your place?"

What in the hell is he up to?

I hesitated a moment, then told him he could come to the apartment. I gave him the address and told him to come around the back. He said he would park his car a block or two away and be here in 20 minutes.

The weather was warm for late September. The temperature at 7:30 was still 80 degrees. Casey was perspiring and a bit winded when he knocked on the back door. It was getting dark.

I offered him a glass of water. He was on my turf now, so I opened a beer for myself as we sat down at the kitchen table.

He wasted no time getting to the point.

"For a number of months, the sheriff suspected a connection between confiscated guns that are missing from his department's evidence locker and guns later used in crimes by the Motorcycle Masters. The guns are from closed investigations locally and are missing from the evidence inventory. The sheriff thinks it's more than a case of bad record keeping.

"How long have you lived in town?" He asked.

Curious question from a detective who earlier today seemed to know a lot about my life in Sequoia City.

"A couple of years. Why?"

"There was murder case downtown on Birch Street a few years back. Husband comes home early one day and finds a neighbor banging his wife. The husband shoots them both, then turns the gun on himself."

"Yeah, I remember hearing about that. It was still being talked about when I got to town."

"That gun is missing," Casey said.

He went on. "Then there was the courthouse incident last year."

I remembered that, too. A woman and her two children were brutally murdered, shot to death, in their home on a quiet street in Sausalito. The suspect, a drifter named Danny Amos from Oregon, was quickly apprehended. The trial was moved out of Marin County to Sequoia County in hopes of finding an impartial jury.

The husband and father of the victims rented a motel room in town and sat through day after day of testimony in the courtroom. Witnesses, including neighbors, policemen, detectives and the coroner, took the stand. There were graphic crime scene photos on display as well.

I couldn't stay all day to report on the proceedings, but I would stop by the courtroom every day to watch for a few minutes. I stayed in the back, where I could see everyone come and go without creating a distraction. Ed had a front-row seat behind the prosecutor.

I made it a point to be in the courtroom when the defendant was on the stand.

It was a turning point in the trial.

Amos said the murdered woman had initiated a sexual relationship with him and that it had been going on for some time. Answering a set of leading questions from the public defender, Amos detailed every alleged sexual encounter with the victim. Every location they had sex: at her home, in her bed, in the shower; while parked by the roadside in her car; in a nearby park; once in a supermarket parking lot, even several times while he was driving her car. Every sexual act. In excruciating detail. Amos described a woman with an insatiable and adventurous sexual appetite. Amos wanted to convince the jury the victim was a frustrated housewife looking for more excitement and fulfillment than she had ever experienced. I nearly gagged when I heard that.

In retrospect. Amos said he realized he was just being used by her, a comment so ludicrous it would have been funny in any other setting. It was the most disgusting comment he had made on the stand. And there were a lot to choose from.

The story, however, was obviously false. Amos was coached. He was following a sleazy strategy developed by the public defender. I cannot imagine how the husband must have felt. He sat ramrod straight in the courtroom. His eyes were riveted on the witness stand. He showed no emotion, but it had to be incredibly difficult to hear horrible lies about your wife told under oath.

The topper to the testimony was when Amos insisted he was nowhere near the murder scene at the time of the crime. He said he "could never harm the woman who loved him." In fact, Amos said they had planned to run away together the following week. Almost as an afterthought, again at his attorney's prompting, Amos said he assumed the husband found out about their plan to run away and murdered his family in a rage.

The prosecutor, with an overwhelming amount of evidence, shredded the defendant's alibi and the whole sexual "affair" story in less than five minutes. None of the defendant's story held up to the scrutiny of the prosecutor. In the days following the murders, investigators spent more than 70 hours scouring the crime scene for evidence. There was more than enough evidence to charge Danny Amos with three counts of first-degree murder.

The jury didn't believe Amos either. The trial lasted 18 days. The jury deliberated less than three hours. Danny Amos was found guilty on all three counts of first-degree murder.

When the verdict was announced, the husband and father of the victims quietly rose from his chair, pulled out a large handgun and shot to death the accused and his public defender.

Two shots.

The stunned bailiff turned and pulled his gun and fired two shots. In less than 20 seconds, Danny Amos, his attorney and the grieving father were dead.

The verdict came in before I could get to court while I was recording my 5:30 newscast. I heard about the shooting from the police scanner. It was big news throughout the country for a couple of weeks.

"The murder weapon, the husband's gun and the bailiff's service weapon are all missing, too," Casey said. "In all, more than 75 guns are unaccounted for over the last five years. And I think I have just scratched the surface."

"But if the case is closed, the guns are just disposed of, right?"

"Maybe 30 years ago, but not today. Any gun used in a crime has to be logged in and accounted for in the department inventory locker. If the gun is later disposed of, a requisition has to be filled out, then reviewed by an under-sheriff. If he signs off, then the means of disposal is also detailed and overseen by an officer. There is no paper trail of any kind on any of the missing guns."

He went on: "If the guns were seized as result of a search warrant, those guns can't be disposed of without court approval. It's part of the state Penal Code. Weapons seized with a warrant are property of the court, not law enforcement. The court's disposal procedure is more tightly regulated, yet there are at least two dozen guns seized with a warrant that can't be accounted for.

"There's even a process required when an officer in charge of the evidence locker retires or is reassigned. Every gun is inventoried, along with a description, serial number, case number, seizure date and any other identifying information. The departing officer then signs the inventory, so there's a paper trail in case any evidence shows up missing later.

"The last two officers, one retired and one reassigned, stated that no inventory was completed when they left. The two officers said they were never asked to sign any documents and their requests for an inventory were ignored by their immediate supervisor. One of the officers eventually talked to the sheriff and that's when I got involved.

"Your buddy Ed was investigating the connection between the missing guns and ones used by the motorcycle gang. Two of the missing guns were found at crime scenes linked to the gang.

Before I could ask Casey how he knew so much, he volunteered "Ed and I worked the story together. I was his source and he was mine."

After a short pause, Casey asked, "You think I could have one of those beers now?"

S E V E N T Y

Later

Casey winced. "So, what was all that tough cop crap at the station this morning?" I asked.

Casey said: "I need to make sure anyone within earshot heard the questioning, because the real reason for my being here is entirely off the books. The sheriff called me in from Redding a few months ago. He needed someone from the outside to poke around and look into the missing guns as well as any other shenanigans going on in his department. Unfortunately, a crooked cop knows all the angles. He's studied and watched criminals for years. He's pretty good at covering his tracks."

It takes one to catch one, I thought.

Casey took a swallow of beer. "Incidentally, your answer to 'How dumb do you think I am?' was one of the best comebacks I've heard. I damn near busted out laughing. And it didn't help that the other guys in the room thought it was funny, too."

I told him he had really pissed me off.

"I could tell."

I asked, "How did Ed fit in?" I choked on the question. It still seemed unreal.

"I called the newspaper one day, introduced myself and asked to speak to a reporter. The call was transferred to Ed. We met for lunch a couple of times so I could decide whether he could be trusted and if we could work together. Ed mentioned you were a straight shooter and a good friend."

Casey hesitated a bit and looked at me squarely. "For the love of God, Mark, Ed's murder wasn't part of any plan. His murder caught me completely off guard. It wasn't anything I expected." He continued looking straight at me. "I would never put him in any kind of physical danger. If I thought there was any risk, I would have told him to bow out." After another hesitation, "I thought he could simply ask a few innocuous questions around the station—talk to some of the people I mentioned. He was supposed to just pass the information on to me. That's all.

"All of my interaction was with the sheriff. The sheriff would request certain files from the Sequoia City substation and forward them to me in Redding. I was going to work in the background until we were ready to present our case to the district attorney and the Grand Jury.

"I also contacted the state attorney general's office. You don't go off half cocked when you start accusing police officers of crimes. Especially the theft of firearms and the possible sale of those guns to criminals.

"Because of the way Ed was tortured and murdered, it provided the perfect cover to show my face around the station. What you were told about my being here 'another set of eyes looking into Ed's death' was all anybody other than the sheriff needed to know about my being here."

Tortured and murdered, I thought.

God, Ed.

Casey finished his beer before I could focus on that sentence and its implications again. "Ed and I talked once a week and compared notes."

"Why did they kill him the way they did?" The question was out of my mouth before I was able to think it through. I wasn't sure I wanted to know the answer. I still can't mention Ed's name with torture and murder in the same sentence.

"I'm sure at first they wanted to find out what he knew." His voiced dropped.

"From the looks of things, I imagine he told them everything pretty early on."

God, why was I even talking about this? It was like driving by a car wreck—I couldn't look away or ignore it, no matter how gruesome it was.

"They couldn't afford to take any chances that he knew more than he was telling. That's when things probably got worse for him."

Realizing my discomfort, Casey stopped for a moment and touched my arm. It was another compassionate touch from a man. Like my reaction at Cameron's funeral home, the gesture made me uncomfortable. Instinctively I stiffened and drew back.

Casey lowered his voice and continued. "Mark, I won't pretend otherwise. Ed suffered terribly. Initially, the psychological fear of what might happen was more frightening than the pain. You saw "The Exorcist": the fear of something unseen or unknown only amplifies the terror."

Casey put his hand on my forearm again. It didn't seem so threatening now.

"Mark, I know you've been reliving in your mind what it must have been like, what was happening to him. I know it's not much comfort but Ed was probably not conscious for the worst of it. At some point, Ed's mind would have shifted from terror to preservation to accepting the reality that he was dying. There is a great deal of peace in that transitional moment, Mark. I've seen it."

"That's hard to believe."

"I was a combat medic in Vietnam. I was at the side of more than a dozen mortally wounded young men in the field. They begin their transition wide eyed and fearful. Some of them are in terrible pain. They are afraid to die. As their life begins to ebb and the reality of their death becomes clear, they make me promise to tell their parents or girlfriend how much they loved them. In their final moments, Mark, they simply drift away. There is no terror and no fear. They simply let go—peacefully. And then they are gone."

For the second time today, I realized tears were streaming down my cheeks again. I couldn't stop.

Casey waited a few moments, then went on, softly but in a matter-of-fact tone.

"Tossing Ed off the overpass was a warning, Mark. A message. If they simply wanted to make him simply disappear, they would have tossed him down the mine shaft with the other two bodies or left his body along a trail. They also would have done a better job of getting rid of his car. No, they wanted everyone to know they had uncovered a source. And they wanted to be sure everyone knew how they would handle a snitch."

His voice drifted off and he was silent for a moment. He realized he had slipped back into "cop mode" and was talking without emotion about Ed's last minutes on earth.

"I'm sorry, Mark."

Then he looked directly at me. "Mark, I need your help. I have obviously come very close to a break in the case. Somebody's nervous. I need another set of ears around the station. You are under no obligation. I would understand if you said no. I would just ask you to keep this conversation off the record if you decide not to work with me."

And, with a statement of the obvious, "because it's now very dangerous."

SEVENTY-ONE

Sequoia City
Friday, September 29, 1978
The Visitors

Kathleen is the part-time front office receptionist at the station.

When I came in just before noon, she wasn't really sure who the men were that stopped by to see me earlier in the day.

"They were dressed in suits," she said, filing her nails. "Suits. In this weather. They asked for 'Mr. Keating,' so I knew they weren't from around here. And they were driving a black sedan. Who in their right mind would own a black car in this part of the state?

"Anyway, I asked if they wanted to wait or leave a message and they said no. They said they would see you later. They looked pretty official," she said and resumed filing her nails.

When I pressed for more information, she said, "That's all I know," examining her handiwork.

Which wasn't really much. But then again, she was just part time. It's not like the job was a career or required a college degree. She was thrilled to be part of "the radio business" as she told her friends.

A business card would have been helpful, I thought.

Kathleen's information could have been more vague, although it was hard to imagine how.

S E V E N T Y - T W O

Sequoia City

"The Last Song"—Edward Bear

Still no word from Emma.

I stopped by her apartment a couple of times and left notes on the door. Some were sexy. Some were angry. The notes were gone the next time I went by, so she obviously picked them up.

I stopped by the Rip Roarin'. Sherry, one of the waitresses, said she had not seen Emma in a couple of weeks. "Her name's not on the work schedule posted in back. I think she and Gerry are out of town. I don't know when they'll be back."

Sherry said she would tell Emma to call me if she saw her. I wasn't sure if the message would get delivered, but actually, I didn't much care at this point.

I just said "Thanks" and left.

Emma never called.

I did get a couple of postcards from her and she said she would be in touch soon. The postmarks were from Sacramento, Redding and San Francisco. She said she missed me. And they were all signed "Love, Emma."

She and Gerry are out of town together and she signs them "Love, Emma"?

One of us is clearly nuts.

"Over You"—Gary Puckett and the Union Gap

MARK'S GREAT AMERICAN NOVEL
Chapter Twenty-Three

Bombay, India
Santacruz Airport
Air India Flight 855 to Dubai
January 1, 1978

As he looked back on the events of the day, Zia remembered searching for other members of the team boarding the plane in New Delhi. None had boarded by the time the cabin doors had been locked and secured for flight.

He tried not to think that he might be the only survivor. Surely some of the team caught a different flight to another destination. For the moment, he took some consolation in that thought.

His concentration was momentarily interrupted when the air from the overhead vents stopped. The plane had disconnected from the ground power source. The air flow began again a few seconds later as the airliner's generators kicked in.

The jet pushed back from the terminal and taxied for several minutes into position near the end of the runway. Until the plane was airborne, Zia knew, the tower could recall the plane back to the terminal.

It was dark outside. Somehow that made him feel more comfortable.

Piloted by Captain M.L. Kukar, the "Emperor Ashoka" had a crew of 23 and a passenger manifest of 190.

Captain M.L. Kukar acknowledged tower instructions to turn the huge jet onto Runway 27 and hold its position. A few moments later, just after 8 p.m., the Santacruz Airport tower cleared Flight 855 for takeoff.

The two-mile runway ends just a mile from the Arabian Sea.

The distance to Dubai is 1,915 kilometers.

The cabin lights were dimmed for takeoff. Zia's heartbeat quickened as the engines came to life and the plane started to move. At any second, he expected the plane to begin an emergency stop and return to the terminal where he would be removed at gunpoint.

The 813,000-pound airliner continued to pick up speed. The engines whined louder and the runway lights zipped by faster and faster.

A moment or two later, as the jet neared V-1 speed, the point where the pilot is committed to a takeoff, Zia felt his heart pounding in his chest. When the jet reached the vertical roll speed of 160 knots (184 mph), it lifted off.

Zia would only relax once they were airborne and out of Indian airspace.

It was 8:12 p.m.

In New Dehli, meanwhile, President Carter had just concluded a conversation with a personal assistant.

SEVENTY-THREE

Casey and I arranged a way to exchange the information I gathered.

At first, I would go to a phone booth at 6:30 every Thursday evening and call him in Redding. I usually carried a couple of dollars in quarters so I could complete the calls without getting cut off. Then we started switching days of the week and times of the day. I also started calling from different phone booths in town.

It felt like I was living in a European spy novel. Robert Ludlum would have been proud.

I really wasn't able to pick up much around the sheriff's office. Reporters are supposed to ask direct questions, so I wasn't used to hedging with lots of verbiage and subterfuge. At any rate, I would pass along whatever conversations or tidbits I might overhear or information I might uncover.

My newscasts included feature stories. These were usually human interest stories and I could devote up to six minutes of my newscast to them. I had interviewed local historians, locomotive engineers, utility meter readers, mailmen, geology professors and astronomers from Shasta College, firemen and seasonal fire tower employees, school principals, foresters, expert fishermen, local authors, miners and men who helped during the construction of the Sequoia Lake project. They would tell their stories, I would edit them for broadcast and turn them into feature stories. I often broke the story up into multiple parts and broadcast an installment every day over a period of a week.

These features gave me a way to fill time with local interest stories instead of state or national news off the UPI teletype.

I decided to do a feature on the process of criminal investigations: detectives, defense lawyers, prosecutors and, conveniently, how evidence was recorded and stored.

It might have been me or what I knew and what I was doing, but the evidence officers were the most reserved and cagey with their answers. They insisted on being interviewed together, which I thought was odd. This wasn't "60 Minutes", for God's sake.

In any case, I was able to piece together a pretty good feature story about the overall process. I made two cassette copies of the original, unedited interviews and mailed one to Casey.

I went to the United California Bank branch and opened a safe deposit box. I put the other taped copy of the interviews and my notes in the box.

You never know if they might come in handy later.

SEVENTY-FOUR

October 18, 1978

Starting in late August, I became aware of odd sounds on my phone at home and at work. Lots of clicks and static.

At the station, it was an easy mistake for someone to pick up a line that was currently being used. Realizing their error, the person would quickly hang up and switch to another line.

But the issue with my home phone was different. Sometimes I would have trouble hearing the person on the other end of the line, then suddenly their voice would become loud and clear like an extension phone had been hung up. Only my home phone was a private line and there were no extensions. And it didn't happen just once or twice. It happened all the time.

By the end of September, it was distracting enough for me to call "611," the phone company repair service number. "The line checks out OK" was what the service rep told me after finishing his tests a day later.

I called my friend Charles "Wes" Stevens at Pacific Telephone Company. Wes had been with the company since the days of operator-placed calls and party lines. He had about six months until retirement.

When I told him I thought someone was listening in on my phone conversations, Wes reminded me federal law required an audible beep on any phone line that was being recorded or when someone was listening in. Wes was skeptical about my concerns but said he would look into it.

In the 1960s and 70s wiretaps were fairly easy to detect if someone knew what to look or, more accurately, listen for.

A couple of days later, Wes called and told me to come by the switching station.

He said it was possible my home phone and maybe the news line at the station were tapped. He wasn't absolutely sure because he was having trouble tracing the source.

"Every time I try to locate what I think is a tap, the source disappears. It's like a freight train on the main line. Someone in a remote location throws a switch and the train heads into a siding out of sight—or, in this case, out of earshot.

"If it is a wiretap, it is pretty sophisticated."

He smiled, and said "It looks like you might be very interesting to someone. What are you up to?" He said with a chuckle. "You aren't cheating on your taxes, are you? Maybe it's the IRS."

I couldn't tell if he was serious or having some fun at my expense.

Maybe I was overreacting. It wasn't that long ago that wiretaps and illegal recordings were the end of Richard Nixon's presidency. The technology was certainly more readily available today.

"For What It's Worth"—Buffalo Springfield

MARK'S GREAT AMERICAN NOVEL
Chapter Twenty-Four

Bombay, India
Santacruz Airport
Air India Flight 855 to Dubai
January 1, 1978

When the plane lifted off, Zia let out a sigh he was sure could be heard three seats away. After the setbacks and disasters today, at least he had made it. Finally a turn of fortunes. Finding out what happened to the rest of the team would have to wait.

In just a few minutes, he would order that drink. And have a cigarette. For the first time since that morning, his breathing actually felt normal.

In the cockpit, as the plane began to climb, Captain Kukar used the Attitude Direction Indicator (ADI), also known as a gyro or artificial horizon, to begin banking the jet to the right toward Dubai. The ADI indicated the plane was banking to the right.

Captain Kukar noted a discrepancy between the ADI and another cockpit monitor. The second monitor had a conflicting reading about the jet's course and attitude. That monitor indicated the jet was flying on a level flight path.

Kukar discussed the situation with his co-pilot and flight engineer. The crew was unable to immediately resolve the discrepancy of the conflicting readings from either side of the cockpit.

Airline pilots are trained to trust their instruments. Modern aircraft have redundant instruments. In some cases, there is redundancy on top of redundancy.

Now out over the Arabian Sea, there was no visible horizon nor any city lights to verify what was happening. Kukar did not check the redundant monitor again. He banked the 747 to the left, believing he was leveling off the plane's flight path.

It was four minutes after takeoff.

SEVENTY-FIVE

Monday before Thanksgiving
November 20, 1978

"What do you mean the …uh…your investigation is closed," I asked when Casey called for the last time.

"The sheriff said he appreciated all the hard work I had put in, but he would take the investigation over from here," Casey said.

"What?" I was stunned. "But why?"

"I don't know why. The sheriff is an upstanding guy—a straight arrow. He and I have gotten to know each other pretty well over the past few months. This came totally out of the blue this afternoon. There was no discussion and no explanation beyond what I've told you. I have my suspicions, but that's all they are. I don't have any hard proof linking the sheriff or a relative or a close associate to the missing guns. But something stinks here, there's no doubt about it."

"But what about the Grand Jury and the state attorney general?" I asked.

"Those have been shut down, too. Nothing, none of my investigation, none of my hard work, nothing is going anywhere. It's over."

He was angry. I was dumbfounded.

"What about the investigation into Ed's death…murder? Is that closed too? Talk to me, Casey. You owe me that much at least. What the hell is going on?"

There was a brief pause. Casey continued in a voice just above a whisper, even though I knew he was alone. "Mark, you're on your own. You need to be very careful from now on. Lay low. Don't ruffle any feathers. Don't ask anymore questions of anybody at the sheriff's office."

He paused. "Mark, at his request, I turned over all of my notes and records to the sheriff. He has probably handed them over to someone else. Please, Mark, and I can't emphasize this enough: Please be careful. I don't think you're safe."

Like I needed to hear that.

"Good luck," he sighed, then hung up.

No "goodbye." No "thanks for your help." Nothing.

That was the last time we ever spoke.

I remember looking at the receiver as if it had something more to say. That's it? All's forgiven? Let's just forget it?

Never mind?

SEVENTY-SIX

My apartment
Sequoia City
Wednesday, November 29
3:30 a.m.

I bolted awake.

Startled, I was disoriented. Unsure of where I was or even what time it was. It took a moment to orient myself. My heart was pounding.

This is the second time this week I've been startled by the sounds of a big motorcycle.

When I got to the radio station Monday morning, I didn't notice the motorcycle parked a half a block away. When I got out of my car, the motorcycle started up, the rider revved the engine loudly several times, then raced toward me. He made a war whoop as he went by and gave me the finger.

I figured he was sleeping off a drunk and I startled him when I pulled in to park my car.

That didn't explain the half dozen motorcycles racing up and down North Bristlecone Street. They raced to the end of the block, gunned their motors, screeched their tires, turned around and raced by the front of the house. This was their third time by the apartment, accompanied by lots of yelling and cursing.

I crouched under the window sill and looked out. I knew better than to turn the lights on.

Then they were gone. All was quiet, but I couldn't get back to sleep.

SEVENTY-SEVEN

Sequoia City
Friday, December 15, 1978

The impromptu meeting called by my boss after my last morning newscast fell on me like a ton of bricks.

"Some of our advertisers have decided to boycott the station. It's aimed at your news coverage." He looked directly at me. "Gerry Apte started the ball rolling. You know, he doesn't like you.

"Mark, normally I resist pressure from advertisers. Over the years, an advertiser might threaten to 'never spend another nickel' with the station because of something that was said on the air. In a couple of months, they're back and act like nothing ever happened."

Where was this going, I wondered.

He was fidgeting a lot. He picked at his fingernails while he talked, never looking up at me. "This time it's different, Mark. A couple of our biggest advertisers are part of this thing with Gerry."

Now I was on edge. Very anxious.

"Even the Chamber of Commerce thinks there's been too much coverage both here and at the newspaper on the real estate fraud investigations. It's not good for business and not good for tourism. Everyone thinks it's time to move on."

I tried to focus while he rambled on. Move on? And who the hell is 'everyone? I thought. I noticed my breathing was quick and shallow.

"A friend of mine owns a Chicken Delight restaurant offering delivery down in the Bay Area. If there's a mistake in the order, the customer will chew out the delivery boy, then call the restaurant and say they will never do business with Chicken Delight again. They also threaten to tell all their friends about the lousy service. And, what do you know, it's not long before they place another delivery order."

Why the hell is he talking about chicken delivery? Where is this going?

"Mark, I guess what I am trying to say is this boycott is a serious business. You know we count on heavy advertising revenue in December. Christmas and all. Around the sales office, we call it 'harvest time.' I'm going to need to make some changes. Well, actually, Mark, I uh, need to make some cutbacks."

He looked down at his desk. "Mark, there's no easy way to tell someone they are fired. Hopefully this check will help."

He reached across the desk and handed me a check. "It includes some extra vacation pay."

Once again the world was moving in slow motion. "What? What do you mean? You're firing me?" I couldn't believe what I was hearing.

He was exasperated and obviously embarrassed. "Yes, Mark, I'm letting you go. Today. Right now. You can come back after 5 tonight and pick up your things. I'll be here. In the meantime, I need your key."

He stood up and offered his hand. "Good luck."

Again with the "Good luck." He could have added, "You're on your own now."

I shook his hand limply.

I undid the station key from my ring, handed it to him and walked out of his office.

The meeting was over.

Everyone at the station must have known I was getting the ax this morning. Kathleen was in the bathroom. The sales people were all gone. Even Charlie Dillon looked busy in the control room, balancing the phone on his shoulder and flipping through records.

I walked out the door of KSBC, got in my car and headed downtown. There was someone I had to see.

SEVENTY-EIGHT

Everglades, Florida
December 29, 1972

Seasoned airline pilots will tell you that commercial airline accidents, other than those resulting from mechanical failure, happen when the flight crew forgets their No.1 job which is to fly the airplane.

Anytime a pilot loses sight of the No.1 job, accidents happen. Many small airports display a picture in their waiting room showing an airplane in a tree with the caption, "Aviation is not inherently dangerous in itself, but much like the sea, to an even greater degree, is terribly unforgiving of carelessness, incapacity or neglect."

Such was the case when an Eastern Airlines L1011 TriStar jet, Flight 401, left JFK bound for Miami on December 29, 1972. On final approach into Miami, the crew could not confirm that the nose gear was down and locked. The crew focused on the landing gear issue in the final four minutes of the flight and lost sight of their first priority. While trying to resolve the issue, the auto pilot became disengaged. The crew was unaware the plane was losing altitude.

Miami tower approved a crew request to make a 180-degree left turn. Just 25 seconds later, the first officer realized the altitude had dropped. Seven seconds later, while still in a left turn, the TriStar's No. 1 engine struck the ground, followed by the main landing gear.

The National Transportation Safety Board said the accident was caused by distraction in the cockpit which resulted in CFIT—"Controlled Flight into Terrain." Of the 176 people on board, 101 died.

My life seemed to be rapidly approaching "Controlled Flight into Terrain."

SEVENTY-NINE

Friday, December 15, 1978
Three Days Before the End
The Rip Roarin' Bar

"Precious and Few"—Climax

Day or night, unless there's a band on stage, the jukebox at The Rip Roarin' is always playing. And no matter what time of day, the bar smells like stale cigarettes and spilled beer.

It was just before 10 a.m. when I came in. I passed Jill, the bookkeeper, on her way out with a bank bag under her arm headed to the B of A branch down the street. She never looked up. I'm not even sure she saw me.

I started up the stairs to Gerry's office. He was standing on the landing and waited until I reached the top.

He shook his head and with a chuckle said, "How's my favorite unemployed newsman?"

News travels fast, I thought. Maybe there are no secrets in town, after all.

"Sorry, but I'm not hiring right now, even though I think you'd make a terrific part-time dishwasher. It would be a perfect job for you. You certainly have the skills." Then, with a particularly ugly sneer, he added, "You were never going to amount to much anyway."

When communities are located near large water projects, engineers produce an inundation map. The map shows the areas most at risk to gradual or sudden flooding by a dam failure. At that moment, the dam in my head burst. There was no inundation map for what happened next.

He sounded like my father. I heard it a lot during the first eight years of my life. I wasn't prepared to hear it again this morning and certainly not from the likes of Gerry Apte. My rage welled up from deep inside and exploded without warning.

"What the hell do you know, you son of a bitch." The bar resonated with my voice. Actually reverberated. Even Gerry was stunned at my outburst.

Humpty Dumpty was taking a great fall.

"Who the hell do you think you're talking to?"

I was out of control, much like the last night I saw my father. I yelled and cursed louder. "You're an old man and a petty crook. You may have beat the system but your buddy Bobby didn't. He's fish food. So's Greg. He was probably a pretty tasty dinner for the buzzards in the canyon."

Stunned, Gerry started to say something but didn't get the chance.

I still can't believe the next words out of my mouth. I have no idea if they were true because the subject never came up. I blurted them out anyway: "And Emma says you're really lousy in bed."

Until this moment, I never understood how a boxer could anticipate his opponent's next move in the ring. Today, at the top of the stairs, outside Gerry's office at the Rip Roarin', I knew. When he started to throw a punch, I instinctively stepped sideways. His rage or his age got the best of him. Trying to adjust to my new location, he lost his balance and tumbled, headlong, down the flight of stairs.

The scene was reminiscent of Scarlett O'Hara in "Gone with the Wind" when she fell down a long staircase after an angry exchange with Rhett Butler. Just like Scarlett, Gerry went over and over, end over end, until he came to a stop at the bottom of the 15 stairs.

It all happened so fast. His last look at me was a lot like Greg's last look. He couldn't believe this was happening to him.

He wasn't moving. God, I think I killed him.

The flood waters in my head quickly receded.

Curiously, too, I am relieved. It took a couple of days after Greg's head hit the rocks to reach any level of relief. And that was after a passionate few days and nights in bed with Emma.

Not so this time. Although I am instantly relieved, I am also nearly overwhelmed with nausea.

I stood at the top of the stairs replaying the event in my mind. I wasn't in any hurry to see if the son of a bitch was alive or dead, but then remembered Jill would be back soon, so I went down the stairs.

"You'll never amount to much either," I said and kicked him as hard as I could.

"And Greg didn't amount to much either." I kicked him again. He didn't grunt or make any sound. It felt like kicking a sack of potatoes.

I stepped over him and left the The Rip Roarin' for the last time.

All the while, the jukebox continued to play. And all I could only think about was Emma.

"...Baby it's you on my mind, your love is so rare. Being with you is a feeling I just can't compare. And if I can't hold you in my arms, it just wouldn't be fair..."

Now I am sweating terribly and breathing in deep heaves. If I don't keep moving, I will start shaking. Shivering. Again I am fighting for altitude.

I need to get away for a while and think.

"...And if I can't find my way back home, ah, it just wouldn't be fair. 'Cause precious and few are the moments we two can share..."

E I G H T Y

Late morning
Sequoia City
Friday, December 15, 1978

I went back to my apartment and looked around.

I was feeling yet another profound sense of loss. I had paid the rent through the end of the month, but there wasn't much reason for staying around.

"American Pie"—Don McLean

No Emma. No Ed. No job. No Grandpa for that matter. Not much of anything left.

I loved this place. It felt more like home than anywhere else since I left Grandma and Grandpa's house.

I packed some camping gear, coffee, small cereal boxes and a couple of cans of Dinty Moore beef stew. I also found a large notebook left over from college. I needed to get away and think. What was it Emma said? "There's a lot going on and I'm trying to get my head straight."

It wasn't like planning for a vacation. I didn't have days to decide what to pack and what to leave behind. I grabbed everything I could think of and I really couldn't think of much. I did grab the Jameson's.

I had smoked my last joint right after Ed died. I wish I had one to take with me now.

I tried calling Emma's house once more.

"I'm not in Love"—10cc

No answer.

"...After nine days, I let the horse run free 'cause the desert had turned to sea... Under the cities lies a heart made of ground but the humans will give no love..."
—America, "A HORSE WITH NO NAME"

EIGHTY-ONE

Early afternoon
Friday, December 15, 1978

Little Grass Valley reservoir is about 90 air miles from Sequoia City.

Since I obviously can't drive "as the crow flies," the trip takes 3 ½ hours and covers nearly twice that distance. The national speed limit right now is 55 mph. Almost everyone drives at 63 miles an hour hoping to shave a few minutes off a trip and avoid a stop by the Highway Patrol.

Right now, the California Highway Patrol prohibits officers from hiding on off-ramps or out of the sight of approaching traffic. The agency believes the sight of a patrol car is enough incentive for speeders to slow down. The agency also uses vehicle decoys: mock-ups of real patrol cars parked along a highway. These decoys are frequently moved to keep drivers alert and avoid the location from becoming predictable.

The CHP can't use radar now either. Discussions to change that policy are ongoing in the state Legislature in Sacramento. The only way to get caught speeding is to have a patrolman observe a car driving at an excessive speed or "pace" you from behind. On some freeways, the CHP uses aircraft in conjunction with a couple of ground patrol cars to nab speeders. A sign alongside the road saying "Patrolled by Aircraft" was enough to get around the speed trap prohibition.

I was on the road just after noon. The weather was cool and dry and I had the windows partially cracked with the floor heater on. Once out of the hills, the car radio could pick up lots of radio stations. For a while, I listened to Jim Eason's talk show on KGO in San Francisco.

I wasn't paying attention to how fast I was driving or even where I was. I was driving on autopilot. Just before 3, I found myself at the Oroville Dam Boulevard exit on Highway 70. I filled up at the Richfield station just off the freeway. The station attendant was listening to KPAY-1060 AM in Chico.

I tuned over to it before I got back on the road.

My mind drifted in and out, lulled by the hum of the road and the sound of the radio on my way to LaPorte. The drought's impact on the level of Lake Oroville was visible off the left side of the road as I drove into the hills toward Forbestown and Challenge.

It was odd, I thought: Everyone's world is mostly the same as it was yesterday. Or even the same as this morning.

　　Not mine.

　　Not by a long shot.

　　What was it that Skeeter Davis sang about?

"The End of the World"

"There's a loneliness that only exists in one's mind. The loneliest moment in someone's life is when they are watching their whole world fall apart, and all they can do is stare blankly."
—F Scott Fitzgerald, "THE GREAT GATSBY"

E I G H T Y - T W O

Plumas National Forest
LaPorte, California
Friday, December 15, 1978
Late afternoon

"Cherish"—The Association

"Sometimes When We Touch"—Dan Hill

Dusk was fast approaching when I stopped to use the pay phone at the Union Hotel.

I wanted to—hoped to—talk to Emma one more time. I wanted to hear her voice again.

"Hello it's Me"—Todd Rundgren

The operator told me to deposit $1.50 for a three-minute call. After depositing a combination of quarters, nickels and dimes, the operator said, "Thank you, here's your call." I could hear the sound of the call going through.

After three rings, I heard "Hello."

I felt my heart race hearing her voice again. It was a tonic.

"Hey, it's Mark."

*"...Cherish is the word I use to describe, all the feeling that I
have hiding here for you inside..."*

"Where are you calling from? Where have you been?"

Funny questions coming from her.

"I'm camping for the weekend." It was an odd way to start a conversation. It had been weeks since we had seen or even talked to one another.

And I certainly never discussed camping in December.

"Wrong time of year for that isn't it?" She asked, somewhat playfully. " Going to be a little chilly at night I would think."

I choked up. The silence on the phone was almost deafening. It felt like an eternity but couldn't have been more than a couple of seconds. I weakly cleared my throat. My eyes teared up.

No song titles running through my head now. I only hear full lyrics playing...

> *"...You don't know how many times I'd wished that I had told*
> *you, you don't know how many times I'd wished that I could*
> *hold you..."*

"Are you still there?" There was a pause. "I'm sorry, Mark. Hey, I didn't mean to kid around. Are you all right?" More silence from my end. A pause, then she said, "Babe, tell me what's going on. You're upset. I know. I'm sorry. Mark, I called the station this afternoon and they said you weren't working there anymore. What happened?"

> *"...you don't know how many times I wish that I could mold*
> *you into someone who could cherish me as much as I cherish*
> *you..."*

"I'm a mess, Emma." I was half talking and half crying. My mother would probably say I was blubbering. "I don't know what to do. Everything is screwed up...I've screwed everything up." Not having anyone to talk to the past few hours did not make my thought process any clearer. The flood waters were raging in my head again. "I've screwed it all up."

"Screwed what up, Mark? What are you talking about?"

And after a deep breath, I said, "I've screwed up my life, Emma. Your life."

I felt like I was trudging through knee-deep slush, "Gerry's dead. I went to see him after I was fired and I...I think I killed him." I choked up again.

The line was now silent on her end.

Then, very softly, deliberately and actually quite kindly, she said "Tell me, Mark, please...What's going on? What do you mean Gerry's dead...that you killed him?"

I was silent, quietly gasping for air. My mental altimeter was in a dive.

Hearing nothing, she the changed the subject but I knew it would not be for very long.

"Mark, I'm sorry I've been out of touch so much recently. I've missed you."

Yeah, right, I thought.

After a pause, "David's father is going through another divorce. I've been staying with David at his dad's house in Redding for a couple of months. We thought it would be less traumatic on David if I were around. David's stepmother packed up and left rather suddenly. David's father is traveling constantly. He has a crazy schedule, so he's not home much these days. It was impossible to get away long enough for me to come home. I haven't told David about you and me—us—so I couldn't call while he was around."

I know she was waiting for some kind of response. For a moment, I couldn't think of anything to say.

"I hadn't heard anything from you. Not a word. Just a couple of damn postcards."

The words came out more harshly than they needed to.

"I didn't know what to think. Gerry wasn't around either."

Another pause on her end, longer this time. "Oh my God, Mark, you thought Gerry and I were out of town together, didn't you? Son of a bitch! For God's sake, I haven't been with Gerry since Greg disappeared in August. Something was different—changed—after that weekend in your apartment. You know that. Everything was different. Different with Gerry. Different with me. God, Mark. Different with you and me."

"The last time I talked to Gerry was weeks ago. I told him what was going on with David and his father. I needed a lot of time off and hoped he could hold my job for me. I was lucky to catch him at Ed's funeral. You know his legal problems keep him out of town a lot, too. I tried to catch up with you at Ed's funeral, too, but you cut out so quick."

For one of the rare times in my life, I was at a loss for words.

"Mark, I've been meeting with attorneys in Redding and Sacramento. I'm trying to get full custody of David. There aren't a lot of attorneys who want to take on the custody case of a single mother working in a bar whose ex-husband is a prominent businessman. It's going to be a real tug of war with his father. I know it's right for David in the long run, even though I feel like I'm kicking his father while he's down. Mark, talk to me."

I wasn't sure what was going on in my head. My thinking felt like more of those square pegs trying to fit in round holes.

"Mark, I tried calling your apartment, hoping to catch you. You never seem to be home. I called the station a couple of times a week. I talked to Charlie Dillon. I also talked to Kathleen more than a few times. I left David's father's phone number with her and the best time for you to call me back. She said she would leave you a message. I guess that was too much to ask. She's a real lightweight. Does she have trouble managing the phone and a message pad at the same time? I think her IQ is about two notches above concrete. Who did she have to sleep with to get that job? The owner?"

Realizing her train of thought had derailed, she quickly got back on track.

"Mark, I've called a lot. I was beginning to think you had moved on…that we were," now she hesitated, "through."

Fumbling for words she said, "Mark, I just got back in town this afternoon. Anna next door had been picking up my mail. She found your notes. They're all here with the mail. They are so sweet.

"Please, tell me what's going on. You're scaring me."

> "…Perish is the word that more than applies. To the hope in my heart each time I realize. That I am not going to be the one to share your dreams; that I am not going to be the one to share your schemes…"

I paused. "I'm sorry, Emma. I've screwed up. It's awful. I don't know what to do. Where to go. I shouldn't have called you. I didn't mean to bother you."

"Mark, wait. Please, hon, talk to me." Then, just above a whisper, "Tell me what happened with Gerry."

"He got me fired, Emma. The son of a bitch beats the system and then gets me fired." I raised my voice a couple of decibels. "I went to see him at the bar. I confronted him outside his office. He reminded me of my father, the son of a bitch. He tried to punch me and fell down the stairs."

"You don't know he's dead, Mark."

"Oh, I know Emma. He's as dead as Julius Caesar. The bastard said I would never amount to much. After he fell, I went down the stairs and kicked him as hard as I could. Twice. I was so mad. He didn't grunt or move. He's dead. Then I left the bar and came here."

"And where is 'here' Mark?"

I didn't answer.

> *"...That I am not going to be the one to share what seems to be the life that you could cherish as much as I do yours..."*

Another long pause and a very deep breath.

"Mark, please come home. We can work this out. Please, I'm sure it's not as bad as you think. Please, Mark, please listen to me. We'll work this out together."

"I can't Emma. I just can't. I'm finished. It's all over. I am nothing but a fraud, Emma. I don't know who I think I am. I have worked so hard to put on a good front for everybody. It's really hard work, Emma. Really hard. I just can't do it anymore. I won't do it anymore."

The line was quiet. The operator broke in and said I needed to deposit 75 cents for another three minutes. I put the receiver down and fumbled for the change in my pocket. I managed to find enough change to deposit and keep my life line open. The operator said "Thank you" and clicked off the line.

Back on the phone again, I was sputtering and sobbing a bit.

"Mark. Please listen to me. We can go to the police. You know the detectives there. And, God knows, they all knew Gerry. You know Seth at the D.A.'s office. Mark, he fell down the stairs. They'll determine it was an accident. Please don't do anything rash, Mark. Please don't do anything until we meet with the police. Please come home. Please. We can sort this out."

And after a pause, I whispered again. "I really am a nobody. A fraud. I haven't done anything with my life, Emma. Nothing!"

She said, softly, "You've changed me, Mark. My life. I'm different because of you. I want you to come home, Mark. Please, Mark, come home...for me."

Then, in the last conversation I would ever have, I finally said the words I had avoided for so long. "I love you, Emma." After all the emotional walls I had built over the years, I couldn't believe how easy it was to say. "I really do, Emma. I love you."

Even after all the times we'd made love, all of the time we'd spent together, it was the only time I'd ever said that.

It was quiet again. I weakly said "goodbye" but as I put the receiver back, I thought I heard her say, "Mark. I love you too."

Quickly I put the receiver back to my ear, but it was too late. The connection had been severed and even another $1.50 in quarters would not bring the connection back.

*"...and sometimes when we touch, the honesty's too much, and
I have to close my eyes and hide. I wanna hold you till I die, till
we both break down and cry, I want to hold you till the fear in
me subsides..."*

For at least a minute I stood there, crying, holding on to the phone like it was a life preserver. Holding on for support. Holding on to what now would never be.

Then I looked around to see if anyone had seen me. I was alone. I took a deep breath, wiped my face on my sleeve and got back in my car.

"I'd Really Love to See You Tonight"
—England Dan and John Ford Coley

MARK'S GREAT AMERICAN NOVEL
Chapter Twenty-Five

Bombay, India
Santacruz Airport
Air India Flight 855 to Dubai
January 1, 1978

The "Emperor Ashoka" continued to climb out and away from the airport at the normal rate of ascent of 1,800 feet per minute. Indian Air Traffic Control cleared the jet to climb to 8,000 feet.

Zia's first ever airline flight was earlier today but that plane was much smaller. Nothing compared to this experience. The feeling of power was incredible. The engines appeared to be the size of locomotives.

Moments after takeoff, the 747 encountered some light turbulence as it cleared land and gained altitude over the Arabian Sea.

Zia was struck by the absolute darkness outside the jet. He was used to the dark skies at home, although there was always some faint illumination from the stars. Sometimes a full moon and the starlight were almost bright enough to read by.

And in the city and at the university, there was always plenty of light.

Not so tonight. Nothing but blackness everywhere except for the flashing lights on the wingtips. He could just barely make out the wings moving up and down ever so slightly.

He strained to see anything else outside the window by his seat.

It was the last thing he would ever do in the last instant of his life.

E I G H T Y · T H R E E

Plumas National Forest
LaPorte, California
Friday, December 15, 1978
Late afternoon

The top of my head felt like it was on fire. There was a tremendous buzzing in my ears.

Little Grass Valley Campground was about five miles away. My car radio was having trouble picking up stations at that time of day and that far back in the mountains.

The signals came and went, but I could just barely make out a few stanzas of one of my favorite songs. It was America's "A Horse With No Name."

There was a lot of static and interference. I lost the signal for a few seconds. The station faded out, then back in again I parked my car outside the campground near the entrance gate, which was chained shut.

I shut the engine off, got out and locked the car. Of course I locked the car. Nobody around for miles, but I locked the car. The irony even made me smile.

I opened the trunk and unpacked the gear I brought. Grandma gave me the camping equipment she and Grandpa bought years earlier. I planned to be here a few days.

Grandpa.

"I Won't Last a Day Without You"—The Carpenters

After a brief moment, I slammed the trunk so hard the car rocked on its shocks and set off to find a campsite.

I looked around and took in the fresh air. It was cool and refreshing. Crisp. The breeze rustled through the pines. What did poets called this? "Bracing."

Whatever it was, it helped clear my head for a moment.

The shadows in the forest were very deep now. I needed to find a spot and set up quickly.

In the past, I loved camping here.

First with Ed.

"Rocky Mountain High"—John Denver

Emma and I spent one passionate weekend camping here last summer. We spent a lot of time in the tent. We had a lot of fun that weekend. After that weekend, we planned other trips but never made it back. This was the first time I'd been camping since. Emma and I kidded about the weekend calling it "Hot Days and even Hotter Nights."

Emma.

God I wished she was here.

"We'll Never Have to Say Goodbye Again"
—England Dan and John Ford Coley

MARK'S GREAT AMERICAN NOVEL
Epilogue

Bombay, India
January 2, 1978

Initial reports said a huge explosion brought down the "Emperor Ashoka -Your Palace in the Air," killing all 213 passengers.

Flight 855 had been airborne less than five minutes.

Viewed from shore, the huge fireball provided a stunning contrast to the pitch-black ocean waters of the Arabian Sea. There was speculation that a bomb was on board. Initially, nothing was ruled out, including a missile strike.

Within 24 hours, Indian and international safety investigators as well as representatives of the plane's manufacturer, Boeing, were on site. Search and Rescue teams combed the waters where the plane went down in less than 50 feet of water. There was a lot of debris. There were no survivors.

Experts and representatives from Boeing reviewed radar and black box data.

Accident investigators were able to rule out an explosive device or missile strike in the early weeks of the investigation.

The investigation determined the fireball occurred when the 747 slammed into the ocean at full takeoff speed, loaded with more than 150,000 pounds of aviation fuel.

Relying solely on the ADI, Captain Kukar started banking the jet to the left. He had not resolved the conflict with other cockpit meter readings. With no visible points of reference, he believed he was leveling off the jet's flight path. In reality, the jet was already on a level flight trajectory when he started banking the jet to the left.

Kukar apparently neglected to check the airspeed and turn rate indicators, sending the huge 747 into a stall. The flight engineer attempted to alert Kukar to the error five seconds before impact.

The jet slammed into the water two miles from the end of the runway.

"*...It felt good to be out of the rain. In the desert you can remember your name 'cause there ain't no one for to give you no pain...*"
—America, "A HORSE WITH NO NAME"

EPILOGUE

*"Forget the former things; do not dwell on the past. See, I am
doing a new thing! Now it springs up; do you not perceive
it? I am making a way in the wilderness and streams in the
wasteland"*
—Isaiah: 43-18-19

Monday, December 18, 1978
Running Deer Campground
Little Grass Valley Lake
La Porte, California
Elevation 5,000
5:16 p.m.

Mozart once wrote his father saying: "I never lie down at night without reflecting that, as a young man, I may not live to see another day. Yet none of my acquaintances could say that I am morose or disgruntled."

Spoken like a true genius. With a lot to show for his life. I, on the other hand, am morose and disgruntled with no acquaintances left to ask or confirm it.

I'm not sure there's anything left to say? I have 30 blank pages left in this notebook. That in itself is pretty depressing. "Not much to report" for my time on earth.

I've been so cold today, too. This fire isn't throwing off much heat. I've been shivering a lot. And I'm so very tired. It gets dark so early up here. The sun set an hour or so ago.

The smoke from the fire is winding lazily upward. It's hypnotic as I watch it drift higher and higher.

Odd, I must have dozed off for a bit. I've stirred awake now.

Funny, but a moment ago, I was shivering and ready to throw another wet log on the fire. Now I am really, really warm. How could the weather change that quickly? How long was I asleep? It couldn't have been more than a couple of minutes.

Even my jacket feels hot.

I can't believe how warm I am.

I probably should have left the Jameson's alone today. My nerves are totally shot. I'm jumping at every sound. Am I hearing something or just imagining it? Is that a branch or pine cone falling? Or footsteps? I am really straining. Do I hear something?

Do I hear a car engine? Voices? I think I'm seeing headlights and flashlights.

What the hell is happening?

Maybe someone will find this and maybe they won't. I can't imagine what difference it would make in any case.

What a statement about a person's time on earth after just 27 years: a profound disappointment with 30 blank pages left.

God it's so hot. I've got to get out of this jacket.

Funny what I'm thinking about: the cockpit recording of a mid-air collision in San Diego a few months back. The accident happened when a passenger jet, preparing to land at Lindbergh Field, collided with a small private plane. Twenty seconds later, the jet slammed into the ground killing the 135 people on board and nine people on the ground.

I remember how calm the cockpit crew sounded as the doomed jet hurtled to the ground. In the instant before impact, the final words from the crew were: "This is it! Brace yourself! Mom, I love you!"

"Well the picture is changing, now you're part of a crowd, they're laughing at something, the music's loud. A girl comes towards you, you once used to know. You reach out your hand but you're all alone in those time passages. I know you're in there, you're just out of sight. Oh, time passages. Buy me a ticket on the last train home tonight."

APPRECIATION

Thanks to my friends who helped with background, insight and encouragement: *William Sager*—Cal Fire Chief, retired; *Kathy Zancanella*—South Feather Water and Power Agency, retired; *Wayne Wilson*—Cal Fire, retired, Oroville California; *Dr. Timothy Huber*—Physician, Oroville California; *Burton Akins*—Butte County California Sheriff's Investigator, retired, deceased; *Stan Starkey*—U.S. Forest Service, retired; *Jerry Jacks*—Northwest Airlines 747 pilot, retired; *Tony Koester*—Butte County California District Attorney investigator, retired; *Mike Ramsey*—Butte County California District Attorney; *Bill Hansell*—California Department of Water Resources, retired; *Jerry Fitzgerald*—private pilot, retired; *Mike Parkison*—Ice delivery business; *Reed McClure*—USAF Airman; *Emmett Pogue*—Friend and fellow writer; *Nancy Weston* whose concept of "strong parents and weak children" is referenced on page 40; *Bob and Brenda Wentz*—CEO Oroville Hospital/Owner Oroville Sports Club (Bob and Brenda purchased a reading of excerpts of this book as well as the first autographed copy. The purchase was part of a charity auction to benefit the historic State Theatre in Oroville, California); *The Serra High School Padres, Class of '68*, who meet at Carl's Cabin every year in Dorrington, California; *Dr. Richard and Frances Rohrbacher* (The Rohrbachers were the first to read a draft of the manuscript and encouraged me to continue. Dr. Rohrbacher passed away before publication of this book); friends *Dave Logasa* and *Mark Wisterman*; professional manuscript editors *David Little* and *Michael Masterson*, who provided insight, direction and corrected a plethora of punctuation errors; and *Dustin Cooper*, Attorney/Partner Minasian Law Firm, Oroville, California.

Copyright clearance of lyrics was conducted by *Joy Tillis* of WJOY Music in Chicago. Joy was easy to work with, appreciated my sense of humor and provided valuable guidance and insight into the music copyright and licensing industry.

Literary copyright clearances were arranged by *Ethel Scholey* of Oroville.

Thanks also to *Claudia Harcourt* of OddDog Design who designed the jacket cover and formatted this book for electronic and printed versions.

I also appreciate *Tim Noonan* of Russell Investments who encouraged me to complete this work, adding "Writing a book requires rivers of tears and gallons of gin."

Additional inspiration, creativity and encouragement came from: William Hill Coastal Chardonnay; Jordan Vineyards 2010 and 2011 Cabernet Sauvignon; Whole bean "Italian Roast Coffee" from Mother Lode Coffee Company in Sonora, California; Perrier Jouet Champagne; Seven Falls Cellars 2012 and 2013 Cabernet Sauvignon and their GPS Cabernet.

SEPARATING FACT FROM FICTION

This book is only marginally autobiographical as I do have a record and music collection that is the envy of my friends. I also have song titles and music running through my head all the time.

I did work in television and radio broadcasting. I did string for the United Press International and The Sacramento Bee. For a time, I worked as an assistant news director for a television station in Yakima, Washington and a news director for KORV in Oroville, California.

Little Grass Valley Campground and reservoir are real places. The facilities are currently under the management of South Feather Water and Power Agency. At the time of the story, the U.S. Forest Service operated the campgrounds.

Life in a fire lookout tower was described to me by a veteran of seasonal work in the late 1970s. What happens in a lightning storm in a fire tower is accurate.

There was no commercial California radio station with the call letters KBSC at the time of this writing.

The weather conditions in Rajasthan, India, including the day of the 126-degree record temperature on May 10, 1956, are accurate.

Professional radio, TV and movie announcer Art Gilmore attended Washington State University in Pullman, Washington. It's estimated he did more than 3,000 movie trailers during his career. WSU is my college alma mater. Mr. Gilmore annually awarded a scholarship to students in the Communications Department. Students submitted an audition tape with a script Art had prepared. Mr. Gilmore announced, via tape, the most promising student announcer at an annual awards banquet. I won the award in 1972. Mr. Gilmore died in 2010 at the age of 98.

There is no Sequoia Surge; however, the foehn, the Chinook, the Satana (Satan's Wind, aka Santa Ana) wind do exist as does the Sundowner along the California coast near Santa Barbara and the Konocti Effect near Clearlake in Northern California. The record swing in temperatures in Spearfish, South Dakota, in 1943, is accurate.

Both the 1949 Mann Gulch Fire in Montana and the 1953 Rattlesnake Fire in the Mendocino National Forest did occur as detailed in the story. The number of firefighter fatalities is accurate.

Hypothermia is real as is the mammalian divers reflex. Hypothermia is known as a silent killer and its effects are hastened and enhanced with alcohol.

The great California floods of 1955 and Christmas/New Year's 1964-65 did happen and the flood flows, loss of livestock, property damage to the lumber mills and state highway bridges are accurate.

President Jimmy Carter did embark on an eight day goodwill tour of Europe, Asia and the Middle East in late December 1977. The president did arrive in New Delhi on the afternoon of January 1, 1978, for a three-day goodwill visit. The itinerary of the entire trip is available online through Mr. Carter's Presidential Library.

The flight characteristics and information on the Boeing 747 were supplied by a retired 747 pilot, who flew international routes.

Air India Flight 855 headed for Dubai did crash into the Arabian Sea on the evening of January 1, 1978, shortly after takeoff from the Santacruz International Airport in Bombay. It was the first 747 Air India purchased as described in the story. The cause of the crash was later determined to be instrument failure and pilot error.

Details about Secret Service activity and investigations relied heavily on my imagination along with a sprinkling of information generally available on the internet about presidential security during the Clinton, Bush and Obama administrations. Historical information came from http://www.secretservice.gov In the early 1980s, I was selected as a member of Rotary International's Group Study Exchange program, representing California Rotary District 519, in India. I spent seven weeks in the country, living with residents of the communities we visited, touring the area south of Bombay (Mumbai today) and speaking to Rotary Clubs in India. It was an experience I doubt could be replicated. I was immersed in the culture of India and grew to love the genuine hospitality of its people and the history of the country and its culture.

The Rotary Group Study Exchange is open to a non-Rotarian under age 35. "Building Bridges of Understanding" was the theme of Rotary International the year I visited. One family I stayed with for a couple of nights wrote my wife after I left and said they set a place at the table for me every night in hopes I would someday return.

Pacific Southwest Airlines Flight 182 crashed in San Diego, California on September 25, 1978. The transcript of the cockpit recording is available from a variety of websites on the internet.

To my knowledge, there was no plot against President Carter during his overseas trip in 1977-78. Any connection between President Carter's visit, an assassination plot and the airplane crash are strictly my own invention.

BIBLIOGRAPHY

Dorr, Robert F.—*Air Force One*. Motorbooks International, 2002. ISBN 0760310556

Hardesty, Von—*Air Force One: The Aircraft that Shaped the Modern Presidency*. Northword Press, 2003. ISBN 9781559718943

Walsh, Kenneth T.—*Air Force One: A History of the Presidents and Their Planes*. Hyperion Books, 2003. ISBN 9781594518331

Information on the gold fields and discoveries in California came, in part, from http://www.cmi-gold-silver.com/blog/10-most-prolific-gold-fields-in-the-world.

While not used as reference material *Young Men and Fire* by Norman Maclean outlines, in gripping detail, the events of the Mann Gulch Fire in Montana.

Information on flooding and inundation mapping came from: http://water.usgs.gov/osw/flood_inundation; http://www.usgs.gov/blogs/features/usgs_top_story/rain-for-thirsty-california/; http://www.usgs.gov/blogs/features/usgs_top_story/the-christmas-flood-of-1964; https://weather.com/science/weather-explainers/news/atmospheric-river-explained

Information on tornado watches vs. warnings came from: http://www.accuweather.com/en/weather-news/the-difference-between-tornado-1/61817

Logging railroad information came from http://www.american-rails.com/

Information on the assassination of Archduke Ferdinand and his wife Sophie came from these sources: http://www.eyewitnesstohistory.com/duke.htm; http://time.com/3880415/margaret-macmillan-on-assassination-of-franz-ferdinand-and-sophie

ABOUT THE AUTHOR

Jim Moll grew up in San Mateo, California, attended St. Matthew's Catholic School, Serra High School and the College of San Mateo before completing his education at Washington State University in Pullman, Washington.

He graduated with a Bachelor of Arts Degree in Communications in 1972.

He pursued a professional broadcasting career at KNDO-TV in Yakima, Washington. He also worked for a broadcast computer installation firm, IGM (International Good Music), in Bellingham, Washington.

Returning to broadcasting, he worked at WRMN and WJKL in Elgin, Illinois, before moving to Oroville, California, in 1974 to work as News Director KORV-AM.

He moved into Sales and Management in 1979 and assisted in putting KORV's sister station, KEWE-FM on the air.

Jim is active in community activities, serving as past president of the Oroville Area Chamber of Commerce and Northwest SPCA. He is on the Board of Directors of Oroville Hospital, and is involved in the preservation efforts of Oroville's historic State Theatre. He is also known as "The Voice of Oroville" for his many duties as emcee.

Photo courtesy of Stifel Financial

Jim began a career in financial services in 1985. He is currently an investment professional with Stifel Financial.

This is his first novel. He worked as a monthly guest columnist for the Chico Enterprise-Record and the Oroville Mercury-Register during 2018. He is a member of the North State Writers Club and California Writers Club.

Jim and his wife, Claudia, have been married 42 years and make their home in Oroville.

Made in the USA
Columbia, SC
05 February 2019